BUDHINI

BUDHINI

Sarah Joseph

Translated by
Sangeetha Sreenivasan

PENGUIN

An imprint of Penguin Random House

HAMISH HAMILTON

USA | Canada | UK | Ireland | Australia
New Zealand | India | South Africa | China

Hamish Hamilton is part of the Penguin Random House group of companies
whose addresses can be found at global.penguinrandomhouse.com

Published by Penguin Random House India Pvt. Ltd
7th Floor, Infinity Tower C, DLF Cyber City,
Gurgaon 122 002, Haryana, India

First published in Malayalam as *Budhini* by DC Books, Kerala 2019
First published in Hamish Hamilton by Penguin Random House India 2021

Copyright © Sarah Joseph 2021
Translation copyright © Sangeetha Sreenivasan 2021

All rights reserved

10 9 8 7 6 5 4 3 2 1

ISBN 9780670093830

Typeset in Bembo Std by Manipal Technologies Limited, Manipal
Printed at Replika Press Pvt. Ltd, India

www.penguin.co.in

To Budhini,
With love and gratitude—for giving me
a place to start from, and to return to

'When journalism is silenced, literature must speak. Because while journalism speaks with facts, literature speaks with truth.'

—Seno Gumira Ajidarma, *Ketika Jurnalisme Dibungkam Sastra Harus Bicara*

Contents

Author's Note

Why Budhini Matters

In 2015, an extraordinary seminar was conducted in Chalakudy under the aegis of the River Protection Forum. It was a seminar to discuss the impact of the proposed hydroelectric project at Athirappilly.

At the seminar, I heard about Budhini for the first time from poet and political activist Civic Chandran, who had written a poem on the same. He asked me if I could elaborate it into a story. It was a theme that touched me deeply. It stayed in my mind for long. Chandran found the story of Budhini in an article, 'Recovering Budhini Mejhan from the Silted Landscapes of Modern India', by Chitra Padmanabhan, published in *The Hindu* on 2 June 2012. I read the article several times and went through a lot of studies related to it.

Crores of people have been uprooted from their soil for mega development projects before and after Independence. It was a disturbing thought that their stories had gone unrecorded. According to data with the United Nations Commissioner for Refugees, people have been displaced for development projects on a large scale in India. Since 1947, 60–65 million people have been uprooted, including 40 per cent tribals, and 40 per cent Dalits

and marginal farmers, and activist Medha Patkar had sought UN
intervention.

On 6 December 1959, then Prime Minister Jawaharlal Nehru
had gone to inaugurate the Panchet Dam across the Damodar
river. A girl chosen by the Damodar Valley Corporation (DVC)
welcomed the prime minister with a garland and tika on his
forehead. The fifteen-year-old girl was ostracized by villagers later,
citing violation of Santal tribal traditions. She was expelled from
the village. Budhini was her name.

Nehru had made the labourer girl who used to carry bricks
and mud for the construction of the Panchet Dam inaugurate the
dam. But after the photo session, she had ceased to be a story for
newspapers.

DVC also dismissed her from her job, perhaps because of the
talk among villagers that she was 'Nehru's wife'! How she lived her
life after the incident wasn't anyone's concern.

Budhini started taking shape in my mind as a symbol of crores
and crores of people who have been drowned in memory during
nation-building, mega projects, including dams, and companies
such as DVC and Bharat Coking Coal Limited.

Even now, people in eleven villages on the eastern borders
of Jharkhand are fighting against the acquisition of their fertile
land for construction of a thermal power plant by the Adanis.
The realization that the story of Budhini is also the story of
uprooted people is what motivated me to write a novel on her.
Her story should not have gone unwritten. I had to develop it
into a story of the Santal tribe as well—a population that lives
peacefully in areas that are fertile and rich in resources, without
exploiting them.

In her article, Padmanabhan mentioned her attempts to meet
Budhini. "All this while, I had debated the merits of meeting
Budhini. Last week, through a friend's friend in Ranchi I got news
that Budhini died last year, disconsolate to the end. She was in her
late 60s," she writes.

In the third week of November 2018, I reached Jharkhand. It was a pilgrimage through the memories of Budhini, who I believed was dead. Also to meet people related to her and gather all available information on her.

I felt Budhini had to be revived from the criminal forgetfulness of the country; she wasn't just a mud block that was broken during the great nation-building process. I felt that she should rise again in the nation's memory along with hundreds of villages, vast farmlands, forests and temple complexes that were drowned in the Panchet reservoir.

Budhini is a novel based on a news article. It is not her life story or a historical novel. I started writing it as a story of Budhini who was dead. While writing it, I took utmost care on how to blend history with fiction, and how to merge news and fiction. The life Budhini lives in my novel may not be the life of the original Budhini. The original Budhini's life wasn't what my character called for. That I left to imagination and possibilities. My assessment is that imaginative power will help make historical facts truthful.

In the course of researching the novel, I discovered that Budhini, now in her seventies, was alive. It was purely coincidental that I got to meet her as well. I could experience the same wonder and happiness I felt all through the writing of this novel.

(This essay by Sarah Joseph was first published in the *Indian Express* on 28 July 2019. It has been translated from the Malayalam by Yamini Nair.)

1

Rhythm! Drums! Drums!
Rhythm! Rhythm! Drums! Dance!
All but the dancing ground!

L et us begin with the woman who persevered. Not how she recaptured the dancing ground, but how she ran incessantly without knowing whose land to set foot in. Waking up in the fourth phase of the night, she lit her stove and boiled some water. If she had a pinch of tea leaves or rice, she would have made some tea or gruel.

'Oye, Ratni, wake up! We have to be there straight away. Please don't wake your baba. The moment he's up he will start whining, "Why toil over something in vain, Ratni's ma? You have been running for a long time now, haven't you? Will your complaints reach their ears? Better get back to sleep than wear off the soles of your feet." But, Ratni, it doesn't work like that; we should barge in and vex them as often as not. In the end, they will be forced to make a decision. Your baba is depressed, but could we endure more than this! Put your blankets over those boys, Ratni. Poor kids, they have been cold all night. Here, take this hot water. It's not likely that Jauna Marandi will wait for us. His tongue has no bones. And if we don't make it on time, he will go on grumbling about it till we get there.'

Languorous but still on her feet, Ratni staggered out of the house. Could this shack covered with asbestos sheets, tattered burlaps and rags, sandwiched between the walls of two multi-storeyed buildings, be called a home? Shoving the ragged fabric covering the back of the house aside, the child squatted on the ground and peed. From the mud *kanda* on the ground, she diligently filled water in a coconut shell and rinsed her mouth and face. She shuddered because of the cold.

'Ratni Mei!' Hearing her mother call out in a hushed voice, she went inside without delay. A little black dog followed her into the room, squeezed itself to make space between the sleeping boys and then curled up on the floor. Looking into her eyes, it wagged its tail in concern.

It was still dark and extremely cold. Dragging her daughter, who was still shivering, she walked out. Fetid odours rose from the leftover scraps of the city from the previous night. Carrying a tiny bundle on her head, the child ran after her mother. When she noticed some stray dogs barking at her daughter, she bent down to pick up a stone. The dogs stood lost for a while and then beat a hasty retreat.

Jauna Marandi had asked them to wait at the spot where the path from Asansol joined the main road to Dhanbad. His jeep would start only after loading people from around Asansol bus station. The rattletrap of a vehicle was the same age as his grandfather. It experienced the same uncontrollable quivers as the old man, not to mention the same case of arthritis! Whenever Jauna started the engine, one was exposed to a clatter that sounded like a truckload of steel plates tumbling down. Well, what of it? The jeep regularly plied to and from Asansol and Panchet. In between, the vehicle transported schoolchildren in the morning and in the afternoon. Audaciously arguing with the bus conductor, Jauna would manipulate passengers into his jeep. Any curiosity expressed about how Jauna kept piling people on board would leave him flabbergasted. And if anyone complained about getting smothered, the motor-mouth would retort harshly: 'Has anyone been choked to death by riding in Jauna's jeep so far? No one! I tell you, people know how to adjust. They will force their way to find a place to stand on their feet. It is not possible to conjure up some legroom out of the blue, is it? If there's a will, no one will have to balance on one leg, and if there's room for the head, Bhaiya, there will be room for the leg as well. We all have to go, don't we? And, oye, look at me! The diesel rate is rising. The cost of rice is rocketing. I have to live, too, Bhaiya, don't I?'

Some worker from the Damodar Valley Corporation (DVC) would lose his patience and say, 'Stop bragging and start your vehicle, Jauna. It is getting late.'

'Will time ever cease to travel? What else has time got to do? Go on infinitely, day after day, night after night, no idea where, for it leaves no clue. No head, no tail! You can't harness time, you know,' Jauna would snap back.

'Sick of him!' By then, the DVC workers, who worked at the Maithon and Panchet dams, would be exhausted.

Jauna would then ask if the DVC would eat them alive for being a few minutes late. 'Oh, don't fret over it. Nothing will go wrong, Kailas Bhaiya. Jauna knows how to pick up speed to make up for lost time.'

'Yes, yes, absolutely!'

'Call me names if I fail to drop you at the gates of DVC a minute before the siren goes off!' Jauna would snap his fingers at them as if he was calling his dog.

'Thanks to our stars we remain alive after each ride in your jeep, Jauna. Have you any idea how people take their lives into their hands when they travel in your vehicle?'

'And how many times has your life fallen out of your hands, Kailas Bhaiya? Tell me. It is not just today or yesterday that you began flying in my jeep; you are on a season ticket.'

This left Kailas tongue-tied. Jauna did give ticket concessions to DVC workers.

*

It was Aghan, the coldest month! People trembled, trees stood chilled to their juices and no animal was to be seen outside. There were but four people on board, all of them going to Panchet. Where were those who went to Maithon? Didn't we need to take them too! There was not a soul anywhere. No one! Also, the thick layers of fog obscured even the nearest objects.

Jauna's one-eyed jeep blinked on and off. The trip would be a loss if he couldn't collect a minimum of ten people. He screamed at the top of his voice, 'Panchet Dam! DVC!'

His shrill call, drilling through the fog, hit the walls of Asansol's Saint Mary's cathedral and reverted to his throat.

'There's no sign of people, Jauna. You should start now. Maybe they'll join us on the way. It is bust-ass cold today. The frost is biting into the bones,' said Dipankar Hembrom, the older gardener at DVC, rubbing his hands together and shivering. A monkey cap marked by holes and a sleeveless sweater were all he had on his body.

'How on earth do you stand this cold in these shredded clothes, Dipu Bhaiya?' Jauna asked him.

'You sound arrogant because of your young blood, dear boy.'

'Go, Jauna, or we'll get out.'

'Is that a threat? Well, you asked for it.' And with that Jauna turned the ignition on. A truckload of steel dishes fell, followed by a small earthquake, making the engine go off.

'It's the cold, brother. The jeep is no different from us. Don't we kick-start our motors, too, with a nice cup of tea in this cold?'

It wasn't easy to argue with that ratchet-mouth. If Jauna's jeep's engine had to be warmed up, there needed to be many more people on board. Grudgingly, the workers stepped out.

'Look at him, Kailas Bhaiya, how peacefully he leans against his jeep while we stand on thorns under our soles.'

Jauna was rolling *chukka* on the palm of his hand. Ever so often, he would shout, 'Panchet . . .'

Babulal, a lanky worker as thin as a thread, walked towards him and folded his hands in request.

'Dear Jauna, I was down with fever for the last three days. Imagine what will happen if I don't make it today either? I will lose my job for sure. Let me roll the chukka for you, but you've got to start.' And then Babulal cried out, 'Panchet Dam! DVC! Maithon!'

Jauna's heart was no stone that wouldn't melt. Life was no joke after all. He knew how Babulal ran his house. The poor man would never make it big in life. Yesterday, he was under the scorching sun, and today was no different. No rain came to cool him. A strange world it was! Basically, people should cudgel their brains for a god who is not prejudiced.

'Hop in, Bhaiya. Stop screaming your head off.' Jauna started the vehicle. This would be a trip with only four people on board.

Some losses are gains, Babulal's sigh conveyed to Jauna. Though he was not content, Jauna did feel grateful.

*

'We are very late, Ratni Mei. It seems Jauna Marandi has already left.' Ratni's mother was dejected. Loosening the knot at the end of her pallu, she took out some coins and counted. 'Jauna had promised to take us for free. What should we do now! I saved these coins to buy medicine for your baba, but now we will have to spend them on bus tickets. But if you can walk, Ratni, there is a shorter route through the forest.'

Ratni didn't say whether she could walk or not. Her teeth chattered, thanks to the cold.

While life saunters, the sun might as well rise in the west one day, marking the end of order. Then daybreak will turn into the hour of darkness. Like time suspended, nothing will be understood. Not everyone will overcome the bewilderment that is yet to come.

As Jauna's jeep climbed up the road from Asansol to Dhanbad, an arm adorned with thick silver bangles suddenly appeared right in front of his vehicle. A strong arm! Nothing else was visible in the fog. Jauna forced his weight down on the brake pedal.

'Get in,' he bawled.

The DVC workers noticed the woman and child get into the jeep through the impenetrable fog. The woman wore a mud-coloured sari with a green border and the girl a crimson sweater. The child carried a bundle of clothes which she hugged close in a bid to protect herself from the insufferable cold. She looked not more than seven or eight. The woman had a grey shaded shawl wrapped around her and a lengthy red fabric bag on her shoulder. There was no seat. They hunkered down on the floor.

It was only the next day that Jauna Marandi realized, much to his shock, that the woman and child had boarded his jeep and alighted at the gates of the DVC to commit suicide. Though the news was not as candid as it sounded, some of the workers near the dam had seen a woman climbing up the steps of the reservoir, holding the hand of a little girl wearing a crimson sweater. Yet, even Dipankar Hembrom couldn't make out who those workers were. Some others had seen them standing on the verandah of the DVC office. For about an hour and a half, they stood there with their faces hanging. Eventually, the cleaning girl who worked there on daily wages—a young girl of fifteen with a sweet look—reported that she had seen them go inside the office room.

Why would she tell a lie? Besides, she was genuinely excited to speak about them.

'I am positive,' she asserted. 'That little girl had a bundle bound in a faded yellow cloth, which she put down on the floor in front of the office door. She kept looking back at it as they went inside. Apparently, something very dear to her was in that bag. The woman was pulling her along forcefully. She had to lift her heels to look at the bag as the woman's arms were blocking her view. She sobbed and tried to pull the woman back.'

The cleaning girl said she had picked up the bundle, mopped the floor and put it back. It was not heavy, but when something had tinkled inside she had felt herself transforming into a child again. Presumably, what chimed inside was a pair of silver anklets with tiny beads enclosed within. There were probably floral motifs and birds and runners chiselled on the metal surface. When she was a young girl, she too had longed for a pair of *itil paini*. Brass would do if silver was too expensive, provided they pealed as she walked. So far, she had had no luck in owning them. After cleaning the verandah, she had lingered there for some more time. She wanted to see the woman and girl come out of the room. How eager the child would be to hold her bundle close to her chest again! She may even open it to examine the treasure inside. However, the cleaning girl recalled, the child showed no particular enthusiasm when they came out. It was her mother who took the bundle from the floor and placed it on her head. She was sure the woman was her mother. The woman, she remembered, carried a red bag on her shoulder.

All of them talked alike about the red shoulder bag, but there was no consensus about which shoulder it hung on. Left or right? Still, no one had seen them jumping into the reservoir, and no one knew when.

A fisherman testified that they didn't dive straight into the water. According to him, they slowly went into the reservoir till they sank. Since he was far away from the scene, he couldn't see clearly. From a distance, the girl in the crimson sweater had seemed to be the size of a small kitten. But what went into the reservoir was no mere silhouette but a real woman who possessed an unbearable calmness of being. The water hadn't stirred, not even a ripple. And hence there was no evidence for this account.

At times, the fisherman tried to flesh out his story in an engaging way. But who was he? That was the first thing that needed to be ascertained. Where did he usually go fishing? A stranger who spun his yarn out of whatever got caught in his net was not to be believed. No woman was found dead and floating over the reservoir. No child was reported to have been seen climbing down the steps crying or wandering near the precincts.

Nevertheless, the woman and child were real. Jauna Marandi, Kailasnath Kisku and the cleaning girl testified to that. The woman and the child, they said, were in Jauna's jeep from Asansol to Panchet Dam. Because of the cold, the child had continued shivering and dozing off against Kailas's knees. Her face was as cold as snow. As a hot desert wind blew in his heart, Kailasnath wrapped the girl's hands in the ends of his blanket.

2

'Our people would like to believe that the woman committed suicide years back,' Rupi Murmu told her friend Suchitra, a freelance photographer. They were talking about Budhini Mejhan on their way from Kolkata to Dhanbad. Rupi had received a text from her cousin, Mukul Murmu, who worked in a crockery shop in Dhanbad, saying that Budhini was still alive. The message had shocked her, literally. Rupi had read Budhini's death report in one of the significant newspapers, as its lead story, in June 2012. The article had hinted at how miserable her last days were, how poverty and infirmity had mistreated her and how she had to die a death deprived of justice. She had read about Budhini's death in some other newspapers as well.

Budhini was a distant relative of Rupi's. But since Rupi had maintained no sentimental ties with her, her death did not strike her emotionally. Rupi had not even seen her in person. Yet, the fact that Budhini was alive moved her strongly. Much before the news reached her, she had started her research on Budhini, her village and the many other neighbouring villages, thanks to her dadu, Jagdip Murmu. It had disappointed her when she had to introduce Budhini's story to the editor. The name hadn't captured his attention so far. 'Who is she?' he had asked.

When Rupi had described Budhini as the wife of Pandit Jawaharlal Nehru, the editor had burst into peals of laughter.

'Illegal?' he had retorted.

Rupi didn't smile, but her colleagues had joined the editor in laughing out loud. She didn't want to make it a laughing matter. She knew her blood was rushing to her face, making her cheeks burn.

'How many years of Indian history do you know about?' she had asked the sub-editors. Eventually, she chose not to equip them with more details. The newspaper was from Delhi, so were the journalists. They didn't need to acknowledge a small Santal village called Karbona, which lay close to West Bengal, near the eastern borders of Jharkhand. However, despite being journalists if they were unaware of Budhini who used to live there, it was unacceptable. For Rupi, Budhini was not a light case. It became Rupi Murmu's purpose to record—with certainty—the death and resurrection of Budhini.

Since there were no more texts after the first one from her cousin, and his cell phone was always out of network coverage, Rupi began doubting the credibility of the news and eventually got frustrated. Even if it was a hoax, Rupi thought, no matter how many years had passed since her death, the country should know how Budhini Mejhan lived the last of her days. Should Budhini's life end just like that, without a trace of reminiscence? Was she but a mud block that was broken during nation-building? No, no, it cannot be so, Rupi determined in her mind. Budhini was not a person; she was a nation herself.

She had then called Suchitra on the phone.

'Where are you now?'

'I'm here in Kutanellur.'

Suchitra was on her sabbatical at home for ten days, recording the festival season there. When Rupi had called, she was with her maternal cousins, clicking pictures of the festivities, perspiring beneath the summer sun. Over the deafening roar of the percussion, she couldn't understand what Rupi was saying. She sent her a text message: *Busy now, call you later.*

That night, Rupi told her the story of Budhini Mejhan. The name Budhini was new to Suchitra as well. Somehow she thought it was the name of a dancer. An Odissi dancer clad in traditional costumes, moving to a slow and confused pace with her left hand persuasively placed on her left hip, the right hand reaching out to it, her right foot dragging her leg backwards in slow motion and her head tilting to her left flashed in front of Suchitra's eyes.

'If the woman who has been marked dead is still alive, we must find her,' Rupi Murmu said.

Budhini Mejhan's whereabouts were unknown except for the vague guess that she was either in Ranchi, or maybe residing in a rented house somewhere in Purulia. Anyhow, she would not be in her native village, for the villagers, including her relatives, considered her dead even though they knew she was alive. Budhini had committed a crime. They had punished her. Now, what if she is dead or alive? After all these years, their verdict had remained unchanged.

The unfortunate part was that they knew she was pure. Those who punished her knew this. Nevertheless, there was a reason for the punishment and the evidence persuasive.

'Our people have their right and wrong, which need not be in agreement with the others. Besides, our jurisdiction and means of execution are different. We don't beg for an appeal from an outsider. For us, our gram sabha is our Supreme Court,' Rupi Murmu had explained to Suchitra.

Suchitra had been to Jharkhand two years back to take pictures for Rupi, who had been researching 'The Other Side of the Great Indian Temples'. Back then, she had clicked many pictures of reservoirs, the debris of Telkupi, the Fort of Panchet, the relics of the Tilkamba dynasty and a sunset overlooking the Panchet Dam.

Rupi was both appreciated and roasted for her research. Her research was based on the Santal villages that were submerged because of the rising of the dam.

It was her dadu, Jagdip Murmu, who had incited her to undertake the research. His village, Bharatpur, was one among the many that were submerged near the valley of River Damodar. There were more than a hundred villages. 'It is not the Damodar but the dam that has drowned the villages,' he had insisted.

'Flood was familiar to us, for it followed every year. The Damodar would race into the houses and settlements and recede just the way it came. But she deposited in our land whatever she brought with her. Between one flood and another, we would farm our areas, grow rice and prepare for the succeeding wave. But with the coming of dams, things changed. The water forced us out forever.'

Rupi Murmu began her research to get to the bottom of her grandfather's story. Nehru was excited about dams as he thought they were the huge structures that would determine the destiny of the nation.

Was there any other place more sacred and sublime than this!

'On the contrary, I ask whether there are any other places more devastating than these,' Rupi's dadu had drawn a ripple of protests. 'I dream of the day when dams will be demolished.'

Rupi knew how awful the tragedy of Jagdip Murmu's life was. It was dense and insistent in the stories he told her when she was a child. She relished the dancing folk of his tales, imagined the lustrous landscape with its forests, mountains, rivers and endless fields, marvelled at the ecosystem where people shared their lives with the departed ones, the Bongas. With great astonishment, she understood the power of fantasy, according to which the dead lived with the living. She walked through the streets of the village cherishing its music, dance, rhythms, paintings and art. She had listened to a melody from a distant flute.

But everything was taken away by the dams, she reflected on her dadu's words.

'Not just Bharatpur, Rupi, your dida's village, Baliyad, sank as well, and the rest of the neighbouring settlements too. Everything is under the water now! The hot springs and temples of Telkupi were no exemption. Everything was destroyed, leaving us homeless!'

But why on earth couldn't we analyse Nehru's words in a different light? What's right? What's wrong? Who is the judge?

The excavations of Nehru's dreams brought out dams, railway lanes, coach factories, steel mills, manure plants, petrochemical units, industries, energy, agriculture . . . and the progress of the nation!

Rupi wanted to shake off the dangerously sentimental influence of her dadu to ensure her research was scientific and unbiased. Nevertheless, she had to face hundreds of people like him, who spoke just the way he did. They came from the slums of the roaring cities, living a life which was not theirs. They were depressed and furious. Their children were unhappy and dissatisfied. In between questions and answers, they drew symbols of unrest on the tree trunks and walls nearby. They seemed defeated thinking of their losses, of how their children had lost the nights where a solitary canoe with its single lantern on the Damodar wafted through the wind that carried the inebriating smell of mahua, the distant star and the saintly silence. Their children were not led by the divine Bongas; they didn't have a *jaher* to go to. And therefore they were bitter and spiteful, their minds never peaceful, their bodies oven-like.

Rupi Murmu wrote: 'They were not fugitives. They were neither Hindus nor Muslims. Nonetheless, their names were registered in the statistics of the victims of Partition. Dams were not even mentioned. They were never labelled as the hundreds of thousands of people from the settlements that got submerged. After which their lives and deaths became the responsibility of no one.'

Rupi's research—the critics opined—brought out barely half the truth, and the other half of her tracks, they said, she had buried away. By amplifying the losses of some of the villages, she had dismissed the winnings of the whole nation.

'I was not writing stories but collecting data,' Rupi retorted. 'And the data I gathered has flesh, blood, marrow and soul.'

Jagdip Murmu hailed from the banks of the river of sadness. At schools, when children are asked to name the river known as the sorrow of Bengal, they jump up from their seats and shout, 'Damodar!'

And though she was not living the life of a Santal, Rupi's roots were buried deep down in the Damodar. She couldn't weigh dams as sacred volumes or massive temples. Joseph Jobon Murmu, Rupi's father, said: 'Today you can think or write the way you want to, but had you been in 1948 or 1949, Rupi, you would be counted as a traitor who was against nation-building.'

Jobon Murmu had been with Jagdip Murmu during the days of hardship and had gone through the same distress. But his dismal thoughts were split into two divisions: 'Before Joseph' and 'After Joseph'.

Jobon Murmu, who had been taught to feel proud of the Bhakra Nangal Dam, had taught the same to his children.

*

The trip to Jharkhand is more compelling this time, Suchitra thought. Except for the assumption that Budhini lived somewhere in Jharkhand, they knew nothing about her house or her address.

Since Mukul Murmu was unavailable on the phone, Rupi began calling her friends in Jharkhand.

'Did someone lead your cousin to believe that she was alive?' Suchitra asked.

'Who is she to youngsters? Fat chance that someone talked of her! What do they know about her! Her life is no big deal for anyone. Budhini Mejhan should rise from the reservoir laden with the mud and stones of history. That's what we have got to do.'

Once they crossed the borders of Kolkata, endless stretches of paddy patches came to view on either side of the national highway.

Those fields, it seemed, would continue seamlessly till the end of the road. Some of the fields were harvested; others unharmed. Dirty-looking people, barely dressed, were working in the fields.

Long rows of palash, sal, banyan, palm, jackfruit and other such trees lined the roads. Goats and buffaloes grazed on the lush meadows, shepherded by children carrying sticks bigger than themselves. Yet, the air was oppressive and the sky overcast. Long before they reached Raniganj, briquettes of coal started appearing on the streets. Entering Raniganj, they saw mountains of coal. Pervasive dust from powdered fuel choked the thick air. Loading coal into sacks, grown-ups, as well as youngsters, tied them to bicycles and forcefully pushed them along. The coal dust was indelible on their skin. It filled their pores, faces and clothes, giving them a shadowy appearance. The trees, too, had given away their green. Even the soil was black.

'Will Budhini Ma be seventy-five now?' Suchitra asked.

'It is said that she married Nehru when she was fifteen,' Rupi answered.

3

A child of fifteen! When she untethered the buffaloes of the kheer vendor, she reminded them:

I wouldn't want you to get into the river today, the current is strong. Ma! Even I had trouble getting out of the water after my bath. Go, go and have your fill on the green grass. Like the miserable Ledda who fled in fear of the tiger, I will wash, wipe and rub the place for you to lie down when you come back.

Scooping up handfuls of droppings and cowpats, she filled a basket.

Aha! Don't forget the case of Ledda who was dear to all the wild buffaloes out there. Poor boy! Running from the tiger that frightened him out of his skin, he took refuge in a hole on a tree. Eventually, he started living with the wild buffaloes. Shouldn't he go back home? Sadder but wiser now, he didn't spare time to ponder over it.

Moreover, it worked for him as long as the tiger didn't pounce at him. He had no bigger fish to fry.

But I tell you, no animal is half so silly as the tiger. It could gobble up Ledda, wild buffaloes and, ha ha, even elephants, but the nitwit was extremely scared of tiny lizards. The small chirping of a lizard would frighten the pee out of it. Terrified, it would act out its dream violently in its sleep and get the forest quaking with a roar. Ah! The lizard is munching on me!

Once, the tiger caught Ledda and said: 'I am going to eat you anyway, hear your bones crunch.'

Ledda begged with a howl of terror: 'Could I do one last thing before you turn me into a proper meal?'

'What's that?'

'Before you gulp me down, I would love to chew on a piece of tobacco stick.'

'My boy! Make it fast!'

Shh! Listen! Buffaloes, as Ledda pounded at the tobacco, the crushed stalks made a sound similar to the clicking of a giant gecko.

'What's that?' the terrified tiger asked.

'It is the lizard that bit the tiger in its sleep,' Ledda answered.

Startled, the tiger ran for its life. As it flew, it yelled out, 'Please don't send it after me.'

Thus, Ledda was free from the monster that wanted to devour him. But he couldn't find a way out of the inner labyrinth of the jungle where the tiger had chased him. Eventually, he ended up in the tree hole near the place where the wild beasts slept at night. He couldn't perceive how the buffaloes managed to sleep in filth like that. Feeling sorry for the animals, he removed the cowpats and manure, dug a tiny trench to drain the urine, fixed a broom of green leaves and mopped the place. Then he retreated into his hole in the tree. Even if the tiger came back, it would not find him. But the buffaloes were startled. Who did this! Ledda didn't come out, nor did he speak. But he did the same thing the next day and on the days that followed. Inquisitive as they were—listen carefully, Buffaloes—the wild buffaloes commissioned a clever cow to monitor the scene.

The clever cow that found Ledda reported that it was a kind human being who lived in a hole in a tree trunk.

The buffaloes went to the hole and bawled in concert: 'Oh, kind-hearted one, please come out.'

They appointed him as their assistant whose job was to clean the pats and pies and scrub and rub their rumps as they bathed in the river. In return, Ledda could taste the milk of every cow in the field and drink the milk of the cow he liked the most.

Ledda, who was tremendously good at his chores, found time to roam around with the buffaloes and play his tiriao that he had made by drilling seven holes in a bamboo stalk.

She dropped the story once she had finished collecting the manure. Laughing and giving her silver ornaments a shake, she fled with her basket as the kheer vendor chased her with a cane.

'Stop, you nasty girl!'

She hopped around his buffaloes without giving him a chance to get to her.

'Come and look at what your girl, this dummy, has done,' the kheer vendor rushed to her house and complained.

'How on earth do you expect me to run my business with the half a litre of milk that I can hardly squeeze out after the calves have had their fill? And, of late, this has become a practice. Why do you torture me like this? The buffaloes have nothing else in their heads these days except running away, snapping the poles and ropes. What can I do? And to top it all, the river acts as a hurricane, only God knows when it is going to wipe everything off! I warn you, if something of the sort would happen, your girl will not be . . .'

The kheer vendor didn't say the rest of it. He was not from the village and had no idea what might provoke them to beat him up. He had had similar experiences before too. But was that an excuse to keep silent?

The girl, who was smart, appeared much more energetic in her own verandah. And she had an audience too!

'You separate the mothers from the calves and keep the poor things tethered all day under the scorching sun. Haven't you seen how, by noon, there is foam coming out of their mouths? But how could you guess? By that time, you are sitting with your head inside the pot of kheer. Kheer Bhaiya, it is not for nothing that they jump into the river without a thought.'

The audience laughed quietly. The girl's family and neighbours were among those who backed her with their laughter. Holding his head with both hands, the kheer vendor sat down, crushed, thinking to himself that maybe he tortured the girl in a past life. What else could explain such animosity?

The girl, meanwhile, accused him of squeezing out even the last drop of milk to make kheer, leaving the calves without their share. She said he made good money by selling kheer to the DVC workers. How else could his wife afford to have a golden nose pin?

'One day I will put mud in your pot of kheer, wait and see,' she threatened him. The audience burst into another round of laughter. Muttering under his breath, the kheer vendor left the place. The girl's mother scolded her and told her not to touch his buffaloes again. But all the neighbours were on her side.

'What's wrong in it, Budhini's ma? He is not a decent man, for we have seen him beating his buffaloes for not giving milk. Sometimes he comes running from the meadow and kicks the buffaloes on their sides. He even hurts them by flinging their tails,' someone said.

'He swears non-stop and spits on the ground,' said Chotroi, a young boy who was remarkably angry.

'The price of his kheer is rising daily. Isn't it unfair?' asked Prasad Hembrom.

Budhini was relieved. She had made no mistake. Her goats were plump and healthy, for they ate all they wanted from the grassland. There was plenty of grass on the riverbank. The kheer vendor should let his buffaloes graze there. Instead, he tethered them to the ground, as he had no time to shepherd them.

It was Budhini who tended her goats in the meadow. Since she had no kheer to sell, she had ample time to attend to them.

Climbing on the branch of a sal tree—it was forbidden for girls to climb trees—she would play her *tiriao*—again, forbidden for girls. If anyone complained, she would have to pay the penalty in the gram sabha, begging for mercy. But how could one resist the desire to climb a sal tree, or deny herself the pleasure of a flute?

The seven-holed tiriao was the flute of the village. Budhini had made hers picturesque using vivid threads, the trimmings of which dangled like the edges of a rainbow. Her goats yielded milk and grazed on the green grass, listening to her play her tiriao.

Sitting on the branch of the sal tree, she gave them instructions: 'And you, come here, mother goat, tend your kid, the grass won't fly away. It will stay there for sure. Don't be selfish. And, kid, don't run into the river for it isn't just another wild river but the Damodar! Ramble only by your mother's nipple. Enough is enough! Now come back, lie down in the shadow and muse on, enjoy the cool breeze that blows from the river to your fill. Look at the sky, how peaceful it looks. Sleep, sleep.'

Her instructions sprung forth through the tiriao. Budhini's goats had studied the language of her flute. They knew they need not be afraid of anything. Budhini was with them. She would take care of everything. But the buffaloes of the kheer vendor were different. An expression of constant fear haunted their eyes, frequently wetted with tears. Had they been in Budhini's care, she would have transmogrified them into a herd of happy animals. They would always smile and entertain no ill feelings about their bodies. She would turn them into perfect dancers by playing her tiriao in their ears. Holding their ears forward, they would absorb the music entirely, provided the kheer vendor did not scream. Budhini thought the buffaloes were more vulnerable than the goats. Their expression was marked with a persistent sadness. When the kheer vendor was not around, she would whisper into their ears, 'Depression is evil. Keep on smiling. Once born, all beings have a right to live.'

It was her young uncle, Kanha Manjhi, who made her aware
of that. He was against the ritualistic sacrifice of roosters and other
animals, which the villagers followed religiously. 'We should stop
this practice,' he said. The whole village had turned against him
except his niece, Budhini. He knew she played the tiriao but
turned a blind eye to the genius he discovered in her.

*

All this had taken place before she started working for the DVC.
Before that, she used to do chores at her own home. She used
to grind rice and ragi using a millstone, light the wood-burning
stove and prepare gruel and spinach. She would slice fish and
clean it. By stringing together leaves of sal tree in patterns, she
would make dishes and spoons and baskets, and by weaving
bamboo leaves, make containers and mats. She would polish the
walls by plastering them with powdered mud and shape cow
dung cakes into perfect rounds, tend a vegetable garden in the
backyard and help her mother distil rice to make *hadiya*. She
would work in the fields where the smell of the newly sowed
water-filled patches of earth excited her. She would tell Mani, a
young boy and her neighbour, how, like tiny green needles, the
tender shoots would come to life over the surface of the water
the following day. Curiously, he would ask, 'Who ate the seeds
that Baba had sowed? Was it the ants or the birds?' He was just
four and didn't know much. Budhini taught him the song of
the crying grain.

The grain of rice cries,
The grain of rice asks,
'When, oh, when is my wedding?'
When the rain falls down from the sky
Comes your wedding day,
Soaking the earth wet and full!

However, Budhini felt no bliss or rapture of a coveted marriage even in monsoon. On the contrary, she grew gloomy and sad whenever the sky was overcast. Some nights she even cried listening to the distant roar of the thunder. Mani, who knew Budhini was wide awake, would not go to sleep either.

'Budhiniji, why do you cry?'

'Mani, can't you see it is raining?'

'Oh!' Opening the door, he would step out on to the verandah. At first there would be a drizzle of some raindrops in the courtyard. Pretty soon, a storm capable of drowning the entire house would follow. Ma and Baba usually slept on the verandah. Sitting on top of a rice sack, Mani would watch the relentless rain.

On such days, Budhini didn't go to the field. She went to the woods with Chotroi Soren. Chotroi was Mani's friend but three or four years older than him. He loved her, perhaps, most of all. He loved her because she knew a lot of stories; in fact, she was a storehouse of stories. No matter how many stories she told, she never ran out of them. She always had one whether you were happy or sad, worried or tensed. Chotroi never got tired of the tale of Inangan who doubled his money. Much too terrified to close their eyes, Chotroi and Mani would sit holding each other tightly when listening to the story of Sivalal Murmu, the *naike* of the village who went to attend a wedding in the neighbouring town. By the time he returned, it was very late. As he walked through the moonlit darkness, he heard a baby wailing somewhere near the creek. The next second, a huge white monster sprang out of the bushes with a piercing screech. It had the shape of a child. Grazing through Sivalal's face, it jumped on to a branch of a tree. Reciting all the hymns and mantras that he knew by heart, Sivalal ran away from there. It was the Sima Bonga who seeded disease and all other troubles in the village.

All the same, while telling the story of the parakeet that had to fly away leaving its milk tree behind, not just Chotroi and Mani, but Budhini too would plunge into despair. The parakeet was living in a mansion with all the comforts. She got everything she desired. But one day she was forced to fly away, leaving everything behind. She flew away in great pain.

Budhini sang:

O, parakeet that flies away,
Kiss the milk tree and fly away!

Budhini's face would fall and her eyes would well up.

'Ji, why does the bird fly away if it is so sad?' Chotroi would ask.

'The parakeet is a woman, Chotroi,' Budhini would answer sadly.

4

Her hands were flushed with blisters on the first day that she went to work at the DVC. By twilight, large bubbles appeared on her palms, leaving her with a burning sensation. The liquid inside them tingled and itched until the following morning. Eventually, the abscesses ruptured and discharged a pus-like fluid and blood, blackening the handle grip of the hammer. The stone dust accumulated between her palm and the handle of the hammer penetrated her flesh, causing unbearable pain. The wounds finally healed but left behind calluses. Budhini resented breaking stones.

From morning to evening, it was just stones, her hands and a hammer. The stones sometimes emitted fire and sometimes blood, but never a god or a piece of poetry or a figurine. Sitting in rows with their heads down, many people, like Budhini, particularly children, pounded away at the rocks, reducing them into gravel-sized chunks. The contractors taking rounds would not permit them to raise their heads. Even when they did lift their faces, there was nothing to look at but the masses of pounded stones stretching towards the sky. All this while, grit collected in the pores of their faces, in their hair, in their clothes and even on their eyelashes.

The wind was grey, as was the sky, earth, trees, flowers and grass: grey birds, grey butterflies—a world of volcanic ash!

Deafening roars that perpetually girded the surroundings were unusual for Budhini. Karbona, her village, had been a lake of silence! At times a stone or fruit, or a flower, may fall into it, but mostly the undertones of bouncing fish or hopping frogs dominated the air. The bleating of goats, the short grunts of buffaloes, the barking of dogs, the squeal of pigs and the crowing of roosters contributed to the louder sounds.

The vibrations familiar to Budhini's ears were the snapping of firewood on the stove in the courtyard, the rumbling of the millstones, the clanging of *lotta*, *batti*, *kanda* and other dishes, the plop-plop of dough being kneaded, the waa-waa of Aunt Phulmone's baby. With the day coming to an end, these noises dissolved in the darkness. The darkness was for the Bongas. The hour of the dead souls! Silence!

However, the night, too, possessed delightful resonances. Out of the blue someone would play on his pipe, accompanied by the beats of distant *tamak*s. The *banam* player would find no rest either. With her heart on fire, feet growing wings, Budhini would come to the street. From the sinews of the banam a pleasingly painful melody would be flowing through the streets. By then, the dancers would have started taking steps. Deep down, they would be singing a song whose lyrics dribbled honey.

Ten drums,
Twenty young girls,
Endless, the dancing ground!
Hey drummer, don't stir me up.
And if you do, I will make you swig,
A river in a mouthful.

Reflecting on the ambiguity of the song, Budhini smiled and then felt regret the next second. Even the voice of the person sitting next to her was not audible as they pounded the stones. The boom-boom of the rocks didn't leave the ears even after one was home. Low voices stopped reaching the ears.

No longer could she hear the jingling of the tiny beads in the anklet as her mother walked around, or the goat-like grunts her aunt's baby used to make when it was suckling at its mother's breasts. She missed the minor explosions of Baba's farts as he slept on his side on the charpoy. She couldn't hear Mani making sounds at the back of his throat after tasting the spicy red ant chutney, or the kisses, like squirrels chirping, Phulmone and Shopon shared on the verandah where they cuddled each night. In the core of her ears, rocks bumped on rocks, hammers hit stones.

All the same, she could hear the unsettling beatings of the heart of rocks shortly before a hammer fell. While the earth was cold, the boulders awaited her with heat in their innards.

'Girl, where were you?' Baba asked.

'Girl, where were you?' Ma asked.

'When the earth was cold, Baba, I savoured the warmth from the bosom of the rocks. I took no count of time, nor knew that it was dark.'

'She is fifteen,' Ma said.

'Still a child,' Baba said.

'Ma, I swiftly jumped across the slimy smoothness the rain had caused by caressing the boulders. Crossing over the wild creek, on the byway, I stood under the shadow of the sal tree and turned back. Amongst the enormous trees by the water reserves, the eternally wet rocks hibernate under the moss green blanket. Ma, I saw them at the end of the road: a group of people, both men and women. They came to the woods to collect mahua leaves and were inebriated after chewing on them. Cracking jokes, laughing aloud, they kissed and caressed each other, and the sounds they made as they petted each other resembled the chirping of lizards. No sooner had they seen me, than they burst into a song.'

Girl, come,
Fill up the heart of the row.
No, no! I will not!

Milk tree, my ma,
Will scold me.
Baba tree, my ba,
Will taunt me.
Deadly flower, my bhaiya,
Will thrash me.

Before she started working for the DVC, Budhini used to frequent
the woods. 'Baba, may I go to the forest to pluck leaves?'

Baba and Ma would say in concert, 'Girl, not now. It's time
to pick the lesser yam. We could go together to collect firewood
and wild spinach. Now we are going to work. Today is payday,
and we are off to work. In the evening, we could go to Chirkunda
to buy salt and pepper and dal. Your aunty no longer uses mud to
wash her hair; she uses soaps these days, for Shopon has taught her
bad habits. We should buy her a soap today, and kerosene for the
lamp.'

The more she walked ahead, the more the forest called her
back, tempting her with promises of new scents and mumbles.
Come, the moisture is new. Budhini longed for the woods.
But if she chose to go, she must get lost, for getting lost is
like unveiling new paths to new timber. Which route is right,
and which wood? Each slip-up got her to panic, made her
anxious—to live or to die! However, she savoured the alarm
that accelerated her heart rate. If she chose to go into the jungle,
she would have to face the fearsome tiger, the sight of which
would make blood clot. Then she would get away without
becoming the prey. In the jungle, she would like to catch a
snake from its hole, and hunt down a wild rabbit, a wild rooster
and a giant squirrel. Now and then, a crust from the mound of
white ants could be detached, or her arrow could chase a sambar
deer down. She would enter the woods carrying a load on her
back, one that was unbearably heavy. There would be plenty of
wildflowers tucked into her hair.

She fancied the game of tossing the fiery red flowers of palash into the wild river, losing track chasing after them and finding the trail afresh, and eventually getting into the woods.

'Baba, let's go to the woods.'

'But, girl, where are the woods?'

The *gormen* took the woods and farms and walled up the river. They said they would give dams instead. Dams benefit not just one or ten villages but hundreds and thousands of communities.

What was the catch? All the villagers had farms near the river. Besides, they engaged in communal farming. There was fish in the river. There were stalks, roots and fruits in the forest. Now, there was nothing. The dam was rising. By the shores, the singers sang of losses:

Me,
A singer, angler, grower,
Oarsman, huntsman, drummer,
Oh, Sephali Haram Budhi,
They took away my song,
My fishing line, my little canoe,
Dhak and dhamak, arrow and bow.
'Go to Manjithan'
Grandam Sephali told me,
'Pick up the bow of Haram Bonga.'

Me,
In Manjithan.
Bowed to Haram Bonga,
Took his bow and arrow.
Ba,
In the woods of sal trees, they checked me.
I checked them from the massacre of trees.
There was no time for bow and arrow.

Ma,
They had guns with them.
Their fingers were white as white.

That was a tough time. They had seen nothing like this before. What would they do now? The people of Karbona were clueless.

Raghunath Haram, the oldest man in the village—a hundred and ten years old—pointed out: 'Take a close look, the forest walks away.'

All of them saw it. Each day, by daybreak, the woods seemed to have marched some miles away. Earlier, the forest was straight across the fields. Later, a view became possible only from the lower dale. And then the forest was seen climbing up the hill. It seemed like the woods had settled on the summit for a while.

And then the forest started climbing down. The blue curtain that had been draped over the village was folded and set aside, leaving Karbona naked.

Each tree and offshoot was the home of the Bongas. Karbona was a double world that bore both the dead and the living. Both the worlds were equal. Both demanded shade and shadow. But presently, in the unbearable light, in the open expanse, the Bongas were getting restless. They were angry. Soon, their wrath would seal Karbona's doom.

The villagers planted new saplings for the Bongas to rest. They pleaded to the Bongas to dwell inside the tiny plants and remain composed. They continued doing this till the gormen appeared to expel them.

'This land belongs to the sarkar. Planting trees here is transgression,' they said.

If you tell the gormen that the world of Bongas needs coolness and shade, and that they dwell inside the water, on the trees and in the folds of the ridges, they will not understand. All they know is that the land belongs to the sarkar.

Hundred-and-two-year-old Dhurgi Haram Budhi, the wife of Raghunath Haram, complained: 'The mountains of Marang Buru are burning.'

Shielding her eyes with her wizened hand, she intently looked up at the sky. 'My head breaks apart in the heat. Such scorching heat is new to Karbona.'

Her daughter-in-law, Hira, agreed saying, 'By all means, Ma, when you brought me to this village, it was closed off on all sides by a lush jungle. The sun reached as a guest once in a blue moon. Sometimes, the trees touched the skies.'

Feeding his child gruel, Hira's son came to the courtyard.

'Trees are now floating down the river, Dadiya. They are on their way to board a ship headed overseas,' he said.

'What's that for, Sidho?' his mother asked.

'What's there to know, Ma? The white folk will make grand wooden cots. And their houses, bigger than forests, will smell of sandalwood.'

After the woods, it was the fields. The government officials summoned the villagers.

'Don't you know the fields belong to the sarkar? Water needs to occupy space once the dam rises. So this time you are not supposed to farm here,' they said. That was a strict order and the beginning of all their distress. Budhini was then a child of four or five. What had caused the entire village to suffer like this?

Everything began with the death of Lokhon, the son of Dasarath Hembrom, said the villagers. A rumour swept over the village like a cyclone of hushed whispers. A mere child of eight years, he caved in on the grazing ground of the goats. He didn't open his eyes or speak a word! Upon the charred grasses under the midday sun, he lay on his side surrounded by his goats. Despite the herbs applied by the village doctor, Lokhon didn't open his eyes. On the fourth day, the child passed away. His mother was pregnant. The baby was due in a few days.

It was Dasarath's niece, Ramdhuni, who attended to Lokhon when he was nearing his end. Through her loud, uncontrollable tears, Dasarath's wife screamed, 'Ramdhuni! Ramdhuni is the cause.'

Her eyes resembled those of an owl as she screamed. Ramdhuni, who couldn't resist peeping in from her room, retracted her head at once.

5

Budhini was terrified to hear Ma talk to Baba about Ramdhuni. She overheard their conversation and couldn't get any sleep. Tearing apart Lokhon's chest, Ramdhuni had taken his liver out and eaten it. It happened on the day before he fell.

'Don't you dare talk without evidence, Budhini's ma? Hold your tongue, no rubbish,' Budhini's baba said.

'Why does she regularly roam around with Sarodha Baski?' Ma asked. Baba didn't reply.

'Are you sleeping, Budhini's baba?'Ma asked. Again, there was no response.

'Yo,' Budhini nudged her mother. 'I am scared, yo.'

Baba once again scolded Ma for talking nonsense in the presence of the child. Then he hugged and consoled Budhini and put her to sleep by telling stories. However, when Baba was not around, Ma exchanged hushed rumours about Ramdhuni and Sarodha Baski with the women of the neighbourhood, again in the presence of Budhini. Horrified, Budhini listened to the whole story starting with Lokhon's mother's labour pains that began at two in the morning.

Lokhon's mother woke up with severe cramps. She had entered the ninth month. Thinking it was the beginning of labour pains, she stirred Lokhon's baba from his sleep. Tanked up on the hard drink of mahua, Dasarath Hembrom was not to be woken.

She sensed an urge to relieve herself. Lokhon was sleeping on a cot on the verandah outside. At the *bither*, where the ancestor Bongas of Jagdip's family line resided and over which the fragile flame of a mud lamp burnt incessantly, she lit a lamp from the burning oil lantern and walked towards her son who was snoring out of fatigue. He, too, did not stir. Ramdhuni slept in a room that was on the other side of the central courtyard. Usually, she latched her door from the inside. Lokhon's mother knew that by the time she reached Ramdhuni's door, she would lose control over her bowels.

She also knew that it was dangerous for a heavily pregnant woman to step out into the yard at that hour. Since she couldn't hold back another second, she opened the back door and stepped outside. Squatting in the centre of the vegetable garden, she peed. A little later, she bellowed in relief of her bowels being emptied. That was when she noticed something moving under the fig tree on the other end of the garden. Her lamp went off just then, as if someone had blown it out. Frightened, she continued to sit in that posture. Then, under the moonlight, unable to contain her curiosity, she crawled towards the pigsty to see who it was and what he was doing there at this time. There was not one but two people under the fig tree. Two women! Sitting with their heads stooped, they were devouring something. The intense smell of cooked meat was spreading loose. Lokhon's mother wanted to throw up at once. Involuntarily, her hands clutched her swollen belly. She leaned against the pigsty so that she would not fall. She heard the pigs grunting and snorting. With a loud clang, a tin can dropped to the ground. The women jumped, surveying the surroundings in alarm. Lokhon's mother could not believe what she saw! Those women were completely naked. And one of them was Ramdhuni, with a stick broom tied to her waist!

Lokhon's mother had no idea how she got inside her house without tumbling. Slapping and kicking, she woke Lokhon's baba up from his sleep.

'Ramdhuni . . . Ramdhuni . . .' she kept repeating mechanically.

'What happened to Ramdhuni?' her husband, still half-asleep, asked. He felt his wife trembling like dry banana leaves caught in the wind. She was pointing towards Ramdhuni's door, her pupils dilated in fear, her body sweating profusely. Lokhon's baba knocked at Ramdhuni's door. Drowsily, she opened the door.

'What's happening, Mamo? Has Bavuji got her birth pangs?' Tying her hair up, she followed her uncle. But the moment Lokhon's mother spotted her, she fell unconscious. Lokhon's mother was not willing to consider that the woman she saw under the fig tree was not Ramdhuni. She didn't let Ramdhuni touch her belly.

'What did I do?' Ramdhuni said dejectedly.

The following day, Lokhon was benumbed. Rumours about Ramdhuni rocked the village. After all, why should Lokhon's mother tell a lie? Ramdhuni worshipped Sima Bongas!

The Sima Bongas were not like the other Bongas who guarded the people and their land. They were incessantly restless and furious. Since they were the Bongas of the margins, they could not enter the village to cause harm. Marang Buru and the other Bongas would have expelled them much before that. Therefore, the Sima Bongas needed to enter the body of someone from the village to breed evil. They bestowed demonic powers and prosperity to those who worshipped them, making them wealthy and unbeatable. Once a person started worshipping a Sima Bonga, he was never able to escape the cult that would mark his doom. But why on earth did Ramdhuni ferry such a disaster into her life? Was it because she was a widow who, after the loss of her spouse, was utterly alone? Was she envious of her Mamo's family, Lokhon's mother in particular? Lokhon's mother was beautiful, and so were her children. Ramdhuni thought her Mamo was just a puppet revolving around them, while his estate was under the control of his woman. If Ramdhuni wanted to continue with them, she should work hard to earn her living. Her aunt made her do all the work.

Ramdhuni, who had lost her mother at a young age, was obliged to go to her uncle's house when her father married again. Those days she had her Dadiya who seconded her always. After her death, life became a constant trek over virgin thorns for Ramdhuni. Fate! Why else should her man leave her so early? There was no one to listen to her woes. It is easy to hook on to such lonely people, the villagers believed. It was said that Ramdhuni met Sarodha Baski by the river. Like moss, Sarodha's hair was spread out to float over the moving current.

'Ramdhuni,' she called in a melodious voice. Her eyes were green. Her body seemed sculpted. Ramdhuni could neither raise her voice nor breathe. She knew Sarodha Baski. No one in the village invited her to their house. They thought she was an enchantress who would manipulate their men.

Sarodha listened to Ramdhuni's sorrows and consoled her by petting her back and caressing her. The moment Sarodha's nipples brushed against her face, Ramdhuni sensed a sea of heat unbridling. With a tantalising discomfort between her thighs, she lay down on Sarodha's lap. Meek yet cold, like a slimy reptile, Sarodha's fingers slithered down her neckline towards the small of her back. Slowly, Ramdhuni caved in.

'Don't look at Ramdhuni, don't go anywhere near her or eat anything she may offer. She craves for children. She sings, tells stories and sits by your side. Don't ever listen to her. Come running home.' This was what mothers told their children.

What had caused the death of a child in the village? The heads of the gram sabha addressed the issue. There was no apparent reason for death or sickness to tour their house. After all, the word 'Santal' meant the tranquil soul. Why would infirmities visit those who lived happily and composedly? Why on earth should they die? The unfortunate souls had perceived an opportunity to meddle with their lives. But how? Ramay Haram, the *oja* and physician of the village, the one who drove the evil Bongas away, was called to find the reason and remedy it.

'Call the oja,' the chieftain ordered.

Lokhon's death had made the villagers anxious and apprehensive. Evil deeds might happen again. By then, all of them had surmised the cause to be Ramdhuni. With Ramay Haram's consent, she was to be brought in front of the village assembly. They were concerned about barging into the funeral home and dragging her out of it. If Dasarath Hembrom tried to protect her, he would be punished as well. They were sure that the ever-sore, ever-deadly Sima Bonga was accountable for the child's death. Though they didn't mention the names of Sarodha Baski and Ramdhuni openly, they all waited for Ramay Haram's verdict. Another death couldn't be permitted. Ramay worshipped the fieriest element, which was dynamic enough to chase any enemy Bonga away. Once they had his consent, they would butcher Ramdhuni to pieces. They no longer wanted the person who offered Lokhon's liver to the Bongas in their village.

Death is filth. Death defiled the entire village, let alone the house of Dasarath Hembrom. The primary commitment of a Santal was to live. Death was always an escape from the promise. No Santal would deliberately disown his life. However, the evil eye of the vicious Bongas relentlessly pursued the Santals and their village. At the first chance, they entered, annihilated and contaminated.

Lokhon was no longer a human being. Soon, he would become a Bonga by embracing their world. He needed a proper burial, following all Santal rites, to make his journey pleasant. Things dirtied by death had to be canonized. The wrath of the Bongas needed to be allayed.

Budhini went to the funeral home with her mother. She put the brass lotta she was carrying on Lokhon's bed. There were other things that had to be sent with Lokhon's body. A pair of clothes, a little flute, a bowl from which he used to have ragi, a slingshot and stones, among other things. Lokhon's baba, Dasarath Hembrom, tied some coins in a piece of garb with a hank string and laid it near Lokhon's right hand, like a cinch to use. Someone was singing.

No cry, no mourn, Moni,
Under the roof,
A houseful of children.
Behold them, stamp out the pain.
How could I forage
The daily bread!
River surges.
How could I cross the river?
How shall I overcome?
River overflows.
No cry, no mourn, Moni.
No bitter rue in excess.
The generous sun
Guards you.

Budhini had heard this song before. She, too, had danced to its melancholic tune with the other dancers. But now, with Lokhon dead, she felt her little heart split because of the same music. The burden that sank like a stone in her bosom was more than what a child could bear. And it refused to budge from there. She hadn't regarded Lokhon highly when he was alive. Now she felt he was a beautiful darling with black curly hair. His lips formed a childish pout, as if he was playing his tiriao. But his face seemed pale without a trace of blood, and there was a blue tinge on his lips. Her mother and the neighbourhood women said that these were the signs of his liver being drilled out by Ramdhuni. Besides, those who had washed his body had spotted a small hole between his chest and stomach. Such a death doubled her anguish. The loss she had seen before this was that of her dadiya. Dadiya had been making plates from the leaves of the sal tree when she had leaned against the mound of paddy straw and died as if she were sleeping, leaving no blow of death on Budhini.

Lokhon was buried on the edge of a pond near Dasarath Hembrom's lands. Though troubled, the villagers returned to their lives after the funeral rites, paying penalties and cleansing. It didn't take much time to realize that what they had encountered with the loss of Lokhon was nothing but the brink of a breakdown.

How were they to continue if they could not farm their lands, as per the government order? The forest, too, was far away. Could a village survive by selling plates made of sal leaves alone? Karbona was moving towards an impediment it had not known before. Moreover, the news of some communities sinking with the rising of the Panchet Dam had led to more panic. Many of the towns in Telkupi were already under the water, their people now on the move, abandoning everything they had. The family of Tapan Kisku had already deserted Karbona. They used to make a living by selling baskets and other utensils that they made using reeds and bamboo collected from the forest.

> Milk tree didn't yield,
> Nor did the black cow,
> Weep not child.
> Strain of a flute from distant plains,
> Tomorrow, at the rise of the sun
> Over the heights of Marang Buru,
> My parakeet would fly back,
> A fig in its beak.

The women of the village sang as they rocked their babies to sleep. Budhini was hungry too. She wandered through the streets aimlessly. But when she reached Ramdhuni's house, she ran for her life.

The first hunger death of the village was that of hundred-and-ten-year-old Raghunath Haram's. As he closed his eyes, he cried, 'Damaadi, damaadi.' By the time a batti of rice water reached from the house of the chieftain, the man had shut his mouth.

'Damaadi, Raghunath Haram, damaadi. Open your mouth, have some.' Rice water dribbled out of the corners of his mouth.

'Don't give him any more,' Dhurgi Haram Budhi said. She grabbed the brass batti with her shivering hands, gulped the liquid down and returned the batti. Naturally, the second victim of hunger death in the village was Dhurgi Haram Budhi, who was a hundred and two years old. This time, the oja said in anger, 'Ramdhuni is the cause of every ignominy.'

That same day, violence broke out in two homes: the house of Dasarath Hembrom and the house of Sarodha Baski, which was at the tail end of the village. Sarodha Baski was having rice water when a mob forced its way into her home. They assaulted her, stripped her naked and chopped her hair. They tossed her bloodied body on the street. Swearing, spitting and throwing stones at her, they made their way to Dasarath Hembrom's house to get Ramdhuni. Sarodha Baski had no one to support her. However, Dasarath Hembrom couldn't stand watching Ramdhuni being attacked. When he tried to resist, they thwacked him too. Carrying the newborn, his wife escaped through the rear exit of the house.

When Sarodha and Ramdhuni ran away from the village, the villagers believed that the vengeance of the enemy Bongas would double. The oja felt that the Bongas who dwelled within the water, trees, rocks, fields and roofs of the village were losing strength. To make them stronger, they slaughtered animals, and on the days of such offerings, they fed on the meat of the sacrificed to keep themselves alive.

Suvir Datta came to the village to take stock of the hunger deaths in Karbona. Unfortunately, the gram sabha was not willing to share this information with a *diku*, a stranger.

'Manji, may I know what is happening here? Are you all planning to die of hunger?' he asked.

The chieftain ignored him and looked in the opposite direction.

'If this continues, people outside will have to hear the most unfortunate news. There is no need for all this. Listen to me. The death of someone who was a hundred and ten years old is not unusual. But have you noticed how frail the children in your village look with their bloated bellies, exposed rib cages, sunken eyes and swollen legs? This is terrifying. These children can't fight off disease, just in case. The state of the mothers is even worse.'

Listening to Suvir Datta talk about the children, the villagers looked dismayed.

'When was it that you had some rice water, Sephali granny?' he asked.

Taking her hand, he felt her pulse. Looking into her crusty eyes, which had lost their shine, he spoke sternly to the manji. 'Things are not the same as before. Do you think we can continue to survive on the woods, farming and hunting? Keep up with the times. Listen to what I tell you. Find some other way to make a living.'

The gram sabha was startled. Suvir Datta had come to capture the farmers who toiled away on their own land, to take them away as slaves. Five or eight of them ran away on the spot. The manji and jog manji exchanged glances; their eyes conveyed something enigmatic.

Suvir Datta continued: 'Hands are needed at the construction site of the Panchet Dam. If you work there, you will get daily wages. Don't you think you can buy something and eat when you have money?'

Taking turns, he looked at those who gathered. Oddballs! They remained seated with their heads down. The jog manji stood up. 'You are DVC's man, Suvir Datta, I know. You talk on their behalf.'

'Who told you this? It is true I work there, but that doesn't mean I can't have sympathy for you. I have suggested an easy way out of this, one off the top of my head.'

'It is the DVC that comes off the top of his head,' the jog manji said. Suvir Datta remained composed.

'I was just showing you a door, think well.' With this, Suvir Datta got up to go.

'It is no good building a dam across the river, Suvir Da. Water is *aadi bhoota*. The flow should not be hindered,' the naike said.

Though he was ready to leave, Suvir Datta continued speaking to clarify things in a better way. 'Indeed, water is a deity, Naike. I also understand that. But there are places in our country where that goddess is reluctant to enter. Do you realize that? Crops dry up there without a speck of water. And here? Here, the Damodar overflows to spread havoc. Jog Manji, there are farmers like you in those places. What else could they do but lament about their parched patches of land? Brothers, dams are not as bad as you think. It is because you don't know about them. The government is thinking of transporting some water, the excess of water that affects you every year, through canals and ditches to those dried-up fields. If we can send out the excess water from the Damodar through waterways, it will benefit both of you. Not just that! Think of electricity. Aren't you living in darkness? Won't you appreciate it if power comes to your village? Will you feel sad when light as white as milk fills up the insides of your homes? Think well. Think how it will be when you enjoy electric views and a loudspeaker for Karma pooja? The street lights will change the face of the night in the villages. Listen, Jog Manji, we could milk current from the water if we can check and tame the river that runs shouting, "Touch me if you dare." Will your Bongas stop us from doing good deeds? They covet the wellness of the village, and so does the DVC. Once the dam is built, the DVC will provide you with electricity for free.'

Looking at the people who were still hunkered down, Suvir Datta said, 'Well, I don't have anything more to say.' And then he walked away.

How could they trust a diku? Their concern was definite. Outsiders did try to capture them, subjecting them to slavery against their will.

'I think we should go to work at the dam. It is better than starving to death,' a young man stood up and spoke.

'We also think the same.' A couple of other youngsters seconded him.

These comments outlined a commotion in the gram sabha. Their faith and fear were solid, but their hunger was even greater. They didn't wish to be victims of the wrath of the mountains, forests and the Bongas. Budhini's uncle Tilka Manjhi was entirely against the concept of dams. 'We should not forget how Viswanath Hasda and his people had warned us about the dangers of reservoirs long ago,' he said.

It was the white men who had first suggested building dams on the Damodar. No sooner had they planned it, than the protests had mounted. For them, it would never be an easy task, Viswanath Hasda had said. He had many people to back him from different communities. It was the villagers who dreaded the dam, who thought of them as dangerous.

'No matter how hard you try, the Damodar will not be tamed. It will get back at you,' Hasda had said. Once the white folk retreated, he thought, their designs, too, would follow them. He was fortunate. He didn't have to witness his own people going to work on the dam after all these years.

'We are not to forget what Viswanath Hasda has taught us. Time is not old enough to ignore his sacrifice,' Kanha Manjhi reminded everyone.

'Firstly, let us fight for our lives, Kanha. Should more children be dying?' the manji asked calmly.

'We are thinking of working on the dam because of our helplessness, not because of our will. Don't you realize that? Can we cheat on aadi bhoota and *Bosumatha*? I don't see anyone from outside willing to feed our children at least once a day. It's we who should save them.'

Kanha Manjhi didn't say anything after that. What the villagers said was right too. The condition of the children was pitiful.

The gram sabha dispersed after taking the decision to let all skilled workers work at the dam.

Budhini's baba was among the first lot of the labourers. On the day that he got his first earnings, he bought home rice, dal and mustard oil.

'I couldn't believe we had to pay for rice! My hands trembled, Budhini's ma,' Baba said.

If Budhini's ma could also join him in work, they would be able to buy many more things, he said. When both her father and mother went to work, Budhini babysat the younger children, grew vegetables in the backyard, tended the pigs and chickens, led the goats out to graze, cooked rice, gathered firewood, prepared cowpat cakes, kneaded mud to polish the walls, tidied up the courtyard several times, washed clothes . . .

The daily wages remodelled the lifestyle of the villagers. They no longer needed to forage in the woods or toil in the farms for food. Money could buy anything. Since there were no village shops in the community, they used to carry their goods—whatever they collected from the woods, farms and vegetable gardens— to the open market outside their village, which was run by the Hindus and Muslims. Now, once a week, they visited Asansol or Chirkunda to tour the shops and purchase essentials.

Most of them were eager to buy things they hadn't used before. Instead of brass lottas, steel glasses flashing like silver soon became common in their homes. Guests were now welcomed with a steel glass of water. Some of the women considered their vanity uplifted when they bowed before their guests and placed a steel dish of water at their feet. Instead of hadiya, some people brought to the village bottled liquid from Chirkunda. The new drink was much stronger and those who devoured it behaved like total maniacs.

A yen for sweetmeats and snacks—not made in the village kitchen—was also on the rise. Samosas from Asansol reached Budhini's house too. It was Shopon, her aunt's husband, who brought samosas home for the first time. The samosas were different from the homemade meat jalpitas, which were basically meat-filled balls of dough wrapped in sal leaves and roasted on embers. Shopon said the samosas were potato-stuffed and deep-fried. Though they lacked the tempting smell of sal leaves, they were spicier and had a much better colour. And once you started, you couldn't just stop eating.

Except for special occasions, Budhini's aunt stopped wearing the *panchi* and *parhan*. Soft saris with polka dots and floral prints substituted the traditional costumes with checks and borders. The new material was synthetic silk, which glistened at every move. It embarrassed Ma and Baba when they saw Budhini's aunt in a sari for the first time. However, Shopon was extremely pleased. 'Phulmone, how beautiful you look! Just like the woman in the cinema I saw in the city,' he said.

Acting cocky, Shopon walked with her through the streets of Karbona. From almost all the houses, women stepped out to witness the show. Nobody seemed happy. New trends, they believed, were warnings of approaching troubles.

'Get inside!' mothers shouted at their girls or the wives of their sons.

'What is there to see with a gaping jaw? Go, go, thousands of chores wait inside.'

The next time they saw Shopon riding with her on a bicycle. She was sounding the bell to shoo away pigs, chickens and kids.

'How arrogant is she! She does not wear mud bangles. Isn't it mandatory for a married woman to wear the *hasa-sakam*? Look at my daughter-in-law, Thini. How painstakingly she keeps her bangles from breaking.' With hushed laughter, the other women listened to Thini's mother-in-law praising her. What had happened to this woman who always found faults with her daughter-in-law?

Phulmone, meanwhile, had no regard for mud bangles.

'Oye, Budhini, what is this? This hasa-sakam? How can I walk around freely wearing bangles that break just like that? Is this a punishment for getting married? Besides, they always get me worried that my child's baba will fly away. Why should I wear them to have them crushed, just in case it happens? How sad that will be! Shopon has told me not to wear them if I don't want to. He said he will bring glass bangles from Kolkata, the ones that have colourful beads and tiny bits of mirrors glued on to them,' she would tell Budhini. In a box she had kept some hasa-sakams big enough to slip on and remove easily. She wore these bangles only to flaunt in front of Shopon's family.

Shopon had bought Phulmone a silver *phuli* from Kolkata. No one in the village owned such a beautiful nose pin, one that sparkled with every turn of the head. A firefly flew from her nose tip whenever she moved, sneezed or laughed. Shopon's lemon-coloured synthetic shirt was also from Kolkata.

One day, Shopon bought Budhini a brass *baju* that glittered like real gold to tie around her arm. Phulmone's baju was silver, yet she sang an ambiguous song to taunt Budhini.

> Of the riverside afar,
> Beneath the sal tree,
> Flows in the melodies of a flute
> Oh! How I fancy swaying,
> Caught in the swirl of measure.
> Chiyo, chiyo, wayward lad,
> Chiyo, chiyo, wanton lass,
> The flute player is your kin,
> Oh! Please don't forget that!

Phulmone sang this song as she rocked her baby in the cradle. Immediately after listening to her song, Budhini's ma seized her baju and locked it away in a chest.

'Wait till your marriage, Budhini. I will give it back to you then,' her mother said and told her not to accept any more gifts from Shopon.

'He is your aunt's husband.'

'What of it?'

'Can't you see that Phulmone doesn't like it?'

Budhini didn't understand that. 'I want it. Get it back to me.'

'I will get you one, but not this.'

'When?'

'When I get my wages.'

Finally, Budhini joined the DVC to earn her own wages, at the age of thirteen.

6

It could not be said that Rupi Murmu was living the life of a Santal. She was born and brought up in Delhi. Her baba, Joseph Jobon Murmu, was a railway officer who was routinely transferred. These frequent transfers were traumatic for his daughters Rupi and Anandi. Broken and resewn, their education limped slowly through the years. Often, provincial languages bothered them. By the time they learned the basics of a one-horse town, he would be shifted to another one. Somehow, before the girls entered college, he managed to build a modest house in Delhi. The children spoke Hindi and English, and their mother, Salni Murmu, spoke Bangla and Santali. Jobon insisted that his children speak only in English. However, Rupi's dadu, Jagdip Murmu, emphasized they all talk in Santali at home. Even unintentionally if the children said something in English, the older man would interject: 'Why speak in the language of the white devil? Is it such a matter of pride for you girls?'

'What's there to get so emotional about, Baba?' Jobon would ask. 'Can't you see how times have changed? Even I speak mostly in English. I seldom get a chance to talk in Hindi, let alone Santali.'

'Buy why *Ingiris* at home?'

He never agreed to call a lotta a glass. 'Lotta. Call it lotta, Anandi.'

For the children, it was fun.

'Yo, give me a lotta of water, yo.' They would call out to their mother mockingly.

Jagdip Murmu would pull a long face. Salni understood his feelings well.

'What your dadu said is right. Make a habit of talking in your mother tongue. As the proverb goes, one word for a million Santals. Do you know that?'

Though the phrase she used was unseemly, Jagdip Murmu was proud of his bahu. She was the only one who reminded him of his village these days. Like Santali women, she draped herself in a panchi and parhan at home. She wore mud bangles on her left wrist. It welled up the old man's eyes to see his bahu wear mud bangles amid the fashionable amusements of city life. Even in the villages, women had given up hasa-sakam. They wore silver or gold bangles these days. Sometimes, memories took over him, especially on the days he saw her wearing her hair in a bun with yellow *genda* flowers decorating the sides and the *danda jhumka* hanging down from her waist. His wife's danda jhumka was the last ornament he had traded. He had sold it to buy train tickets. He had bought them for her during a massive seasonal harvest, from a jeweller in Chirkunda.

My father-in-law has suffered a lot, Salni used to cry listening to his stories. Hours later, she would sob in bed, remembering the past. Once Jobon went to work, the children to school and she had finished her work around the house, she would come with a winnowing sieve, with spinach or some other vegetable in it, and sit by his side.

'Tell me your stories, Sosur,' she would say to her father-in-law.

'It is full of sorrows, Bahu. Why do you want to hear it again?'

'Your stories ring a bell. I remember my village where I lived until I turned twelve. My baba went to the fields with his buffaloes, and Ma sang sweetly as she ground rice in the millstone.

Your stories bring back to my ears the sweet note from the bamboo stalk that has seven eyes on it, and reminds me of the massive tree with silver limbs and small fruits.'

She would talk with her eyes fixed on the sieve. Her voice was low and sweet. Her fingers always worked like a machine. Either they plucked the moringa leaves or peeled the onions or something of that sort.

'Tell me more about your village, Bahu.'

'It was in the midst of the mountains, under the blue shadow. My village looked like rows of grass baskets turned upside down beneath the shade of gigantic trees. The young bard of our community used to sing for me:

Give the glad eye,
Oh, delightful miss.
A peacock on my rooftop.
Flying low, it perches on my roof.
I will fly it,
Adorn its wings in vermilion.
Down dale, beneath the sal tree
The flute lets out its strain.

I left my village when I was twelve. It was the time of a famine, Sosur. Ma took me to a convent of sisters in the town. After that, I never saw my mother or my village. I heard my baba left my ma and married some other woman. I don't know if it is true. Then your son married me, and for that I am heavily indebted to you.'

*

One day, inside the convent kitchen, Jagdip Murmu spotted a girl wearing yellow genda flowers close to her ears. Exhausted after cleaning up the yard, he came to the kitchen to ask for a bowl of rice water. The girl came outside with a big pot.

'Damaadi,' she said aloud. He was startled to hear Santali instead of Hindi. Smiling bashfully, the girl went inside. Later one day, he asked her name. By then, Salni Murmu had been baptized as Mary Salni. She frequented the church and had learnt the catechism.

Joseph wanted an educated girl with a government job. Yet, unable to counter his father's insistence, he decided to pay her a visit one day. At first sight, his conceptions were shattered. The nuns said to him, 'Give her life, Jobon. There will be a lot of people willing to marry young and educated working girls. But Mary's life will end up inside the convent kitchen, waste away to nothing.'

Jagdip Murmu never called his bahu Mary. She was Salni Murmu, a perfect Santal. You won't believe how the old man had travelled all the way to a Santal pargana to get her a pair of hasa-sakam! But there, he was told that mud bangles were becoming a rarity. Women wore other kinds of bangles these days. Jagdip's wife, Somnita, had worn hasa-sakam till the day she had passed away. It was when her body was taken away that he noticed the broken pieces of the mud bangles lying scattered on the floor where her body was.

'Tell me about my sosuma, Sosur. Let tears cleanse my mind.'

At that time, Salni would be hanging the washing on the line and the older man would be mopping the floor.

'In the village, our life was far better, Bahu. Back then, one did not need a lot many things. We had farms, the forest and the river. I toiled with my wife and five sons. By the shore or beneath the shade of a tree, someone would play the tiriao. The music would seep through the silence of the paths, reaching every ear in the village, making hearts leap,' Jagdip Murmu said.

Jagdip Murmu's village, Bharatpur, which contained a hundred and twenty houses, was located near Telkupi. Facing each other, the hundred and twenty houses stood on either side of the street. The street itself was the village. All the important events took place on the street. The manjithan, where Manji Haram Bonga dwelled, was in the centre of the street.

Haram Bonga was the first manji of the village. When the streets were unkempt, the Bonga deserted the place. Hence, people were careful not to leave scratches on the streets. Women would sweep the paths clean many times a day. Kneading mud, they would cover the walls on either side, making them look sleek and smooth, drawing pretty pictures on them. People entered the streets of Haram Bonga as if they were in an art gallery. Every house was obliged to keep it beautiful.

'There were artists in the village who worked on raw mud, Bahu. My eldest son, Surjan, your husband's elder brother, carved figurines of dancing maidens on our walls. What an adorable artist he was! People stood wide-eyed before them. It was such a joy living in a spot of elegance.'

Salni felt upset thinking about the dust, din and dirt on the streets of Delhi, where they now lived.

'In the village, I used to dance, Baba. When the nuns sang, I tried to step softly to their tunes, but they didn't like it.'

'All those who are born as women are dancers, Bahu. That's a simple fact, as plain as creepers blowing in the wind. The moment a strike falls on a drum, she gives her beautiful rear a shake. Each drumbeat is like a call from the dancing ground. Someone would blow wind through his tiriao, or beat on his dhams, building up rhythms enough to sweep both men and women off their feet. Somnita was an excellent dancer. Everyone loved to see her dance. Forming a half-circle with their fingers interlocked around each other's waists, the women and girls used to dance lightly in a row. Facing the percussionists, they would form waves like an enormous garland. Two steps to the side and one to the front. And the singers? They made the girls go crazy.

Your brother-in-law, Durgi,
Climbs up the big fig tree
Bees bump into him.

'Most of the songs were composed in the spur of the moment. How many songs I made up for Somnita in my youth! And at seventeen, she came home with me.'

A dancing community! What the devil was it supposed to do without a dancing ground? What if they had their songs, rhythms, gestures, cymbals, gongs and bells but no platform? It happened in Telkupi and in its neighbourhood when the government directed the people living there to quit their land. Many of the communities were living in the area that would come inside the dam. With the rising water level, everything would sink. The government insisted they leave at short notice as their lives were in jeopardy. If they were not willing, the government would have to evacuate them.

To where? And how? The people panicked. Many had warned them of such a potential downspin, but they had never thought it would affect their own village.

The manjis and chieftains of Dhabakkal near Bharatpur, Bonkatta, Sarkkudi, Gamarkkudi and Baliyad assembled in the presence of Marang Buru, the leader of the Santals, whose decision they considered final. From mountain to mountain, Marang Buru travelled with his people. During rockfall and landslides and extreme tempests, he showed them the way by cutting down rocks and trees with his axe. It was he who had instructed them how to build a perfect Santal village, how to make jahers, how to conjure up the Bongas to dwell in there, how to make them happy, how to have sex, how to hunt, how to be humble and how to brew the perfect rice beer. And Marang Buru, the Bonga of the mountains and of hunting, was the most powerful of all Bongas.

'If we desert the village as the sarkar says, the jaher will be abandoned. Forsaking the jaher is forsaking Marang Buru,' Sivnath Hasda, the manji of Gamarkkudi said. The others couldn't agree more.

Marang Buru was not the only one. Their world consisted of an even-larger world that embraced the supernatural world of the Bongas, where the sleepless Bongas spent time watching over the

Santals in every walk of their lives, in laughter and in sadness, in happiness and in anguish, in pain or while eating and drinking. Dwelling inside the forests, mountains and river, the Bongas stayed awake, staring at the living. They were there on the rooftops. They were on the bithers inside their homes; they were on the stepping stones and on the branches that leaned against the roof. It was just a matter of becoming invisible after death. The villagers felt their presence in every breath of life. They kept up their responsibility to appease them. Under the clouds and just above the village, the Bongas floated in the vacuum. Without the dead people to witness, life would be fatal.

Leaving a village behind meant that only the people living in it were leaving; as if a part of it was getting separated. Neither the forests, trees, mountains, rivers nor the Bongas were going with them. Those who were selfless yet incompetent were moving out. Like bottle gourds emptied out, the people were surrendering every single thing that had made them who they were.

The manjis and chieftains of the fourteen villages sat under the sal tree of Marang Buru, in the jaher. There were three sal trees in a file that represented Marang Buru, Jaher Era and Moreko-Turiko—the composite spirit of Five and Six. Next to them was the Gosae Era, the benevolent spirit of the virgin forest. Jaher was the sacred grove of the holy souls.

'All we need is an answer. Help us make a choice.' They prayed in unison.

Johar, Johar
Marang Buru
Johar, Johar
Jaher Nayo . . .

The songs, dance and prayers continued till the morning. A cold wind preceding daybreak swept across the land. The leaves of the sal tree fluttered. Icy dew rained upon them like the words of Marang Buru.

'We are not going anywhere,' the manjis declared. 'We cannot leave just like that. Let us face the worst.'

They returned to their villages and continued with their lives. The women cooked, the men went to the fields, and the women reached the farms with pots of porridge for the men. Young girls gathered firewood and made cowpat cakes. In the afternoon, they went to the pond to do their washing. Sitting comfortably under the shade near the banks, the boys either played on their bansuri or sang equivocal songs. The girls, though they wanted to hear more, feigned anger. Little goatherds climbed up the hill shouting 'hoi, hoi, hoi'. The chickens that were pecking on the streets and the geese were dispersed in several directions. The jog manji sat inside the manjithan telling moral tales—that was his job—to a group of youngsters. The fragrance of boiling rice surged to the streets, resonating with the tak-tak sound of the millstones from the houses.

At night, some person who became rhapsodic after downing a bottle of hadiya took hold of his musical instrument and began sprouting melodies of happiness. The dancing ground summoned. Both men and women came out on to the street. The street itself was the dancing ground. The percussionists played on their *dhak*s, tamaks, *damsum*s and *madol*s, followed by the bansuri and banam, and the singers sang in ecstasy. Women and girls began swaying, holding each other by the waist. A young man and a girl exchanged glances and moved stealthily towards the cover of the shade. There, they stripped each other. The vigorous youngster pushed her down. He got on top of her, keeping up with the rhythms of the percussionists. The pleasing sounds they made in their rapture were drowned in the beats of the drums. Everything was going on as usual. But slowly, something not-so-usual was happening as well.

7

'Oye, Kanu, why did you open the ditch to my patch of rice?' Chungi Soren lashed out at his younger brother, Kanu Soren.

'What do you say, Bhaiya? Come over here and look. It's my patch of rice that is under water.'

'But how can that be possible? Who the heck could open a channel to a patch of yellow paddy? It hasn't rained. Not even a drop. Can't you see how well the sky shines?'

Chungi Soren and his wife walked towards Kanu Soren's patch of paddy. What Kanu had said was true. His rice, the golden grains, had sunk beneath the water.

It wasn't just them. Water had entered the fields of many villagers.

'Is this a real flood?'

'Without the rains?'

They hoped the water would recede after a day or two and they would be able to salvage whatever was left. However, the water level didn't lower even by an inch; on the contrary, it rose. Standing in waist-high water, they lifted festered spikes of rice from the mud. Weighed down by grief, they threw them back. Before their eyes, the fields, wells, canals and lakes coalesced into a single water body that began to spread out and spill over.

All through the day, the sun flamed over that stretch of water, like solid silver. The hope that the water would retreat was lost.

By the time the water from the fields invaded the streets, a much darker and despairing fear had grabbed the villagers.

'This is no play, this is no flood,' the older people said.

'We have been deceived.'

Those who climbed up the hill to check the status had dark reports to offer.

'What the gormen's people said was true. Our village is inside the dam. Not only ours, but many of the neighbouring communities are inside it as well. The temples of Telkupi are sinking. Soon it will be our turn,' they realized. Sorely, they accepted the truth. They would have to leave their village. There were no two ways about it. Either they abandon everything, or they drown.

In the street, the water was up to their knees. It had entered the courtyards too. The villagers grabbed everything they could and moved to a higher plane before the houses sank.

'Take the sheep and cattle to the top of the hill first,' the chieftain said. Binding stems of banana plants together, people made rafts. They laid planks above them and loaded these with rice, pots, clothes and other essentials. They locked the chickens and geese in crates and carried them on their heads. Children, baby goats and piglets were ferried across on small country boats.

The last ones to leave the village were the chieftain and his family. In the manjithan, standing waist-down in water, he prayed for a long time. 'We have to save our children and cattle. Be with us. We do not quit this place by our will. Life, for us, is in the street where Haram Bonga resides.'

The jog manji, the naikes and the other chieftains were there with him. The columns of the manjithan were shaking in the haste of the water. The straw-thatched roof was shivering.

Taking leave of Haram Bonga, the chieftain and his family boarded the boat. It was Surjan Murmu, the eldest son of Jagdip

Murmu, who rowed the boat. He said, 'Marang Buru will never forsake us, Manji. We will come back. We will rebuild the manjithan. Until then, Haram Bonga will remain submerged, waiting for us. Dadu will wait for the return of his children and grandchildren, won't he?'

Surjan, eighteen years old, was a healthy young man whose body was hard as iron, as were his words. The manji touched the youngster's head and bestowed his blessings.

The morning shone over the top of the hill. The heat was severe. Looking down from there, they saw their village, fields and lakes stretching out as a single, mute water body. Their houses seemed like vague mounds of mud under water. Silver curls lapped over the edges.

The women gathered stones to set up stoves. Children, scampering over the hill, collected firewood. The youngsters captured little animals that came floating over the water. The aroma of boiled rice descended over the mountain in search of the village. Cattle grazed wherever there was green.

Ma,
You served a brass bowl of cereal.
I saw only water in it and no cereal.
Ma,
Wherewith did you prepare it?
The cereal that cannot be gulped drain.
My eldest son,
It is the milk of the black crow.
Drink it, down it to your fill.

Sitting at the head of the boat, Surjan sang. Sitting at the other end, Dhorbo Hembrom was fishing. He, too, sang.

Bavuji popped in one day,
Hunkered down on the courtyard charpoy.

Up came the sun, up came the moon.
Bavuji! When are you going back? When?
Bagna, I came here forever and a day,
Treat me as no guest, please.

Likewise, the water was here for no sojourn. It was no flying visit like the floodwater. Each day, the men who ran to the village to check the water level returned shattered. They rowed their boats over the roofs of their own houses.

Over the next four to five days, the supply of rice, ragi and other provisions dwindled. Many people succumbed to illness. The biggest problem was drinking water. Women came down the hill and climbed up carrying pots on their heads. Though there were reserves for grazing, the cattle also climbed down in search of water. The gloom of the people was affecting them as well. Not just the villages, but endless stretches of the woods were also confined within the dam, the manji said.

The forests were sinking. Crowns of small trees could be seen swaying over the water like blades of grass. The undergrowth was entirely swamped.

The seventh day was the day of the full moon. Everything was encompassed by water. Moonlight reflected on still water.

'We are on a dark islet that is about to sink,' they told each other. The radiance of the moon saddened them even more. A young man played his tiriao. Raising their heads, the goats stared at him and the buffaloes sharpened their ears. A girl faced the moon and sang:

By the bushes where the white flowers bloom,
My beloved strays, his buffaloes roam.
Pick me a white flower, sweet and gay,
Let me adorn my hair and back away.
I will get you one, wild and fair,
Put it on your hair, fresh and pure.

But what do I get in return, beau,
There is a flower I desire, though.

She rested her face against her mother's shoulder. Someone sobbed aloud. Was it the mother or the daughter?

They had nothing to eat. Children slept between bouts of crying. The piece of burned fish they had had at noon had flared up their hunger. At night, the wolves were attacking pigs and sheep more frequently. To ward off the beasts, the young men started a fire, kept it alive through the night and played on their drums.

The day the mountain where they took refuge sank halfway, the manji called the young men to his side and said, 'Listen, Surjan, Dhorbo, Jadunath, Chetan, Chunnu. I don't think we can stay here any longer. The children are sick, the women are weak, and we cannot predict what's in store for the older people whose condition is uncertain. This mountain is on the verge of sinking. The gopuras of the temples of Telkupi cannot be seen any more. Most probably, they have sunk already. You should lower your rafts and boats. I entrust you with everything we have. Take the animals, women and children to the shore. Where there is land, there.'

So far, Jagdip Murmu had not faced an embarrassing situation in his life. His youngest son, Jobon, was three or four years old, and his elder brother, Jolo, was six. Both of them fell ill on the hilltop; Jobon was down with fever. It had been two days since they had eaten. Carrying the sick child in his arms, he went to the first house that he saw, one that belonged to a Hindu family.

'Please give us something to eat. The child is sick because of hunger.'

The woman shooed them away. 'Go, go . . . there is nothing here.'

'We lost everything when our village sank. We are no beggars. At least, for the sake of the children . . .'

'Are you no beggars? Why did you show me the palm of your hand then? If you are no beggar, you must be a thief. My husband has warned me.'

Indignantly, the woman shut the door. Jagdip Murmu walked on, his eyes downcast. The Muslims and Christians behaved the same way. 'Get the hell out of here before you let us step on your poop,' they said and drove them away from their premises.

'You are mistaken,' the villagers repeated. 'We had a better life in our village. Our village was the tidiest.'

*

They needed food, water, a place to sleep and clothes to change.

'We can complain to the gormen, the *paranik* said.

'Gormen?'

'Wasn't it the gormen that put us inside the dam? Let the gormen say what is to be done next.'

No one believed a word of it. There had been many rows with the gormen even before the dam materialized. What was the use! Had their wailing sirens reached the ears of the sarkar? 'Manji, should we wait around and die of hunger until the gormen shows up? Let us put a brave face on. No matter what, life is valuable. The world is vaster than this little village. There are many ways to enter it. Somewhere, we may meet again,' someone said.

Jagdip Murmu's family joined those who had decided to leave for Chhattisgarh. They had heard that there were many companies there that exported iron to Japan. To earn a living was any day better than wandering through strange places, getting insulted. Jagdip Murmu's brother, Viswadip Murmu, went to Sindhri. The fertilizer production plants of Sindhri needed workers. A large group of people from Telkupi moved to Bhilai. Hands were in demand in Hazaribag, Neyveli and Singa. There were job opportunities.

Jagdip was always proud of having five sons. His sons, along with his fine buffaloes, could one day till the soil and reap enough to feed an entire village. What active hunters they were! Whenever Jagdip went to the woods with his two elder sons, they returned with heavy loads on their backs. They were never after rabbits and porcupines. They tracked wild buffaloes and hunted down wild boars and sambar deer. It had been a huge celebration when they had once come back from the forests with three gigantic wild boars. The village had feasted on their game. The women had dried the leftover meat with salt and turmeric. Later, they had hung it above the stove to smoke it. All the while, they had sung praise of Jagdip Murmu's mighty sons.

Securing a job at the steel plant had been a dream in vain. After a series of sufferings, Jagdip Murmu and his family had secured a low-rent accommodation. They had sold their buffaloes to the farmers in Karbona, the land which had somehow survived while its neighbouring villages dropped one after another. Jagdip had sold the brassware and his wife's silver by weight in the stores in town. The fact that all the money he had saved so far would not be adequate for a month's rent had surprised him. The rented place was an old shed where junk had been deposited, and which was not far away from the main house where the owner, Kedharnath Gupta, lived with his wife. Jagdip had to manage sleeping, cooking, eating and living in that small space.

Jagdip and his wife remembered their house in the village. The main door opened into a large courtyard where the family used to have drinks, food and other merry gatherings. They dried, milled and prepared rice in the same yard that had roomy verandahs on all four sides, where they stored sacks of rice and ragi. They hung their washed clothes on the clothesline there. From the verandah, doors opened into rooms that were spacious and spotless. A unique area was maintained in the master room, the bither, where the ancestor Bongas of Jagdip's family line resided and over which the fragile flame of a mud lamp burnt incessantly. The family didn't eat without offering a portion to the rightful Bongas. Jagdip and his wife slept in the verandah, while the children rested inside the rooms.

'We have only four rooms, Jobon's father. Where will Jobon sleep when he gets married?' his mother baby-talked to the four-year-old sitting on her lap.

'Somni, let us build a room for Jobon in gold,' Jagdip Murmu would say as he played with his son.

Kedharnath Gupta managed to get Somnita the job of a domestic helper at the house of Thakur Gopichand, where she had to mop the yard and look after the cattle.

'Is this slavery, Thakur?' Jagdip asked nervously.

Thakur frowned at him in sullen contempt. *Look at the nerve of someone who had not a drop to drink.*

'Do you want to live or die?' Thakur lifted his eyebrows.

Though Jagdip feared slavery, he couldn't speak a word more.

'Jobon's ma, for whatever it's worth, do not borrow a single rupee from Thakur. We won't be able to pay it back. You know, we no longer retain our old standing. Thakur will say, "The loan and its interest has become a prominent figure that I know you can't afford to pay back. But I would like to be of some help somehow. Do one thing, continue for another year and pay your debt." And that will go on forever. Eventually, we will end up as slaves in this foreign land,' he told his wife later.

Jobon's mother had never worked for strangers. They had never needed to. Thakur Gopichand had six cows and three calves. Two of his cows were pregnant. Though her primary duties were cleaning the shed, scrubbing the cows down and feeding them, she had to report whenever Thakur's wife called her for some other work.

'Split these logs, Somni. Wash the dishes, mop the floor and wipe the brass lamp well . . .' she would say. Though Somnita would be too busy already, she knew this way she could secure something to ensure her family ate once a day. Most of the time, she picked up morsels from the leftovers that were given her to put in the cow's feeding buckets. The vital thing, she thought, was to not die.

Jola, her fourth son, who looked pale and thin, was always down with a headache or stomach pain. He needed to eat something to regain his health. But how could they eat the leftovers from feeding buckets? Especially when it came from the house of a diku? Somnita was indecisive at first, but later she thought that if the cows could eat it, so could they. On her way home, she would collect wild spinach, water spinach, babuniya leaves and nettle from the roadside. In fact, those leaves were the staff of their lives.

8

Chhattisgarh presented Jagdip Murmu with great sorrows. Surjan, who went in pursuit of a job at the iron mine, did not come back one day. He didn't come back the next day or the day that followed. Somnita cried her eyes out.

'He will return. He will come back the moment he gets a job,' Jagdip Murmu consoled his wife. But there was no news of Surjan. Jagdip Murmu didn't know where to look for him in a strange land with no money or help at hand. The house-owner said, 'Isn't it common practice for boys his age to run away, Jagdip? What's so strange about this? He must have gone to the city. Let him make a living there. Won't he return one day?'

But how could they endure this loss? Jagdip asked everyone he met. 'Have you seen Surjan?'

Sathyajith Babu, the tobacco vendor who sat outside the gates of the steel company where Jagdip worked, said, 'It is better not to go after him, Jagdip. What's lost is lost. We can't tell the sticky situations youngsters get into these days. Go, save the others at home instead of banging your head against the wall.'

Jagdip's wife folded her hands in prayer and stood before Thakur Gopichand. Tears ran down her cheeks. 'Help me find my son, Babuji.'

How generous the Thakur was! He said he could find Surjan. 'Go home and fetch me a photograph of your son, Somnita. I will file a complaint with the police.'

Jagdip Murmu was astounded. They had no photograph of Surjan. In case Surjan was not going to come back, they would never see his face again.

'Our village was submerged.'

'Oh! What can we do then?'

Thakur told them that he really wanted to help and that his younger brother was working in the police. 'But who are they going to search for? How many people there might be who call themselves Surjan! Don't they need some identification signs?'

'He has the picture of a blue buffalo tattooed on his left arm.'

Thakur stood thinking of something for a while and then consoled Jagdip's family. 'Maybe Surjan is roaming around somewhere in search of a job. He will come back with good news. You try to calm down.'

Thakur was walking up and down his large verandah, while Jagdip's sons and wife stood on the ground below. Thakur was indeed a good man. However, his thoughts and prayers didn't yield any positive results. Besides, the family ended up being more traumatized.

The twins, Barka and Kanha, who went in search of their elder brother didn't come back either. They were the strongest and tallest of Jagdip's children. Jagdip and his wife were shattered when their children didn't return after three days. It worried Jagdip to find a note that bore the address of a person in Sugma in the trouser pocket of his fourth son, Jola, who had no idea how it landed up in his pocket in the first place.

'Who is he? Who is this Monsingh?' Thakur asked.

Jagdip's family knew no one by that name.

'Surjan might have written this to let you know about his whereabouts.'

'Surjan doesn't know English,' Jagdip said.

'Couldn't he have asked someone else to write for him?'

Jagdip did not buy this logic. Surjan was a very straightforward person. Why would he run away from his people?

'Do one thing. Go to Sugma. Meet Hariprasad. He acknowledges anyone who sets foot in Sugma. Maybe he knows this Monsingh.'

Thakur Gopichand gave him Hariprasad's address, the directions to reach there and some money for the travel.

It was night by the time Jagdip Murmu reached Sugma with his wife and two sons. Though they had no trouble finding Hariprasad's shop, it was of no use as the shop was closed. The tailor next door informed them that Hariprasad had gone home for the day, which was in a village far away. 'People close their shops early here. I couldn't go home as I have to deliver some dresses for a wedding tomorrow. There are no more buses to the village now. Sometimes, you may get vehicles plying to the village.'

'When does he open his shop in the morning?'

'He opens by eight in the morning. There's no change in that.'

'Let's sit here till then.' Jagdip Murmu climbed on to the verandah of Hariprasad's store while Somni stood hesitant and confused. The street was almost deserted, except for the light from the tailor's shop. It was not quite dark though. The frightening, gloomy moonlight played over the strange landscape.

The children, however, were tired, Jola in particular. They hadn't eaten anything in the morning. Jagdip had bought some bananas when they reached Sugma. Though the verandah was dilapidated, it was large enough for them. The children went to sleep after eating bananas. Jagdip and his wife lay back against the wall without a word. Soon enough, she thought, she would get to know something about her missing children. Her heart began beating faster.

The moment the tailor turned off the petromax, there was darkness. It was only gradually that her eyes found a way around the dull light. The moonlight was pale and ghastly; it cast huge shadows around. Buildings stood on each side of the street in clusters. Occasionally, dogs barked. Emerging out of the darkness, they scampered to the other end of the deserted road. Sniffing, some of them stood in front of Hariprasad's shop. Jagdip Murmu shooed them away. Somnita was afraid that they might attack her children. She covered the children with the end of her sari. By then, she was literally in tears. Jagdip Murmu patted her on the back in an attempt to console her.

'Please don't cry, Jola's ma. Our children will come back.' Jagdip found it difficult to trust his own words. He thought he would never get Surjan and the twins back. With this thought, his heart started thumping wildly, so loud that he could practically hear it.

Fatigued, Somnita lay down beside her children in a foetal position. She placed her head on top of Jagdip's feet, who was still sitting leaning against the wall. The warmth of her tears soaked his feet. Stroking her hair that was as rough as coconut husk, he sang.

Don't cry, Somni,
No cry.
The sky blazes,
The earth burns!
I will give you a ride on my buffalo,
Its tail long and stout.
It'll take you to a land, rare and cold.
Don't cry, Somni,
No more tears!

He supported her head till his feet stiffened. Then he rolled his turban and placed it under her head. Stretching his legs and leaning against the wall, he sat with his eyes closed. He couldn't sleep; he was afraid that someone would pick his pocket. From the darkness between the buildings, he panicked, some shadowy demons may emerge and target his children; or some hungry dogs may drag them away.

He decided to keep his eyes open through the night. Yet, he fell asleep. And then he jumped back to consciousness when he felt a cold touch behind his ears. He felt something brushing against his face while racing into the semi-darkness. Frozen with fear, he saw that it was an unusually white and pale child. With rolling eyes, it looked at him. It was beating its chest with its short arms and wailing. Its voice was unbearable, matching the penetrating sound of some wild bird. Jagdip Murmu clasped his children firmly.

That was the night he lost his children's mother. Who put sleep in his eyes even though he forcefully tried to stay awake? When did he sleep? He slept profoundly, clutching Jola and Jobon. He paid the penalty for that deep sleep. When he woke up, the day was yet to break and Somnita was not beside him. The children were still sleeping. He climbed down to the street. The roof of the tailor's shop was slightly wet in the early dew. From the place where he was to the other end, there was no one on the street. It was an impoverished street. The squalor was apparent from the dirt and waste that was scattered all over. The dogs from the previous night were sniffing and scratching over the waste mounds, hunting for food. He thought Somnita might have moved to some coverings to pee. He waited for her for some more time. Then, calling out her name, he started running through the street. Barking, the dogs ran after him.

Jola and Jobon woke up. 'Where's Ma? Where's Baba?' Jobon started crying.

'I think they too have gone like Surjan, Barka and Kanha,' Jola said.

Jobon's cries grew louder. To console him, Jola took him by the hand and climbed down to the street. Hariprasad's shop was some four or five steps above the road. When Jobon continued crying, reluctant to jump down, Jola said, 'Ma is at the other end of the street. I can smell her.'

He slung his mother's cloth bag over his shoulder and held his baba's sandals in his hand. 'Come, let us go find them.'

The notion that those who went in search of those who disappeared never came back eventually disheartened Jola. He looked back. Who would come after them just in case they went missing too? He saw a dog climbing up the verandah of Hariprasad's store.

*

Hariprasad came to open his shop at ten minutes past eight. The tailor said, 'Prasadji, a family came to see you last night.'

Frightened, Jagdip Murmu, who had come back and was sitting inside the tailoring shop, clutched his children close. Hariprasad asked, 'Are you the one Gopichand told me about? I got his trunk call last night. Sorry, I am late by ten minutes. When they said there was a body of a woman near the weekly market again today, I ran to have a look. It has become two bodies a week. Is there no end to this? I am late as I waited to inform the police.'

He supported his bicycle against the verandah and fastened it to the chain hanging from the pillar. 'Such things will keep happening. Come, friend, what's your problem? If there's something I can help with, I will. Gopichand is a dear friend.'

Jagdip Murmu didn't hear anything. 'Where is the weekly market? Which way should I go?' Seizing the tailor, he shouted like a mad man.

'Come,' grabbing Jola, the tailor ran out of the shop. Taking Jobon by the hand, Jagdip Murmu ran after him. Hariprasad was stunned.

'What happened to them?'

'His wife went missing last night,' the tailor's assistant said.

'Ma Durga!' Hariprasad made a vague gesture of exasperation.

Somnita had been attacked. Someone had covered her body with a piece of soiled cloth that was not hers. Like the calves that struggle out of the tether, Jola and Jobon fought their way towards her. Jagdip held them firmly in his grasp.

Jagdip Murmu had no idea where to go. With his children, he wandered about the railway station at Bilaspur for almost a whole day. Then he got into a train. That journey ended at Jharia.

9

Jharia! Earth keeps burning there. As you walk, there is a mountain of fire beneath your feet. Or a river of fire! But how is the heat under the soles going to affect someone in whose heart an entire forest burns incessantly?

A lot of people got down at Jashpur station, leaving the seats empty. Unmindful of the damp stench, Jagdip Murmu and his children remained seated on the floor near the lavatory of a third-class compartment. He looked for Surjan, Barka and Kanha among those who came and left. At each station, he thought Surjan would get on to the train, or the twins. His wife was not separated from them. From the world of the Bongas, she continued looking at him without blinking.

'Please get up, Jobon's father. Look how dirty the floor is! Sit somewhere else. The kids are hungry. Now you should attend to their every need. I will always be here, right above your head,' she kept reminding him.

Jagdip sat on a vacant seat with his children. He had no ticket. He was lucky that he didn't get caught. Even if he got caught, it wouldn't have made much difference to him. Jola and Jobon started pushing and pulling each other to sit near the window. Finally, Jola gave in. Both of them came to an agreement to share the world outside the window.

Many people boarded the train from Gumla station. Smiling at them, pretending familiarity, a person came towards them. Jagdip Murmu didn't know him; he didn't look like a Santal either. He was a tall man with a sharp face.

'Beta,' he patted Jobon's cheek, lifted him up and sat down with Jobon on his lap. Jola's face fell. Now, he won't be able to see the views outside. Jobon, meanwhile, was making every effort to escape the clutches of a stranger who held him tight.

'Leave him,' Jagdip Murmu said.

'It's all right. I will get up if you don't want me to sit here. But my legs hurt so badly that I don't think I can stand.'

It was frightful to look at his feet. They looked like overboiled roots. When he started to get up, Jagdip put Jobon on his own lap. Maybe he has a ticket. In that case, the seat rightfully belongs to him.

'Where are you getting down?' he asked. Jagdip didn't reply. He had no answer for that question.

'I am getting down at Dhanbad,' he continued. 'My house is in Jharia. I will find a truck or jeep going there.'

He then opened his cloth bag and took out two orange-coloured jalebis from a paper packet. Jola's and Jobon's eyes opened in awe.

'Are you travelling alone? Where's their mother? Are you going to her?'

Jagdip Murmu raised his hand. The children's mother was right above his head. Jagdip felt that the sorrowful expression he saw on the stranger's face was genuine.

'What can we do, Bhaiya? Sometimes life takes strange turns. May Durga Ma guard you all.' He caressed the children on their heads. His name was Sudarsan. He was a farmer in Jharia who now sold coal to make a living. He got down at Dhanbad. As he walked towards the door, Jagdip Murmu thought for a minute. Then he too got up and followed him with his children. He got down at Dhanbad. What Sudarsan had said was right. A truck was waiting there to take people to Jharia. It took a rupee for each person.

'Are you going to Jharia as well? It is strange, you didn't tell me. You don't talk at all, do you? What's your name?'

'It is better if I don't talk much about what happened to me. Let it happen to no one else.'

'If you don't feel like sharing, please don't, Bhaiya. We should keep it to ourselves.'

By the time they reached Jharia, Jagdip Murmu had begun liking him. He decided to ask for help. 'I have nowhere to go in Jharia. I have no house or relatives there.'

'Then what do you plan to do?'

'I want to live. I want to raise my children.'

Sudarsan put his hand around Jagdip's shoulder. 'Jharia is not something that you may expect. But still, you can come with me.'

What expectations did Jagdip Murmu have? That his fields would yield a massive harvest this time? Or that Surjan would kill a tiger with his bow and arrow during the yearly hunt? Or that Barka and Kanha would bring home beautiful brides from the neighbourhood? Or that he would play on his tamak under the shadow of his favourite village trees? Or that once again he would row his boat on a moonlit night, all alone, through the Damodar? That he would listen to someone playing a tiriao from the distant jaher? Or that Somnita would lie trembling under his burning weight on their bed in the verandah?

In the distance, thousands of infernos were flaring up. The truck ran parallel to this unusual sight. Was it a wildfire? Jagdip couldn't believe that a crematorium could be so vast.

'This is a coalfield,' Sudarsan corrected him.

'Why does it burn like this?'

'It's been burning like this for the past hundred years, my friend.'

Sudarsan laughed at Jagdip's shock. 'It would be a considerable loss to turn this fire off, Bhaiya. The fire must go on. Won't you abandon your house when a river of fire starts flowing beneath it? Thousands of people sold their homes and fields for whatever small sum that was offered and moved on. But you may ask, won't the BCCL reach their new place? They won't let the fire die, after all.'

'Who are they?' Jagdip asked.

'Bharat Coal Company Limited. Do you know that they found out that we had been living above a treasure mine of the best coal ever, with no speck of ash? No fuel is better than this coal to melt iron, Jagdip, to melt our lives down.'

It was an incredible sight. The closer they got to Sudarsan's house, the closer the burning mines seemed.

'I am afraid I cannot give you decent accommodation, Bhaiya. Mine is a dilapidated house. In fact, we cannot call it a house any more.'

Sudarsan was a Hindu, a diku, and it was taboo to eat at the house of a diku, or to sleep there. Jagdip Murmu begged pardon from all the Bongas that dwelled over his head.

Sudarsan's wife served them roti and sabzi and gave Jagdip an extra piece of chilli and a red onion. The house consisted of two little rooms and a kitchen, the roof and walls of which were broken in several places due to repeated blasts from the mines.

'When it rains, this place becomes a sea,' Sudarsan's wife said. She spread out a charpoy for her guests.

Jola and Jobon ate jalebi once again, this time with Sudarsan's children who had coal on their faces, clothes and fingers. Fine coal dust had gathered around the corners of the floor and the uneven surfaces of the walls. The heat inside the house was unbearable.

At night, Jagdip and Sudarsan came out of the house and stood in the yard. Sudarsan said that if Jagdip could come with them for work the following day, he could get a minimum of five rupees for sure. Life would not be difficult if Jagdip and his children could work at the mine.

'I work for the company and for myself as well,' Sudarsan said.

Working for oneself was pilfering. They sold coal without the company's permission.

'If we get caught, we will end up in jail. They will whip us, but we need to live, don't we? And imagine the scanty wages the company pays for loading coal into their vehicles! I go with my wife and children to collect coal. Not just us, all the people in these houses you see around do the same.'

They caught sight of several burning mounds spreading out towards the distant skies in front of them.

'Life has no surety, Bhaiya. Living with a cauldron of fire that may erupt any time beneath you calls for trust. Some life! At night we pull out our charpoys and try to get some sleep. We console ourselves thinking that it is unlikely that such incidents will happen here. And sleep? How on earth can we hope for sound sleep? There are minor explosions intermittently, the house trembles and waves of heat rush in. Getting up, we make sure that the blasts didn't take place anywhere near and go back to sleep.'

Jagdip Murmu couldn't sleep that night. He was on the verge of tears, thinking about how his life had transformed.

'Why did you drive us to this inferno?' he asked, lifting his eyes towards the world of the Bongas. His wife touched his brow with her forefinger, allowing the coolness of the entire water in the Damodar to race through him. He got goosebumps all over his body. He was frightened that she might have turned into a restless, vengeful Bonga who was stuck between the worlds. Her death was one of a kind, fuelled by negative energies. Could that be the reason why she dragged him into this kiln of the dead? Jola and Jobon were sleeping. Would she disturb the children? If only they were in their village, the naikes would have taken care of her. The entire world of the Bongas would have lined up for him to fight her earthbound spirit. Here, he was all alone. And she stood above his head with honeyed words in her mouth, leading him to his doom. She was spiteful that she had to die a disgraceful death because he fell asleep. Maybe, she had cursed him not to be able to sleep any more. Jagdip Murmu got up with a start. There was a burning hearth under his feet. It felt like the earth was going to split up and toss fire and embers out. He, along with his children, would burn to death. She was using Sudarsan to achieve her goals. Grabbing his children, Jagdip Murmu ran out.

'What's happening?' Sudarsan, who was lying on the charpoy outside, asked. 'Are you afraid? What's the use of getting worried, Bhaiya? It is not worth running away either. Your children will soon be hungry. You may endure your own hunger, but what about your children?'

Jagdip Murmu was convinced that his wife was persuading him to continue there. She was worried about her children, for she was a mother who had lost three. If Jobon and Jola were not fed, she would attack him.

*

The burning fuel! Bathed in coal, the children, women and men appeared like coal. They flounced through the mounds of flames, filled the baskets and sacks with coal, carried it on their heads through the dangerous slopes that ran both upward and downward. The scorched earth felt like it would rupture anytime. It had ruptured before, according to Sudarsan.

'When you sense an intolerable heat under your feet, move away from there quickly,' he had advised Jagdip Murmu.

Giving a small iron pickaxe to Jola, Sudarsan had showed him how to break coal. Jobon's task was to gather the fuel pulled out by Jagdip and Jola. Sudarsan took them to the coalfields in the afternoon. With each step, fear, heat and fire pulled Jagdip back. He remembered how he used to walk happily with his feet immersed in the cold mud. If needed, he could even sleep there, in the mud.

'Come fast, Bhaiya, or else the favourable places will be occupied.'

Picking Jobon and Jola up by their hands, Jagdip ran after Sudarsan.

'Can you carry the children like this every day? How will they work?' Sudarsan asked.

Digging against a long wall with his pickaxe, Sudarsan plucked pieces of coal. He asked Jagdip to do the same. 'This coal, Bhaiya, once it reaches the nearest town, will sell in no time. Oye, Jola, pick up the pieces fast. Look around. Can't you see children younger than you working quickly? At this rate, I don't think your baba could sell coal for even two rupees.'

Jagdip Murmu looked at his children. They were covered in black dust.

In the strange heat under their feet, the children balanced themselves on one leg first and then the other. Jobon picked up small pieces of coal and put them in the basket. Jola was striking hard against the wall with the pickaxe in his hand. Did Jola have the strength to do that? He was jumping up as the coal burned his skin.

Before nightfall, Sudarsan stopped working. His wife and children came to carry the coal-filled sacks. The children took big baskets of coal on their heads. With a heavy heart, Jagdip Murmu watched them dash through the mounds of fire. The road was far above the coalfields. Like ants in motion, children, women and men carrying their loads clambered up the path.

'Faster, faster,' Sudarsan kept saying. 'If the company people catch us, they will not leave us. They will call the police.'

Jagdip was really frightened. 'So, are we stealing?'

'Stealing? Who's stealing? This is the coal that lies under my house and fields. Would it be theft if I took it?'

'How come your house is here? Your house is over there, isn't it?'

'Who said? That's a pigsty. Did you seriously think it is a house where people can stay, Bhaiya?' Sudarsan asked. 'Here, precisely here, was my house. On the spot where we stand now was my home with five or six rooms, with a lovely verandah, with flowerpots and a goat house in the front yard. And there, in the corner, was a storehouse for firewood, where we used to keep our plough and hoe. We had jackfruit and mango trees, ramaphal and sitaphal. My mother used to dry paddy seeds on large *chikku* mats, while my wife hung the washed laundry on liners that ran across the length of the front yard. Our bullock cart was always parked in the centre of the yard. The children would pretend to be King Dasarath. Invariably, it was Jayanti Didi who played the role of Kaikeyi by thrusting her forefinger into the cart wheel (pretending it was the king's chariot) and saving Dasarath's life. Not once did she give me the chance to be Dasarath. It was Dhananjayan who took on that role. "You are not tall enough, Sudarsan, not handsome either. You should drive the chariot, race the imaginary horses, whip them with lashes and jump into those fancied pits." She thought I was fit for those roles only, whereas Dhananjayan was eligible to be a real king. Eventually, Jayanti got married to her Dasarath. And what became of it? Both of them now make a living by carrying coal on their heads.'

Sudarsan laughed as he walked. 'Can you imagine, Bhaiya? If you can, try to draw some pictures like kids do—the images of fields, trees, ponds, temples and houses over the coalfields that are as vast as the skies. Then you will see our village. Ah, draw a *dhobistan* at the west end. The din and commotion of washing forever dominate the surroundings. Like white cranes, dhotis as white as snow flutter in the wind. But who owns a white dhoti these days, Bhaiya? Dhoti smeared with coal! Shirts soaked in coal! Coal faces! How could you ever differentiate us from coal?'

10

'Wasn't this bulk of coal sleeping calmly beneath the soil until the BCCL came? By digging coal, down and wide, the company proclaimed: "There is a flood of fire beneath the ground. Anytime, it may surge upwards and explode. You should leave this place at once." Could the villagers live in peace after knowing that there was a mound of fire underneath? Was my wife the new incarnation of Sri Parvathi to observe severe penance amid Panchgani? Not just I, the entire village moved out to flee from the fire. The more we moved forward, the closer the company came after us. Bhaiya, we were forced to choose between death by burning and death by hunger,' said Sudarsan, fastening the sack of coal to his cycle. Jagdip Murmu followed him with the load on his head.

Giving a share of three rupees to Jagdip Murmu, Sudarsan said, 'Bhaiya, get what you need from the market. From today, cook your own food. My wife is somewhat like a demon at times. No one can tell when smoke and fire may rise out of her mouth.'

Rice for ten annas, dal for two annas, onion for one anna, oil for one anna, kerosene for one anna, green chilli for half anna, spinach for half anna!

In total, Jagdip Murmu bought groceries for one rupee and four paise.

'Are you not buying flour?' Sudarsan asked.

'Do I need to buy that?'

'Yes, only if you wish to make some roti.'

As he was about to say no, he remembered that he needed a pot to cook rice. If Sudarsan's wife was a fire-spitting demon as he said, how could he borrow a bowl from her? Sudarsan took him to the potters. He bought a small pot, three battis (one big and two small), a wooden spatula and a large pot for water. 'Enough for now,' he told Sudarsan.

Before leaving the market, Sudarsan bought candy for his children. Poor Jola could barely climb up the road with the coal on his head and was gasping for breath. Jagdip Murmu paid an anna to the confectioner and bought red, green and yellow candies for Jola and Jobon. It was the first time he had seen such candies. He felt depressed, thinking that there would not be another trip to the weekly market at Bharatpur. How festive those days were! The youngsters went to the weekly market as if they were going to the carnival ground, armed with bow and arrows, drums and bansuri. Wearing all their ornaments, best clothes and genda flowers in their hair, the girls and women would set out, playfully cracking jokes. Children would have their expectations—sweetmeats, candies, toys and dresses that were not available in the village! They would be talking loudly and playing pranks till they reached the market. All of a sudden, the girls would start dancing. The fair had something to make everyone happy. His wife would buy pots and pans for the kitchen, clothes, soaps and sindoor for herself and incense sticks for the bither. She would fill her bag with oil, salt, green chillies and sweets for the children.

When the villagers set out to the market, the Bongas would accompany them. They would move parallel above their heads and would partake in the revelries. Though the Bongas were invisible in the daylight, they could be seen faintly at night, when the villagers returned from the market. On their way back home, when they would walk in a row through the fields, like an extended garland, the Bongas, in a dimly illuminated lengthy line, would float over their heads, suspended a little below the sky level. Notably on moonlit nights, when they would pass by the jaher, thousands of fireflies could be seen flying upwards to the Bongas, from the leaves of the sal tree that belonged to Marang Buru. A scented breeze would float around the village.

While giving water to Jagdip Murmu for making the gruel, Sudarsan's wife said, 'Tomorrow onwards you should bring the water you need, Mamo. I've been breaking my back bringing water here. Who knows when my sufferings will end? I'm at the end of my rope! I want to flee from this fire and coal and smoke. Whenever I say that, the children's baba gets upset. He thinks he cannot make a living without coal. How many ways are there to live! However, isn't it their homeland? Will their land rise out of this fire pit? People should have intelligence. They should know how to live. What can I do? They think women have neither logic nor brains.'

She went on complaining. Jagdip cooked some rice and spinach. Jola was fast asleep because of fatigue from the unusual heat, dust and exertion. His hands seemed burnt out; Jagdip Murmu had to feed him by his own hand. Though Jobon was playing with Sudarsan's children, his face looked exhausted too. His children were not born in fire; they bloomed in water.

As he lay down to sleep, Jagdip Murmu thought that he must leave. It was a dangerous place.

Earlier Sudarsan's wife had said, 'Do you know, Mamo, people here die because of either the fire or maladies. Which other land do you think may have such stories? There's no one here without cough and asthma. How many children have died! I am worried sick for my children who can't sleep soundly because of those suffocating coughs. One day, I am going to run away from here with them. If their baba wants to come, let him run after me, or else let him burn out and die here. What else can I do? This area was a cremation ghat. Do you know, Mamo, games are being

played over that. Will the dead keep quiet if they are not allowed
to rest peacefully?'

*

Sudarsan said the three rupees Jagdip had earned that day may rise
to five the following day. There were people who sold coal for
eight rupees a day. They lived comfortably.

Jagdip Murmu thought that he would somehow make enough
money and settle elsewhere with his children. But for that he
would have to work till he broke his back.

The blasts were audible from far and near. There were mounds
of blazing fire storms, piles of smoky coal, dormant fireballs, pits for
burning and slaking, cracks through which the fire flowed! In front
of Sudarsan's yard, darkness spread out like an ocean with hundreds
of islets of fire quivering in molten fury.

Jagdip's wife woke him up the moment he closed his eyes.
'Why do you make Jola work like this, Baba? He is a fragile child.
Can't you see the soles of his feet? They look withered like flowers
placed near the fire. Is Jobon old enough to carry head loads? He is
only four. Your spinach was too salty, and the rice was not cooked
properly,' she said.

She touched his forehead with her frozen finger. Striking fear
into his heart, she kissed him on the lips, which felt like someone
pressing a piece of cold metal on him. The kisses of the dead, Jagdip
thought, would chill people to the bone. Those kisses were onerous.
Jagdip decided to sell coal for five rupees the following day.

Jola seemed too tired to walk. Sudarsan said, 'It may be difficult
during the first two or three days. After that things will fall into
place. Isn't it better to work than starve, Jola?'

With small pickaxes and baskets, the children followed the
adults into the sea of fire. However hard he tried, Jagdip could
sell coal for only three rupees. But still, he could save something
out of it. The idea of getting sweets by trading fuel prompted Jola

and Jobon, too, to work harder. Baba took them to the fair and permitted them to ride on the giant wheel. It was their first time.

Jagdip Murmu stayed in Jharia only for thirty-seven days. Those days ended with a crown of fire being placed on top of his miseries. He was led to Jharia to meet his doom. Sudarsan, he thought, was not a good man but an earthbound spirit in the form of a human being. He was sent by the enemy Bongas to deceive Jagdip Murmu. He had boarded the train, trapped Jagdip Murmu's children by giving them sweets and chided them. 'Stand straight, Jola. It's been days now and you still can't hold your head up? Look around, children younger than you carry bigger baskets. Aren't you ashamed of yourself? Let me put one more piece.' With that, he had put yet another large chunk of coal in Jola's basket, making his neck tremble once again.

Jagdip Murmu said, 'Jola, get the load to the top somehow, and then rest there. No need to come down again. I will come to you once I fill this sack.'

Helplessly, Jola agreed. His face, as Jagdip's wife had said, faded like a flower placed near the fire. His legs were shaking. Sudarsan advised, 'Why are you upset, Bhaiya? This is how children learn to live.'

He put the coal-filled sack on top of Jagdip's head. Asking Jobon to follow him, Jagdip Murmu started running. He wanted to get to Jola. Suddenly, the grounds trembled, the foundations shook. Hissing out fire, smoke and red coal, cracks ripped the earth apart with a loud bang. Before his very eyes, Jola disappeared into the burning belly of the earth. Jagdip Murmu stood stiff for a while, unable to understand what he had seen, whether it was real or unreal. Then he ran forward. Sudarsan tried to hold him back. 'Don't move, Bhaiya. There's nothing except boiling red lava.'

*

Jagdip Murmu had no clue how many days he had spent in bed, mumbling unconsciously. When he opened his eyes, he heard a song in a soft tune.

Believe in Jisu,
Salvation comes through Jisu,
Hang on to Jisu,
Take pleasure in Jisu.

He noticed an old nun sitting by his side, swinging to and fro in her chair, singing in a shallow voice. She saw him moving and trying to open his eyes.

'Jog Dip! Oh, Jog Dip!' She pushed him gently. Suddenly, he saw a flood of fire. The fire, just the fire! Boiling and rising fire! From the sky, Jola fell into it.

'Jog Dip!' The nun rubbed his shoulder to console him.

'Jola!' He cried and looked around. When he remembered what had happened to him, he fell unconscious with a loud cry.

'Baba.' A cold hand caressed over his face and wiped his tears. 'Baba, please open your eyes.' It was Jobon.

'Open your eyes, Jog Dip. Look at Jobon,' the nun said.

*

'My life changed then, Bahu,' Jagdip Murmu told Salni who was still crying.

'They asked me to forsake Marang Buru. Had I done that, they would have dealt with the enemy Bongas and restored my peace. "Abandon Marang Buru, believe in Jisu," they said. I tilled their land, cleaned their gardens, farmed in their fields. Instead, they sent Jobon to school and gave us a small place to live in. I didn't believe in Jisu. But I couldn't keep Jobon from praying to Jisu,' he added.

'That is my luck, Baba!' Salni sneezed and wiped her face with the end of her parhan. 'And that's how your son came to the orphanage to see me, brought me with him, and Rupi and Anandi were born.'

'That's true, Bahu. Life is a meandering river. Sometimes it overflows—utter ruin. Sometimes it is peaceful—beautiful.'

11

Two years back, on a flood day in July in Murshidabad, the place which was then under water, Suchitra met Rupi Murmu for the first time. The amount of rainfall received each day in the Chota Nagpur Plateau was alarming. Cloudbursts took place very often. Neither the rivers nor the valleys could handle the devastating downward force of water that carried with it large quantities of mud, stones, boulders and trees. The Damodar and its branches especially couldn't take it at all. During a flood, the Damodar ran unpredictable courses. Whipping its loose hair back and forth, the river would gush forth with billows of mud, debris and boulders. Dumping its headload in the valley, it would run in strange directions.

The floods came every year. This time, the situation was frightful.

'It's like the floods of 1943,' the villagers said. Many were killed in that awful flood that had occurred when they were children. It had been a long time since, but the horror still lingered. Whenever the wind or rain gained strength, or thunder came down louder than usual, they panicked. Petrified, they searched for means of rescue. A whirlpool of fear had taken root inside them, which lay hidden inside their minds. A tiny opening was enough to devastate them, causing landslides of anxiety.

Suchitra had come to photograph the floods of Murshidabad with her camera crew and a reporter from a Hindi channel. Suchitra's Malayali friend, Vinayan, was behind the camera; the reporter, Javed, was from Lucknow.

The people there were angry. 'No one wants stale bread! Give back our homes!' Though they were hungry, they felt that the food packets thrown from above were degrading them to the level of beggars.

'This is a sarkar-made disaster, Behenji, this drowning of hundreds and thousands of houses,' a youngster who evaded Suchitra's camera said with contempt. 'Who is going to believe the statistics of the sarkar? When a hundred people die, they say it is ten people. Who will give the exact number of those who were dead? Can you do that? Aren't you a journalist? Won't you dare to do it?'

No law requires the journalists to answer people. They are the ones who ask people questions; the people answer them.

'The DVC is responsible for this flood. Do you know that? They opened the dams. They know the sarkar won't raise even a pinky finger against them. What's it to them if some poor people die? What is it to the sarkar?' The people were raging, and they didn't show any cordiality to the journalists either.

'You came to photograph disasters! For what! To frame it so that you can put it on display?' another person said.

The people Suchitra saw were not under the shelter of a relief camp. It was a rundown school building where people were angry and restless, and the children cried non-stop.

'They have lost everything; I don't expect them to behave differently,' Vinayan said.

At night, when the rain and wind thrashed Murshidabad, they were sitting in candlelight in a room in Hotel Sonali Bangla, discussing the sufferings of people and the secrets of nature.

'There lurk some mysteries behind the onslaught of the water,' Javed said. 'Not all is known to man. It comes from behind the curtains of time. There's something beyond the physical presence of its coming—consider a tsunami—there's something more to it.'

Javed talked slowly, punctuating his sentences with pauses. As he was slouching in his chair, his long hair touched his shoulders. 'Floods on earth are interactions between man and god. Not just Noah's ark, but the Red Sea that parted in front of Moses also tells us something. Who sends the dove with a sprig in its beak after everything is devastated? What is the message of that sprig? Is it just a signal that the shore is not so far away? Each leaf contains words for the future. All those things defiled by you have been washed clean by the water. Start afresh on earth, each and every single thing. You were in ignorance. The floodwater has washed your eyes clean. Start looking at things from a different view, start from the beginning. After the flood comes peace. Begin with a peaceful order. Consider everything, for nothing is above or below. That's what water tells us, water on your right and left, water over and under you, water is the same everywhere. Floods descend to the earth to talk about the future,' he said.

Javed rubbed his hands together and leaned back. Though his face was enveloped in darkness, his palms, with a hint of red, were visible in the candlelight.

Vinayan told them a story called 'In the Flood'. It was about the story of a dog on the roof of a house that was sinking. The dog was staring at certain death and whimpering helplessly. From horizon to horizon, there was nothing around him except water and the dense darkness. In that vast and frightening water body, he was the only thing alive. The wet nose of death had sniffed him out. The hut on which he was sitting was slowly submerging.

'He might have hoped his master would come and rescue him,' Vinayan said.

'He couldn't take his eyes off the horizon in that hope. He might have hoped for this even while sinking,' Suchitra said.

'A dog's faith in its master is its innate feeling.'

'He might have believed that the innate feeling of the master was the same.'

'The master must have picked: children or dog? Man or animal?' said Javed.

'Even if both were dear to him, there would be circumstances where one of them would have to be abandoned,' Vinayan responded.

'But why does the question of the dog never arise?' asked Suchitra.

'Discarding the weak is the law of nature,' said Vinayan.

'Who decides the strength of lives? Which is the strongest, what strength goes with which life?' Javed interjected.

'That dog was unfortunate. The master had forgotten it in his struggle to rescue his family,' said Vinayan.

'The dog might have believed that he was also a member of that family,' Suchitra pointed out.

'Thus, his sorrow becomes two-fold. It was not just death he was facing. It was a death with the intense anguish of being forsaken.'

'Each time I read the story, I cry for him.'

*

The city was in complete darkness. The telephone lines had been cut off. The wind was still active and there were sounds of trees breaking apart. From the rooftops, tin sheets flew down only to land with banging roars.

'I heard that the entire Birbhum district has caved in. It will be difficult for Suchitra to reach there,' Vinayan said.

Javed and Vinayan planned to go to Midnapur early the next morning. Suchitra, meanwhile, had to photograph the floods in Birbhum for an English newspaper. Before he went to sleep, Javed said, 'It's better you come with us, Suchitra. Won't it be a nice idea to postpone Birbhum?'

But that was not possible as Suchitra had already committed to the task.

The weather only got worse. Listening to the panic-stricken racket of rain in the dark, Suchitra wondered how such massive torrential downpours could continue for such a long time. She didn't feel like eating or resting or sleeping. Whenever she dozed off, she heard the feeble yelping of a dog and woke up with a start. She heard it from far and near, and even from within. Somehow, she pushed through till daybreak.

A young man called Ramakrishna agreed to take her to the flood-affected areas for a rate of five hundred rupees per hour. He was a rickshaw puller in the premises of Hotel Sonali Bangla. The road, however, had already transformed into a river. In several places, the water came up to the shoulders. He decided to take Suchitra on a makeshift raft he had made using two old tyres and some planks.

'You should carry your raincoat, Madam,' Ramakrishna reminded her. He himself had no raincoat, but for Suchitra and her camera, it was a necessity.

'Keep your balance, Madam. There might be a rush of water at times,' he advised. People around them were making their way through the floodwater. Many of them were moving on makeshift rafts like the one Ramakrishna had. Some had small boats while others were using big coracles.

'This year's rain is awful, Madam. Ten years' worth of rain poured down in just this year. But the flood has other reasons, too, even the sarkar agrees. It's the DVC; they opened the dams without notice. And the sarkar won't reveal the truth, Madam. By my count, the flood must have washed away at least a hundred thousand homes. You may ask who am I to collect data, but one thing is for sure. The flood always carries away the houses of the poor, and the poor alone number around hundreds of thousands. I know only their data,' Ramakrishna said.

Suchitra was having a hard time keeping her balance and clicking pictures. She captured the image of a pregnant woman

rowing with her two children. She was not strong enough to pull
hard on the oars. Her wet and tainted sari clung to her, exposing
her belly. Though the rain kept impeding her vision, she couldn't
lift her hands from the oar to wipe the water off her eyes. When the
raft started bobbing up and down, the children clung to her legs,
screaming in fear. The murderous look of the water, combined
with a dismal, viscid sky formed the background of the picture
Suchitra took.

Suchitra took many more images that captured the tragic depths
in detail. The last photograph was that of Ramakrishna, a picture
of him rowing alone, after dropping Suchitra, through the endless
waters. His words had provoked her thoughts. That probably was
the reason why, later, she decided to help Rupi Murmu.

*

'Before they built the dam, the Damodar was merely the cause of
tears in Bengal, Madam. Now it has become the eternal sorrow
of Bengal. What to do! Rich people live in mansions, go out
for movies and drink foreign spirits. Their houses will never get
washed away in floods, for they resist the water. Water loves to toy
with little huts, to sweep them away,' Ramakrishna had said.

He was right. The sarkar, too, criticized the DVC openly. The
chief minister had said, 'The DVC is causing significant troubles in
these areas.'

The DVC had replied saying, 'There's something called an
emergency period that demands action and gives no chance to
think. If we hadn't opened the dams, the scale of disaster would
have been greater.'

Angrily, Suchitra put the newspaper on the table. No one
builds dams to generate floods. The consequences of doing so
should have been well thought of.

The manager of Hotel Sonali Bangla had arranged a truck for
Suchitra to go to Birbhum. Darkness was gaining upon the massive

clouds of the day, even as the rain continued pouring down. The wind was exceptionally chilly and filled the mind with a sickly sensation. The truck driver was to reach only after ten in the morning. Suchitra decided to order breakfast. Where do blunders begin in history? If not like this, how it would have been? Once again, she went through the pages of the newspaper. A young woman in light blue jeans and a red T-shirt came towards her table.

'May I?' she asked before sitting on the chair opposite her, the corner seat by the window. Suchitra didn't feel like responding to the show of false modesty.

'In fact, that is my seat,' she said and pointed to where Suchitra was sitting. Suchitra looked at her questioningly.

'Today, I am a little late. I used to do a lot of work sitting there,' the woman continued.

Suchitra smiled for the sake of courtesy. Anyway, she had no intention of giving up her seat. Looking up from the newspaper, she examined the slender figure in front of her, of the woman whose long hair seemed to flow out of her ponytail. The pastel blue butterfly hairclips that she wore to keep her hair in check gave her the look of a school-going girl. *She is a bit behind the times*, Suchitra thought when she noticed the large gold hoops in her ears. *Though the crimson lipstick goes well with her plump lips and T-shirt, the nose pin doesn't suit her soft, petite nose.*

'Are you a professional photographer?' She asked with childish curiosity, pointing her finger at the camera.

The history of the infinite photographs, captured by Suchitra's Cannon 1DX for Rupi Murmu, started from there. Initially, Suchitra had no plan to stay in Murshidabad for more than two, or maximum three, days. She had decided to return to Delhi with Vinayan and Javed from Birbhum. However, things took a turn at that breakfast table.

Rupi Murmu had almost finished writing 'The Other Side of the Great Indian Temples'. She had been there for the last ten days and completed the last chapters of her research sitting in her room in Sonali Bangla.

'Could you please help me?' Rupi asked Suchitra. She was looking for a good photographer who could travel with her for at least a week. Suchitra, meanwhile, had always fancied going to strange places.

'I feel you could help me for sure,' Rupi said again with hope. Suchitra showed her the photographs she had taken the previous day.

'You are an excellent photographer. I don't think I can offer you a considerable amount, but I can give you a fair remuneration,' Rupi said.

Then she talked about the places they would have to visit and the pictures needed. Maithon, Panchet Dam, the debris of the sunken temples of Telkupi, the fort of Panchkot and some interviews. 'I would like to interview the elders who survived the floods, and I want their pictures to be taken. I want to talk to the DVC officials as well,' Rupi told her.

Soon, Suchitra understood that Rupi was not the kind of person who wasted even a minute—she wrote, read and took tours and interviews. To Suchitra's surprise, Rupi was quick at solving puzzles too. While Suchitra was clicking pictures of the Telkupi temples that had been submerged for decades and reappeared recently when a landslide covered the surface of the reservoir with gravel beds, she noticed how easily Rupi Murmu was transforming into an excellent tour guide, detailing at length about each stone. 'These are the Jain temples of Telkupi, known as Bairavastan. Telkupi was the capital of the Tilkamba dynasty. First-century AD . . .'

A bizarre conglomeration of temples in such a small place! Suchitra found it hard to believe that all these temples, tremendous and humble, had been underwater for all these years. She circumambulated the temples in awe.

'Though I haven't seen this before, they don't look any different from what my dadu told me about them. With these temples lie my dadu's house, fields and village somewhere in this reservoir,' Rupi told Suchitra.

Suchitra looked at her in shock. Rupi was collecting tiny black pebbles.

'I want to give them to my dadu when I get back to Delhi.'

Suchitra, too, picked up a stone and pressed it against her cheek. She could feel its refreshing energy. 'It seems my heart is trapped in Bairavastan. I will come back,' she said.

'I will also have to come back. Seventy-five thousand families. It was not even ten years after India had won her freedom. The welfare state had given these people a taste of freedom by capturing their fields and villages. There was no thought given to rehabilitating them. Seventy-five thousand families. It is not an insignificant number, Suchitra,' Rupi said.

12

Rupi had a Budhini in her mind, who she had conceived in her imagination based on Jagdip Murmu's stories—the brave Santal girl who presented the Panchet Dam to the country, standing side by side with the then Indian prime minister, Pandit Jawaharlal Nehru. However, when she saw the picture of the inauguration of the dam in a yellowed page of a national daily, which was dated 6 December 1959, the legendary figure in her mind caved in. She had come across that picture quite by chance during her research for the 'The Other Side of the Great Indian Temples'. She had collected a photostat copy from the archives. It was a frayed black-and-white picture. Rupi couldn't find the young and vigorous girl from Jagdip Murmu's story in it. It was a face too frightened to wear a smile! Her body language reflected the uncertainty and predicament of a girl who happened to be in a world that didn't really belong to her. Certainly, she was inexperienced; the fear of doing an unknown task lurked behind her brooding look and doleful posture. Her extended arm, adorned with silver bangles, was muscular. Like a dancer's pose, her forefinger and thumb pressed against a lever. She was in the traditional panchi and parhan of a Santal girl, wearing flowers in her hair along with a silver flower clip, *pagra* in her ears and a phuli on her nose. Her nose pin glistened even in such a faded picture. Her look was intense, unyielding, and at the same time, sorrowful. Her deep black eyes were more profound than her puerility.

Rupi Murmu couldn't figure out how the girl in the picture might have changed after fifty years. She had booked a room in Madhulika Inn near Janta Market in Dhanbad. Not long ago, when she had come to attend a conference in Sardar Patel Nagar, she had stayed there. Before reaching Dhanbad from Kolkata, she called her cousin ten or twenty times. His phone, still unreachable, worried her.

'I am afraid we are after a piece of fake news, Suchitra,' Rupi said.

'What of it! There might be scope. We can come out with a touching story on Budhini, can't we?'

Mukul Murmu stayed in Dhanbad with his family. He had a wife and a child. Before his marriage, he had stayed in Rupi's house for three months to attend some training in Delhi. It was a hands-on training for loading and firing a kiln, painting ceramic pottery projects and other techniques. Rupi and Anandi were schoolgoing children then. On his return after the training, he gave them each a ceramic coffee mug, one blue and the other red. Both the cups had pictures of scattered jasmines on them. Her memory of him included a musical instrument that he used to play. Dadu called it a banam, which some people pronounced with a stress on the first syllable. Sometimes, the thin youngster used to sing while playing on his instrument. He would sing sitting on the white garden bench on the terrace of their Delhi house, where the scent of the *raat ki rani* that Jobon Murmu had planted filled the air. As he sang, she thought about the petals of moonlight being showered upon him. Had he continued playing for some more time, Rupi would have fallen in love with him.

Girl, you walk through the street,
On each side red and yellow genda flowers in bloom.
And you! You don't want a single one.

As Mukul Murmu sang, Rupi walked through the street of genda flowers, taking in the delicate, evocative scent.

Mukul's biggest admirers were Jagdip Murmu and Rupi's mother. Jobon seldom joined them. 'What happened, Rupi's ma? Your eyes look wet?' he would ask his wife. She would wipe her eyes with the end of the parhan and say, 'This Mukul has taken me back to my childhood.'

Rupi felt a strange vacuum when Mukul Murmu went back after finishing his training. Sitting on the white garden bench on the terrace, she hummed: 'Girl, you walk through the street . . .'.

That feeling, however, lasted only for a brief period. By the time Rupi joined college; she forgot to remember him.

After his wedding, Mukul visited Delhi once with his wife, Padma. Rupi was not in town then. Anandi reported: 'It's hard to recognize him as he has put on a lot of weight. Ma says his wife is beautiful. Who's not appealing to Ma! And that woman was consistently following mother about, calling her Salni Aunty. She didn't pay any attention to me at all. And you know, Rupi, Ma gave her the new Dhaka sari that was in the closet, the one Papa bought for her. I had planned to wear it to college; I hadn't asked Ma thinking that it was new and a gift from Papa. It's our luck, Rupi, that she didn't give her your gold bangles.'

The moment they reached Madhulika Inn, Rupi Murmu wanted to start working. However, after the long journey, Suchitra couldn't wait to lie down for a while. Stuffing her bags into the shelves, Rupi said, 'Let us make sure to catch him before he leaves the factory. Or else we will have to wander in search of his house. What kind of a man is he! Still no response to my calls.'

Not wasting a second, they stepped out and locked the door behind them. Rupi's anxiety was not in vain. Mukul had already left for home. However, finding his home was not very challenging. He lived in the quarters of the factory workers, which were long rows of dwellings that resembled matchboxes. They were of the same structure and shade with a small road between two rows.

The houses had numbers on them. The only difference among the houses was what the residents grew in their front yards. Apart from the two papaya trees, a drumstick tree, basil and a bed of spinach, Mukul had no flowering plants in his yard.

Mukul took time to recognize Rupi Murmu. He said she had changed a lot. With his greying hair and receding hairline that exposed some protruding nerves near his temples, he too had changed quite a lot.

'What happened to your phone, Bhaiya?' Rupi asked.

'It is dead. I need to get a new one.'

Mukul didn't know Budhini Mejhan's current whereabouts. Like Rupi, he had not seen Budhini in person either. The news about Budhini had come from his wife, Padma, who had gone home for her second delivery. Her home was in Chirkunda, and both her mother and father were workers at the Panchet Dam. She had heard about Budhini from Panchet, which was only twelve kilometres from Chirkunda.

'But I left it at that, Rupi. You took me by surprise,' he said with a tint of regret. For a second, the good old banam player flashed on his face. He said there was a story doing the rounds at the DVC that Budhini Mejhan was bedridden, but he had no clue about its source. A lot of the people were blaming the DVC, who, they said, was responsible for ruining her life. But the people of Karbona refused to hear of it. For them, Budhini had died a long time ago. How then could she die again after fifty years?

*

'I would love to return to the village,' Budhini had told some people from Karbona, but they hadn't replied. They pretended not to hear.

'I am getting on in years, and sick too. What's life without one's own village? I have no money, no savings. You didn't let me live in my village. At least let me die there, can't you?' She said her life was somewhere between the sky and earth. Shouldn't people live with their feet firmly fixed on the soil? She had a village where she was born and brought up, where she had a house, friends and relatives. But she wandered outside it for no mistake of her own.

The young people who worked at the DVC were learned. They came to work in pants and shirts. Some of them even wore sunshades.

'Can't you convince them? Why do you want me to continue as an outsider?' Budhini told them.

But what could the youngsters do? These were things that had happened long before they were born.

'Yes, yes, Budhini Ma, but what can we do when the gram sabha is too headstrong to change its decision?' the youngsters asked. They consoled her that it was her luck that the DVC let her work after all these years. But that didn't comfort her. She longed to get back to her village. She tried many times but failed.

*

Padma had no particular interest in Budhini's case. By the time she came of age, Budhini had sunken into forgetfulness like the temples of Bairavastan. But, of late, she had been making bubbles with her tantrums. Padma's family also partook in the gossip. In fact, her mother had a row with her father.

'Well, may I ask you something, Padma's baba? Isn't it the DVC that's responsible for all this? Wasn't it them who made her dress up and put the garland around a diku's neck? And when the gram sabha exercised *bitlaha* and expelled her, what did the company do? Did they protect her? No, they dismissed her from the job. What was that for?'

Padma's baba laughed at his wife's idiocy. 'How could the DVC let her work there? They knew how the people talked about Nehru behind her back. Who could make them shut their mouths? They would speak of Nehru as well. Won't the DVC be frightened,

Padma's ma? They must have decided not to let her continue there so as to not stain Nehru's name. Nehru is also innocent, isn't he?'

'Nehru is innocent? What are you saying? Can't Nehru understand the gravity of the problem? How can you believe that? When the village expelled her, did Nehru consider her? When the DVC removed her from work, did Nehru protect her?'

'Well, but why should Nehru save her?'

'You can't shut your eyes to something and say it is dark outside.'

'Will it be dark if the eyes are shut for a while, Baba? It is said that Nehru is gormen. Couldn't he possibly have given her a house of her own? Or a job? He did nothing. He might have thought that she would get lost somewhere. The poor little wretched girl! Where could she possibly go? The village left her, and so did Nehru. How long could she survive on air alone?'

'Maybe. But will the gormen have time to go through all this, Padma's ma? Mainly when they have other headaches to attend to?'

'A headache severe than this? I don't buy this. I am saying something and you are hearing something else!'

Such were the arguments that took place in Padma's house, to which she had stopped paying attention. Yet, whenever Mukul called her on the phone, she gave him an exaggerated version.

'Well, I suppose a pregnant woman who sits idly at home needs to talk about something, doesn't she?' Mukul Murmu laughed. He invited them for dinner from a hotel. He didn't cook much in Padma's absence. He made some ragi porridge or gruel in the morning and had lunch at the company canteen. At night, he ate papaya or other fruit. But that day he had two special guests.

'The treat can wait for some other time, Bhaiya. There isn't much time. Could you please give me Padma Didi's address? I'd give anything to reach there right now. I need to go to Chirkunda.'

It was only forty kilometres from Dhanbad to Chirkunda, not more than an hour by car in the same direction where they had come from. 'Chirkunda is a comparatively large city now,' Mukul explained. But Padma's house will be inconvenient for you. They have just one toilet which is outside her house. But why bother? There are nice hotels around.'

Mukul Murmu went out for a while and came back with some food from KFC and cola, saying that they might feel hungry on the way. Rupi looked at Suchitra in embarrassment. She knew Suchitra won't eat either of those things.

'I am sorry, Suchitra. I will get you bhelpuri. And when I am hungry, I don't give a damn about being politically correct.' Greedily, she tore into the chicken.

13

Padma's baba took them to Chotroi Soren. In Karbona, Chotroi was the one who still remembered Budhini, the one who reminisced the most about her. Often, he had to pay penalties for defending her in public. The villagers thought that he still maintained contact with Budhini, though they had no proof. Maybe he would know where she was.

They met Chotroi Soren at the jaher, where the villagers were performing a puja. The jaher seemed like an extension of the forest, a timber island sanctified by the trees of Marang Buru and the other Bongas, in the midst of an open space that was marked by the irregularities of its surface. The three sal trees in a row belonged to Marang Buru, Jaher Era and Five and Six. The mahua tree that stood alone a little distance away belonged to Gosae Era, the god of sex. Manji Haram also had a sal tree there. The sight, Suchitra thought, was reminiscent of the sacred snake groves back at her native place. Her camera captured the images with great enthusiasm. The vessels for the puja were made of sal leaves or mud. New winnowing fans, grass brooms, earthen pots, paddy containers, bow and arrow, spears and agriculture implements like ploughs, yokes and sickles were spread around the trees of Marang Buru and the other Bongas. A mud pot filled with water was placed under each tree, incense sticks burned uninterrupted in front of each Bonga. At the end of the puja, when the naike brought his knees to the ground and leaned forward to salute Marang Buru, the others followed him. They sang in a soft tone, accompanied by the tiriao, banam and dhamak:

Johar, Johar
Marang Buru
Johar, Johar
Jaher Nayo . . .

Padma's father told them it was Chotroi Soren who was playing the tiriao. He was a fantastic performer and sometimes he would go out of the village for programmes. People called him 'Tiriao on the Hilltop'.

'Oye, Marang, I heard you are going to Kolkata tomorrow?' Padma's baba asked Marang, Chotroi's elder brother.

'Yes, Bhaiya, sarkar's programme! How should we not? The party heads are very particular about having a Santal dance at their function, though they will simply walk off while we dance. But they pay us money, though it is not much. You know, my mamo is there in Kolkata. I told him that if we get two thousand rupees each, I will get him a pair of new shoes and his wife a sari with a red border. But my mamo said, "Why do you dream so big, Marang? You've got to start with five hundred rupees."' Marang Soren laughed as he said this. He was the leader of the group. There were thirty people in it, including the dancers and percussionists.

Chotroi was a remarkably gentle person. They talked to him sitting under the giant banyan tree that was on the east of the jaher. The roots of the tree had become soft because of people sitting on it for so many years. A young boy came with his flock of sheep. Seeing Rupi and Suchitra, he stopped for a while. His sheep ran about.

'Chotroi Bhaiya, they come from Delhi. Don't you know my daughter's husband? Mukul Murmu? He sent them here. He said you would help them. So . . .' Padma's baba said.

'How can I help?'

Rupi Murmu opened her bag and took out a picture from a blue file that contained news reports and photographs of the inauguration of the Panchet Dam. Chotroi Soren looked mildly shocked and couldn't take his eyes off one of the pictures.

'Chotroi Bhaiya, we would like to know about this,' Rupi Murmu extended the picture towards him. Denying her with a 'no', he moved backwards.

'Why can't you tell them what you know? You tell almost everyone in the village about Budhiniji, don't you? What's the use? Tell them and let the world know the truth,' Padma's father persisted. But Chotroi remained silent, looking down at nothing.

'Look, Chotroi, it's been a long time now. Budhini has suffered a lot. You were a little boy at that time, and so was I. But you used to spend time with Budhini. Now your hair is grey and your teeth black. I have also changed, and she must have changed as well. Why should we hide the truth any longer? The villagers may not agree, but that doesn't matter. Let the world understand Budhini.'

Chotroi took out a tiriao from his bag. It was wrapped in red silk. It had many tassels, faded and smudged, hanging from it. It was so tarnished that it seemed only laments would rise out of it.

'This tiriao belongs to Budhiniji,' he said.

Chotroi said Budhini had carved it with her own hands. It was her uncle, Kanha Manjhi, who had taught Chotroi and Mani how to play a tiriao and banam. Budhini had shaped her tiriao by watching those who made flutes. She broke an austere Santal law that forbade girls from playing the tiriao. But how could she hold herself back when there were bamboo forests, bansuri and music within her? Stealthily, she would take her tiriao out and play. It was a secret between Chotroi Soren and her goats.

'She used to tell me: "Chotroi, run down and stand guard at the valley." And then she would play her tiriao. "Chotroi, can you hear me?" she would ask. "Yes, I can," I would answer. "Go further away then," she would say. She would make me run till the end of the cornfields. From there, I would hear her voice and the sound of her instrument as vague as a suggestion. I would wait there till she would wave a bunch of green leaves at me, a signal for me to return. "Chotroi, come." Later, I thought about it many times. I wondered whether it was because of her indulgence in that secret pleasure that her life ended up in misery.'

He continued. 'She knew lots of things, stories and songs. How she used to make me laugh with her stories! We laughed our hearts out telling the story of a fox who went to fetch a bride for the gardener from whose garden he stole watermelons. But the story of the girl who was given away to the tiger in marriage was a sad one. By the time it was morning, the girl had run away from the tiger's den. Sitting on the topmost branch of a tree in her mother's front yard, she had sung in anger and sorrow:

> Ma, you wedded me to a tiger,
> Threw me to the bear.
> Now I throw the necklace you gave me.
> I throw the bangles you gave me.
> I throw the jewels, the pearls,
> Take it all back.

'We used to go to the woods to collect herbs. "Chotroi, do you know what these roots are used for? If you have them around your neck, no evil Bongas will come near you. Mischievous Bongas hover above the huts were women stay alone during their monthly time. No evil Bongas can trouble you if you have these roots around your neck," she would say. I smelled those blue roots. Horrible it was. We dug the soil to take them out. Those roots were delicate and didn't travel deep. But there would be earthworms burrowing through the dirt, and when the roots were being pulled out they would get caught in between, their bodies split into two halves, each half wriggling to begin again. For me, it was a disgusting sight. I was scared of them. I despised the sliminess of their skin.

If at all I happened to touch them, I would jump and shake my hands vigorously.

"'Chotroi! Don't be afraid of worms," Budhiniji would scold me. "It's so sickening, Budhiniji. I hate it," I would tell her. "Hatred! Hmm. Chotroi, have you any idea what would have happened if there had been no earthworms?"

"'No."

"'There would be no me and no you. That's it."

"'Ji?"

'She would most respectfully take a wiggler and place it on her palm. And I would scream aloud. "Chotroi!" she would cover my mouth with her hand. "Haven't your baba and ma taught you anything about worms?" It was she who taught me many things. In the beginning there was nothing. She had asked me to close my eyes and imagine the world as an absolute vacuum. No matter how hard I tried, I couldn't possibly do that. All of a sudden, flashing through my imagination, a chirping bird or something else would fly across or a peapod would explode. Or the story of two tiny stars that set out to walk would come to my mind, or a boat would go fast on the Damodar; or on the rooftop, my rooster, Chokko, crowed. I failed the second I try to conjure up nothingness. Everything would turn into a hustle and bustle. What was emptiness? What did it look like?'

"'Oye, Chotroi! Please shut your eyes."

"'Shut."

"'What's there?"

"'Darkness."

"'That's nothingness. Now, imagine darkness is full of water. Just water. Nothing else."

'Suddenly, the trees, plants, villages, houses, mountains, the Damodar, everything sank. Water spread out and spilled over endlessly. "Yes, that's it," she said. "There was only water in the beginning, Chotroi." Spreading her hands out, spinning around, she convinced me how big the world was. "Water everywhere!

Oye! The creator was upset. Where would people live? Chotroi, can you live in water?"

"'Never, I will suffocate to death."

"'Me too. I would choke. The creator knew this. So he created some species that could live on both land and water. Crocodiles, alligators, crabs, frogs, eels, tortoise, earthworms . . . As they multiplied and began living in clans, the creator called their chieftains. The seven chieftains stood before the creator who said: 'Chieftains, I am going to make human beings. They will live only on land. Who out of you can make land for them?' The chieftains didn't quite understand. Land! What's that? What does it look like? How do we make it? What kind of animals are human beings? Why can't they live in water? One by one, the chieftains backed out. The creator was worried, what could be done? Then the chieftain of the earthworms asked the creator: 'God, may I try?' The creator looked at the chieftain and smiled brightly.

"'The worm plunged into the water. For the next seven days and nights, it ate the soil under the water, non-stop. On the eighth day, it rose to the surface and crapped non-stop for the next seven days and nights on the shell of a tortoise. Just imagine, Chotroi, could you or I take a shit for seven days and nights continuously? The tortoise didn't move or shake till the soil was hard. That's how land came into being. Look, Chotroi, the ground sits on top of the tortoise. You, I, our village, goats, the sal trees, everything lives on that! The moment the tortoise gets a backache and decides to lie supine, everything finishes!" After that, I never regarded worms with disgust. But I couldn't love them. At bedtime, I would pray to keep the tortoise away from back troubles. Even now, I do that! How uncertain is life! Anything can happen any time. On what assurance do they keep raising all this on the mere shell of a tortoise? So, I tell you, pray that the tortoise doesn't get a backache.

'I had a lot of misunderstandings. It was she who cleared them. I thought trees didn't walk; she said trees walked on the earth, on the sky and on the space in between. She taught me to listen to the heartbeats of the wild boulders and salute the bhut tree where the Bonga Bhutrang resided. I remember, I used to hide whenever I saw Jog Manji Buhra. "Chotroi, why are you afraid of Jog Manji Buhra?" she would ask me. He had bloody eyes and long hair, and he rolled his eyes whenever he looked at me. The villagers knew something would befall the person at whom he stared for long. On some days, he would stand in front of the manjithan, gawking at both ends of the street. Then, rubbing his nose with the palm of his right hand, he would gape at the sun. He would repeat this seven times. And then, standing in front of the manjithan he would declare: "A woman, too lazy to go to the woods to bring firewood—I know who she is—will come to manjithan without me bidding her. She collected dry twigs and sticks from the jaher. She will have to pay penalties for her two mistakes. First, for breaking the twigs from the jaher, and second, for climbing on the trees of the jaher. The trees of the jaher are sacred, the abodes of the Bongas. Don't you know they don't appreciate women climbing on their heads? She has to pay the fine, has to pay it, and has to pay with life! I know in which houses the *mami* makes *bagna* drink water. And I have found out in whose houses the mamo is sending arrows towards the daughter-in-law and the father-in-law is climbing up the fig tree in the absence of the son."

'The jog manji controlled the actions of the people, ensured they stuck to the dos and don'ts. And that's why his eyes fell on everyone, always. "Is everything all right, Jog Manji?"

'"No, no. Nothing is all right. You should've thought of it before committing the crime. Shouldn't the penalties be paid? The villages living in peace will now get punished for the mistake of someone else. Either the rain may gain strength or the crops may dry up."

'Those who made mistakes, no matter how small or big would panic. Definitely, a woman who climbed over the rooftop to fix a leak would have to pay. Bongas dwelled on rooftops. She walked all over it! Like one who reads minds, the jog manji probed into the eyes of the one who made a mistake. He earned the power for doing that from the eyes of the sun. Like one cannot look directly at the sun, one could not look into the eyes of the jog manji. But Dasarath Hembrom, the former jog manji, was not like this. He was always peaceful. He taught and convinced the young girls and boys how to live. Unlike Jog Manji Buhra, he didn't have a habit of giving warnings. He never said the flood would engulf everything while everyone slept soundly.

'Jog Manji Buhra had other powers as well. The villagers believed that he was aided by Kalsingh and Bhutrang, whom he worshipped and who gave him warnings. The people revered Kalsingh and Bhutrang. Since they thought that Kalsingh and Bhutrang peeped into the world from the jog manji's eyes, they were fearful of him. Unquestionably, these Bongas seemed to be saying things in the jog manji's ears. *Look, the river surges, ask them to abandon the houses, forget about the produce, set the goats, geese and chickens free, take rice and clothing! If anyone is reluctant to leave their homes, doubting the prophecies of the jog manji, then that would be their end. Rolling them into coils, like mats, the river would take them away.*

'What was unusual about a jog manji like him frightening the kids off? Well, he only needed to crinkle his nose at a child for something to befall him or her before they got home. At the least, the child may fall into a small pit or trench.

'"Chotroi, these are wrong things," Budhiniji would try to calm me down. "The jog manji is giving us warnings, which is good. Suppose you are going to fall ill. Won't we do something to stop you from dying? What's wrong in the jog manji warning you about it? Think, you have been bitten by a centipede. If the jog manji warns us beforehand, won't I prepare medicine for you by grinding turmeric and birthwort and keep it till the days of warning are over? By the time your ma reaches the manjithan, crying to Haram Bonga that her son has been bitten by a worm, I would arrive with the medicine and make the leeches suck the poisonous blood out. Warnings are very good, Chotroi."

'Though I was convinced of what she had told me, I looked down whenever I had to walk in front of the jog manji's house. Or, like an arrow on its way to the boar's neck, I would dash past it.'

There was sadness and soreness in Chotroi Soren's smile. 'Some story!' he sighed. And then he started playing his tiriao.

Johar, Johar
Marang Buru
Johar, Johar
Jaher Nayo . . .

Such a magician he was! The entire jaher, along with its flora and fauna, slipped into a flute. Those who were in the jaher came close and sat around him. Some played the banam, some played on their drums. Shoulder to shoulder, one step to the front and one to the back, the girls stepped up to the music, the birds and squirrels grew tranquil on the branches of the banyan tree, the leaves of which whirled in time with the drummers. The Bongas that lined the sky united them in the miracle of happiness; Marang Buru, Jaher Era, the five brothers and sister and Gosae Era were pleased. As they sang, the village prospered in music. With ease, they ascended the heights of ecstasy. No hustle, no pressure and no indulgence. Chotroi played on his flute for more than an hour. In high spirits, people bid farewell to each other.

'Do you know where Budhiniji is now?' Rupi Murmu asked. For a moment, Chotroi looked at her. And then he shook his head.

What could I have done to darkness? Darkness had devoured it all. It gulped her, gulped me, and gulped the river . . .

14

A heavy rose garland trembled in Budhini's hands. She felt bewildered climbing up the steps to the podium. Had Robon Manjhi not held her, she would have tripped for sure!

A DVC officer had told her earlier: 'Budhini Mejhan, you should put this garland around his neck; and Robon Manjhi, you should give him this bouquet. He is a significant person, the prime minister of India, do you understand? You should behave with respect. Now, you stand here. When I call you, come this way.'

'Who is he?' Robon Manjhi asked Budhini quietly.

'Gormen,' she said. Robon was stunned. Solemnly, she stood there holding the garland for the gormen, deadpan and tight-lipped. She was holding the garland just how the DVC people had given it to her, as if the slightest of movements would make its petals fall. They had been made to stand behind a blue curtain from where they couldn't make out what was happening on the stage. Only the shadowy silhouettes of people scampering around were visible to them.

There had been a flow of people to Panchet since morning: all kinds of people, several vehicles, fair women wearing expensive dresses and jewellery. By the time the function was about to begin, they had spread out like the water in the dam. Standing behind the blue curtain, Budhini and Robon heard the roars of the people, the sounds of vehicles and announcements on the microphone. Such a wonder! Panchet, which was quiet so far, started heaving and swaying in delight. Robon Manjhi seemed to be tired. He put the bouquet on a table.

'Chin up, Robon. Pick it up,' Budhini said.

'Ugh?'

'We should behave. Be attentive. They will call us anytime.'

It wasn't long before a loud cheer erupted from the gathering: *Pandit Jawaharlal Nehru ki jai!*

Budhini and Robon craned to listen to the speech, but they couldn't make head or tail out of it. However, they understood that someone was speaking on the mike and caught the 'jai' that the crowd roared. An official from the DVC signalled to them. 'Oye, Budhini, Robon. Come up.'

Seeing the huge crowd, Budhini and Robon were taken aback. There were too many people! And so many colours! There was so much happiness whirling around, almost like a hurricane! A man in white ran up to the stage in great excitement. One of the DVC officials who was on the stage asked Budhini to put the garland around that man's neck. Surprisingly enough, the gormen's figure she had imagined was different. For the villagers, the gormen was invariably a bitter pill. Their harrowing experiences had taught them a different story, based on which she had given him a long face, frightening mass of a body, bulging and bloodshot eyes and an offended look. Strangely, this man in white bore no resemblance to that figure. The red rose he wore on his chest was incongruous with the figure she had imagined. The homeliness displayed by the present gormen, the one in front of her, could not be replaced just like that.

With a generous smile, he bent down to help her garland him and reached out with both hands to take the bouquet from Robon. The mob applauded as if it would never stop. They shouted victory to the leader. The auspicious ceremony was in honour of giving the country the newly constructed Panchet Dam.

'At last, the sorrow of Bengal will be the joy of Bengal,' said the person who had been talking all along. The people cheered. He continued vigorously. The gist of it was this: 'We have tamed the Damodar and won our wrestling match with nature. Now the Damodar cannot come and go as it fancies, ravaging everything, sowing death. The DVC has put it in chains. Where will it surge now! Nothing is impossible for man. Man is undefeatable. He has the wisdom and expertise to discipline the powers of nature. It was his scientific awareness and technical knowledge that helped him harness this river. I tell you, the scientific era is born in India. The country is becoming modern; we are making progress. Forge ahead! Forge on; let that be our only objective. The old world is no more, for we are new people. The Damodar is no more the tears of Bengal but its laughter. It will yield energy for the nation, the light it generates will reach the villages covered in darkness, parched farms will be quenched of their thirst, we will run industries with electricity, and people, from today onwards, will live in peace. From now on, the floods will not trouble us . . . this is modern India.'

The mob applauded wildly. With calls of 'jai', they waved their hats, napkins and flags. The percussion instruments banged. Budhini wondered why her mind felt like it was sinking looking at the masses that swirled like the turbid waters of the Damodar during monsoon. She wasn't enjoying it even a little bit. What could be right? Was it the right thing to tame a river, or should it continue to flow without any hindrance? The benefits of a dam could not be neglected. The DVC said electricity could be produced out of water. Budhini imagined electric lights gleaming in all nooks and corners of Karbona, which was otherwise enveloped in darkness. There would be lamps inside the houses too. The DVC said they would give the villagers electricity for free. Not just to Karbona, but to the neighbouring villages also. That seemed to be a good thing.

She looked at Robon Manjhi. Maybe he was also thinking of electricity. She, however, couldn't find the jubilance of the mob reflecting on his face.

The DVC officials had asked her to dress up like a traditional Santali woman. 'Budhini Mejhan, wear all the ornaments you have, on your ears and your neck. You are the lucky one to receive the prime minister tomorrow.'

She had obeyed them. She didn't have all the ornaments. There were no coin necklaces or silver anklets, yet she had decided to dress up.

Budhini's ma had mud bangles and a necklace made of burnt mud beads. Even when they had had enough money to buy silver bangles, Ma's first request had been a pair of *itil paini*. Budhini and the elders had gathered around to see Aunt Raymani adorn Ma's ankles with itil paini. Mami tweedled the others in. 'Oye, Teju's ma. Oye, Damini, what are you doing there? Come fast, Aunt Raymani is here to put itil paini on Budhini's ma's feet. Look how beautiful it is! Pure silver engraved with flowers and peacocks! No one owns such sweet chimes in Karbona. Come, come fast if you want to see.'

Teju's ma was breastfeeding him. She came with the child still suckling on her breast. Damini came with her elder sister, Jugita. To cut a long story short, all the girls and women in the village filled Budhini's courtyard. Aunt Raymani massaged Budhini's ma's feet with oil. First, she tried to put the paini on her right ankle. But since the paini was small in size, she felt some pain. Even though her skin was massaged with oil, it bruised. Budhini's baba had bought his wife itil paini when the corn and ragi had yielded well that year. Budhini had a silver *kanta* to wear on her bun, a silver phuli for her nose and a silver *silha* to wear above her ears. Ma had bought her silver *bala-sakam*, a wide bangle and two thin ones, after last year's harvest, when she had earned it by reaping a field outside her village, where Budhini had also accompanied her.

That day, Budhini wore a white blouse with faded black stripes and dark polka dots between them, and a panchi and parhan the colour of milk. When she had started from home, all dressed up with flowers in her hair, Ma had daubed black ash collected from under the mud pot on her cheek to ward off the evil eye.

The DVC officials were delighted that Budhini had done everything she was told. They had the perfect Santal girl to represent her tribe in front of the prime minister.

The crowd was quiet and attentive during the prime minister's speech, but Budhini couldn't follow what he said. She had heard the DVC officials talk about how the prime minister described dams as the magnificent temples of his dreams. 'It's not I who should inaugurate the Panchet Dam; the thousands of workers who worked here should have the honour of dedicating it to the nation. Come, child,' he called Budhini to his side. She felt nervous, but he was so tender as he held her close to him. 'Look, child, when I say "press", press this lever down. Do you understand?' He helped her. Budhini Mejhan had set the Damodar free of the DVC's shackles. *Go forth, my beloved river, flow peacefully. Go wherever you would like to.*

It was impossible, however, that the flow would be as peaceful as she had imagined. There was no other way for the river to go except to gush down the precipitous slope of the dam. As it ran to its freedom with the wrath of being chained for so long, its motives were destructive. It carried with it a maddening flow, a desire to devastate anything that came near. Discontented, it flowed writhing in pain, not where it liked but through the channels allotted to it, controlled in many ways.

The DVC officials whispered in her ears. 'Budhini Mejhan, now speak through this mike. Say that the Panchet Dam is dedicated to the nation. Say it loud and clear.' Budhini couldn't believe it. She? Her legs shivered, her throat parched up and her palms grew colder.

'I don't know,' she said.

'Talk casually, like the way you talk to your friends or family.'

An announcement was made. Santal girl Budhini Mejhan would soon dedicate the dam to the nation. Curiously, the mob waited for her to speak.

She spoke in her own tongue, Santali, and was applauded with great zest. Her language had not yet been included as an official language in the Constitution of the country. In the decades that followed, it had to roam around in the margins without getting permission to enter.

Drumming hard on the dhak and dhamak, with roars, all the boys and girls of Budhini's age returned to their village after the ceremony. The elders had already left for home without waiting for the function to end. Like they did to celebrate the festival of Karam, the girls collected the flowers they spotted on the wayside, decorated their hair and necks and danced in front of Budhini. The boys played on banam and tiriao. They had other instruments as well. Chotroi pushed the others away to stand close to Budhini. He didn't leave the end of her parhan at all.

Karbona should celebrate! After all, the prime minister of the nation had told the girl to declare the dam operational. He had said, 'Come with me. Open the dam.' She had released the river, Karbona's Budhini Mejhan. Swilling down pots of hadiya, she must dance till the end of the night. *Race, beloved river . . .*

Nevertheless, the festivities ended abruptly. The village looked like the house of the dead. Even the wind had deserted the place. The lamps were not lit; the street was lifeless.

15

Mothers dragged their daughters away before the rollicking crowd could enter the village. It was on its way to the neighbouring community. But what was happening there? Why were the women and children running in panic? Why were they leaving the place in groups?

'Chotroi, come with me. Let's go and see what's happening?' Holding his hand, Budhini ran home. As they entered the street, Jog Manji Buhra came in their way. With a sudden blow, he separated Chotroi and Budhini. Pushing him out of the way, he ordered, 'Run home! Quick!'

Looking at Budhini, he rumbled in anger and then walked towards the other end of the street. As he walked, water spilt out of the mud pot he was carrying, leaving behind a trail of wet soil. With each step he took, he swayed—the obese, pot-bellied dwarf!

The fear and bafflement visible on Budhini's face, who had never been afraid of Jog Manji Buhra, confused Chotroi. He lingered around and didn't go home. He followed her.

Budhini's house was near the village well, marked by a sal tree that sprouted on its own by the grace of Haram Bonga. Once Jog Manji Buhra was out of sight, Budhini hurried home. She stopped at the well, panting. The moment she lowered the bucket into the well to draw some water, a group of youngsters jumped out of nowhere and surrounded her, shouting 'setta'. There were nearly eight or ten of them. Chotroi swiftly switched to the hideaway in between the houses. Marang Soren, his elder brother, was the leader of the pack.

'Don't dare to touch the well,' Marang yelled. He seized the bucket and rope from Budhini.

'The gram sabha is gathering, you bitch. You may not need to drink water any more.' Standing around her, they called her names and walked away to the other end of the village with the bucket and rope.

Chotroi Soren remembered that day.

'I still remember how Budhiniji stood under the sal tree, crying. She was young and trembling and surrounded by bullies. How could anyone ever forget that?'

Chotroi Soren talked in a feeble voice. His words tumbled out like withered flowers. As he spoke, he persistently ran his forefinger over his tiriao.

'Marang was furious. A wind of heat blew over me as he passed by with his thugs, shouting curses. I was afraid to come out. I saw Budhiniji going inside her home. Running through backyards of other houses, I reached the back of Budhiniji's house. I called her in a hushed voice; she didn't hear. No one was inside the house. I saw a pot of half-cooked rice on the clay stove with some burnt out firewood scattered around it. There was a ball of dough half-wrapped in a sal leaf, placed on a bamboo tray. Maybe her ma kneaded it to make meatballs for the evening. An upturned pot of water had left small puddles on the kitchen floor. The floor, coated with cow dung, had developed cracks because of the water. The clothes from the clothesline in the verandah were in the central courtyard. Cowpats, which were stored inside a crate, were all over the floor.

'"Ji?" I lowered my voice and called out to her. When she didn't answer, I looked for her in the rooms and on the verandah. I wondered if her mother too might have run away with her like the others. Mani's blue dress was lying near the door. When I stooped to pick it up, someone touched me on the shoulder. It was Budhiniji; I almost cried.

"'Chotroi!" she said and pulled me into a room, closing the door behind her. The room had a tiny window that opened towards the street. I saw Budhiniji's frightened face through the light that came in.

"'Chotroi, what's happening outside? For what did the gram sabha meet? Why did they ask me not to touch the well? Why did your brother grab the bucket and rope from my hand?"

'I had no answer. I, too, was upset with Marang. What had happened to him? I had never sensed any spark of anger in him for Budhiniji. In fact, one day, he had whispered a secret in my ears. "Chotroi, I am going to war over your Budhiniji. Not just any tug of war, but a real war against all the youngsters in the village. Who wouldn't fight for a woman who glows like a wild strawberry? Why, Chotroi, why do you hang with her all the time? Better you stop it. Listen, I am going to take my buffaloes to the place where she comes to pick cowpats and to the woods where she plucks leaves. Listen, Chotroi, it will be neither the snake nor the Bongas who touch her, but I, your brother. Later, she will remember affectionately how my poison was deadlier than that of a snake." I noticed the bashful smile on his face as he said this. And I felt it was good. If Marang wed Budhiniji and brought her home, I would be happier than Marang, for I would then listen to her stories every day. But still, how could he behave like this with her? How could he seize the bucket and rope from her?

"'Where are my people? The house is in utter disorder and the village is silent! What's all this, Chotroi?" Budhini asked me.'

Both of them continued looking at the empty street through the tiny window. Was there anyone coming from the other end of the road? The evening sun, like slabs of gold, had fallen on the ground through the leaves of the sal trees. Chunki Hembrom's dog, Fatak, was sniffing around. He lifted his head at times, trying to catch smells and looking around, as if he had received some kind of information. He had forgotten how to wag his tail. It felt as if the dog was in a dilemma.

'Something horrible had taken place,' said Budhini.

Chotroi was feeling the same. It was in the air, even though it was hard to grasp. It seemed as if everyone was angry: the jog manji, Marang, his friends and even Chunki's dog. Holding on to the bars of the tiny window, Budhini surveyed the street. When Chotroi snapped his fingers through the bars to catch Fatak's attention, she stopped him. 'We are hiding here. Don't you know that?'

At that moment, they heard the dhamak. That was the beginning.

Here, the tiriao player became soundless all of a sudden. The creases of feverish memories became noticeable on his forehead. His eyes, their sparks already dead, were yellowish. There was a black scar at the corner of his lips. Rubbing the green tattoos on his arms, he spoke in a voice that belonged to the past.

'Not one or two, we heard the racket of countless drums. It was frightening,' said Chotroi. The dhamak could be played for many reasons. It could capture the mood of pleasure, sorrow, anger and hatred. Back then, it was scary.

When Budhini held his arms firmly, he sensed that she was shivering. The two sat close to each other. Her body felt so hot that he felt like he was sitting beside a hearthstone.

'Ji, don't you want to light the lamp?' Chotroi asked.

'No,' she whispered.

Looking at the darkness outside the tiny window, he grew more restless and worried thinking about why the drums were being played so loudly. Closing his ears with his fingers, he spoke again.

'I am scared, Ji. Let us light the lamp.'

Budhini pushed him aside. 'Didn't I tell you not to? Go, go home, you wretch!'

She drove him out. Startled, he stood by the door. She had never behaved like this before, or called him a wretch, or pushed him out of her house. Until then, she had been the one who had asked him to speak only gentle words. According to her, strange birds that migrated from the east and the west picked up kind words from the earth to chew on. Sitting on the boughs, they sang sweetly once their stomachs were full of the right words. Developing goosebumps all over their trunks from listening to those melodies, the trees sprouted a profusion of blooms, sending scented breeze to fill up the earth. But the birds that migrated from the north and the south picked up the dirtiest words people could utter. Invariably, they got chronic diarrhoea since more than half the words people used were revoltingly absurd. Leaving smelly droppings in the fields, mountains, rivers and on people's heads, they hovered tirelessly. As their stomachs were always in distress, their songs too were intolerable like the wail of the Sima Bonga. That is why, she said, no one should utter curse words. But if you have no other option, always try to beat about the bush. For instance, if Chotroi had to call Marang names—Chotroi should never do that in the first place—he should say, 'Dog barks looking at the butt of elephants.'

Chotroi adhered to the life lessons Budhini taught him. He never said a bad word to anyone. If at all he said something evil, he dreaded the birds. But Budhiniji had called him a wretch without beating about the bush. She had asked him to get out of her house. Though he was afraid of the darkness, he decided to obey her. He climbed down to the central courtyard without stumbling.

'Chotroi!' Budhini called out to him from the darkness. 'Where are you going?' She had lit a mud lamp. It saddened her to see him on the verge of tears. 'Not just one, Chotroi, there are a lot of drums. I can hear the dhak and dhamak. Listen carefully; the beat and rhythm are not regular.'

Pressing his face against the tiny window of her house, he remembered the story of the river that had a row with its mother and stormed out of the mountain saying it would never come back. The mother stayed there, thinking the river would flow back one day. But the river could not flow backwards. Chotroi, however, was no river that could not flow backwards; neither had he had a row with Budhini. Closing his eyes, he prayed to Manji Haram; he prayed to the Bongas in the bithers. *Save us from fear and danger.*

The vast field outside the village was being prepared for bitlaha. The air trembled with the shouts of people, followed by erratic drumming. It seemed like they were heading for a big hunt. Bitlaha, too, was a hunt. It has an animal, sticks and lances and armed hunters.

By then, the field was full of people who were building up the spirit of a native carnival by drumming on the tamak, *tumdak* and madol, blowing through *singa*s and *sakwa*s, playing on banams and other instruments like the *karatala*s and *junko*. Hunting, too, was a carnival. Not just the people of Karbona, but those from the nearby villages who received an invitation to join the bitlaha also came. All of them were men. Women and children were not allowed to participate. They were, in fact, required to immediately abandon the place where bitlaha was taking place. Men, inebriated with mahua and hadiya, sat in circles. Shouting aloud, some of them went towards the percussionists to cheer them up.

Five of the manjis from the nearby villages were invited as per the mandate of bitlaha. The manji of Karbona received them and their followers with due reverence.

Dihri, the chief of the huntsmen, came with loud hollering. People who were spread all over came running, enclosing him. The heavy-hitting strikes grew louder, the hard beats rocketed. When the crescendo rose to its zenith, some of the men stripped and jumped into the centre of the playground. Nudity made them incorrigibly excited and bitter. Standing in rows in front of the percussionists, the naked men started dancing, sending up shouts of hilarity to the skies.

When Dihri jumped into the pushcart parked in the centre of the playground, loaded with four of the drums, the mob lost its poise. More and more people stripped and danced in front of Dihri, who capriciously thrust his hips forward. When, at the height of the massively heated drumming, he lifted his loincloth from around his waist, the drums in unison echoed the thunder. His nudity was appalling. It seemed as if something had been fastened to his member.

The singers grew uncontrollably excited.

Drumstick of the priest,
Twelve-inch long,
Girls,
Go nowhere near him.

The men shrieked in ecstasy. Without their clothes, they were delirious. Thrusting their hips forward, taking their penises in their hands and shaking them hard, they shouted at the percussionists: 'Fuck . . . fuck . . . fuck . . . fuck . . .'

Like the flagstaffs of wrath, some of those penises were erect. Any sexual gesture that was possible through body movements was on show. The singers added fuel to this.

Bees in the butt of the priest.
Girls,
Go nowhere near him.
Give us your leaf plates.
Drumstick of the priest
Is gross.
Girls,
Go nowhere near him.
Drumstick of the priest,
Twelve-inch long,
Is Gross
Girls,
Go nowhere near him.

16

When Karbona's manji began his speech, the drumbeats and hollering died out gradually. As per the mandate of the bitlaha, there needed to be questions from the manjis of the five neighbouring villages, which would be answered by the manji of Karbona. Both the queries and the responses were dramatic.

The manji of the nearest village asked, 'What justifies the rabbling crowd in Karbona?'

'A Santal girl has defiled her clan. She has married a diku by putting a garland of flowers upon his neck.'

'A Santal girl is not supposed to marry a diku, is she?'

'No, she is not. It's a custom since the beginning of the seven Santal tribes. That's law and justice.'

'And what are the law and justice?'

'A Santal girl is to be joined only with a Santal. Be it a man or a woman, the one who marries a diku should go out of the clan.'

'What's the penalty for breaking the law?'

'Nothing less than bitlaha.'

'So?'

'So, I seek permission to ostracize the woman called Budhini Mejhan.'

With this, the hollering, dancing and heavy drumming began again, much stronger than before.

Fuck . . . fuck . . . fuck . . . fuck . . .

The yelling was furious. Through the tiny window of her home, Budhini and Chotroi saw the group of men advance like a torrent of muddy water. Oh, the gruesome dance of nudity in the light of the burning torches! Lances, spears, bows and arrows rose up and down with the rhythm of the percussions.

As the procession came closer, they saw the naked Dihri dancing in a frenzy to the rhythm of hunting, sitting in a pushcart stacked with drums. The monstrosity of his stark nudity frightened Chotroi. Budhini, too, stood dumbfounded.

Indeed, there is an animal before the eyes of the hunters, blanched with fear and running for its life. Is it a bear, tiger, or a wild boar that they are running after, armed with lances, spears and hoes to chase it to a trap? Chotroi felt they were running towards him. *I am the prey! My face is stuck on the square of the tiny window, and my limbs are numb. I am about to get caught.*

The manji and Jog Manji Buhra walked in the front. Chotroi couldn't identify them since they were naked. But when he did, he stared at their nudity with disgust, fear and despair. That was the first time he was seeing the nakedness of a grown-up. He had never thought that the sight would be such a dark mystery. In the torch lights, all their faces looked fierce. He was worried that the evil Bongas were coming to the village in concert.

Karbona's manji was holding up the bough of a sal tree that had just two leaves. One was shaped like a long pipe and the other was folded on each side, pinned at the centre, looking like a flat plate with a groove in the middle. Chotroi learned the significance of that bouncing bough of a sal tree much later, when he came of age. It was cruel and disgustingly insulting. The long pipe symbolized a penis and the flat plate a vagina. What the procession had taken out was a flagstaff purporting the licentiousness of the accused. As they got closer to Budhini's home, they became an indocile mob that dashed forward, losing restraint altogether. The sal tree in front of her house quivered from the roots to the branches; the water moaned in the well. With a start, Budhini withdrew from the tiny window and hid in a corner of the room.

Fuck . . . fuck . . . fuck . . . fuck . . .
Dhuk . . . dhuk . . . dhuk . . . dhuk . . .

Shouting thus, they gained strength in their steps and danced wildly in front of her door. To his dismay, Chotroi found Marang to be in the lead. It was disgusting to see him slide his hands between his thighs, hold his pecker up and yell 'dhuk, dhuk'. Chotroi gaped at how his member grew so big. Yes, he hadn't seen it recently, but the last time he did it was no bigger than a hibiscus bud.

The mob grew silent when the manjis of the neighbouring villages stood on the threshold of Budhini's door. The dance of the possessed ceased, as did their vulgar songs and drumming.

'Let this not befall on any house,' said the manji of Karbona. He put the bough of the sal tree on the roof of Budhini's house. 'Let no house be marked like this.'

They fixed a bamboo pole to the entrance on which a burnt-out log of wood, a worn-out broom and some used leaves have been tied. And then, like a hurricane set free, they stormed into the house. Those who raced in urinated on the walls, floor, stove, pots and other utensils. Some of them squatted low on the courtyard to take a crap. They entered every room and defiled everything. They wetted the cots and sheets with their urine. Pulling out clothes from the lines, they relieved themselves all over them. They barked at the percussionists to play the rhythm of taking a leak. The pipers presented the sound of passing water, triggering mysterious rumbles of laughter.

Chotroi hid under a charpoy. Budhini stood frozen in a dark corner. Before she could resist, four or five of the men had hauled her into the courtyard. Loud, animated cheers rose as the hunted animal fell. The rhythm of hunting grew more raucous.

They danced, lifting their long sticks, bows and arrows, roaring boisterously all the while. Marang and his friends were under the influence of arrack. They held their members in their loose fists, moving their hands up and down the shafts. *Dhuk . . . dhuk . . . dhuk . . .*

The manji ordered them to stay away from Budhini. The noisy merrymaking came to an end. In the courtyard of her childhood home, she stood helpless and pale with her head bowed to the ground. The chieftain talked calmly.

'This Santal woman called Budhini has married a diku in her own interests and thereby violated the customs of the clan. Many people in the community witnessed her putting a garland around the neck of a Hindu called Nehru. He may be a prime minister or whoever; for a Santal, he is just an outsider, a diku. The penalty for marrying a diku is banishment from the tribe. Everybody knows this. I repeat once again for those who do not know of this. The gram sabha has decided to ostracize Budhini by the execution of bitlaha. Our well-wishers, the five manjis from the neighbouring villages, have given their permissions. Bongas, dead and buried, who dwell left and right, up and down, and inside every living and non-living thing have bestowed their approval as well. Hence, it is determined to purify the village by expelling this Santal girl who has defiled it. Seeking forgiveness, a sacrifice in penance would be given to the Bongas who guard the tribe. Each of the houses in the village, along with the streets, fields and water, will be cleansed. The chieftain will beg pardon for the misdeed that has taken place during his time and later purify himself.

'From this moment, no one should have any contact with this woman, be it inside the village or outside. Nobody should talk to her or help her in any way. She should not be given food or water, or clothes to change or a place to sleep. She can't touch our water. She is banned from our wells and ponds and animals. She should not step on our soil to defile it. Just in case her people or relatives take pity on her and transgress the rules, they too will have to pay the same penalty. Marriages, births, deaths, funeral rites and yearly festivities will be denied to her. No Santal child will marry the diku's seed that she will give birth to. From this day, her place will be out of the precincts of the village. So, close the doors on her with loud bangs and block the paths. The gram sabha's decision is not to be violated. If at all anyone oversteps, the rest are obliged to report it.'

When the manji stopped speaking, the jog manji, the one who was responsible for the demeanour of the youngsters, came forward. 'This is a warning to those youngsters who behave of their own free will. No one should try to bring the outsiders to the village. They have their eyes not just on our women, but on our land, woods and water too. Once they are satisfied, they will discard our women. But by then the seeds of other clans will have been born among us. The outsiders will demand the women of their land, and thus, our grounds will be usurped by them and their children. And by mingling with the blood of the others, our clan will lose its indigeneity. The outsiders will compel their women and children to follow the culture and the ways of their tribes, striking discord in the rhythm of our social life. Our habit of living as a single unit, as we do now, the character of living in groups as villages will give way. It will lead to a dispute between the other clans and us, and the conflicts will end our tranquil lives. We are peace-loving; we are Santals, Sant-Al—the quiet soul. Our villages, fields, forests, rivers, singing, dancing, tiriaos and everything else give us pleasure, but an encounter with an outsider will rob us of our joy. So, be it man or woman, you should not think of marrying an outsider and bring him to our clan,' he said.

As he finished his speech, the huntsmen took positions behind Budhini, ready with their bows and arrows. 'Out,' they shouted. Still not comprehending what was happening, the embarrassment vivid on her face, Budhini walked forward. Behind her, the lewd jeering of the men grew more offensive.

She stood in front of the manjithan for a while. But the people pushed her forward. From somewhere, a stone was hurled at her. It hit her forehead. Covering her temples, she ran for her life. The villagers chased her till she traversed the streets and the jaher, reached the boundaries of the woods, crossed the stream and was lost in the forest.

Hiding behind a kadam tree near the river, she saw them retreating, hollering noisily. Her eyelashes were wet because of the blood flowing from her forehead. She thought the red light of the distant torches, moving further away with every second, was splintering. For a long time now, she had been encircled in the whirlpool of deafening roars. Now, the sounds and lights were bursting away into fragments.

At a distance, she could see them sitting in a circle. Now, light, as if in a well, was trapped inside that circle. A dark man-wall was barring it from leaking. They were seeking forgiveness from Marang Buru, Haram Bonga, Jaher Era and all the other Bongas, by giving sacrifice, thereby ensuring their village remained free of any blemish.

The sound of the drums was now like chantings or whisperings. The chieftain walked to the centre of the circle, to the heart of the light, and stood there. With a pot of water and penalty money, he sought mercy for the stigma that had befallen during his period. The five manjis of the adjacent villages accepted the penalty money and cleansed him of the blemish.

'Haram Bonga, please accept this,' the chieftain said, lifting a black rooster that was to be given in sacrifice to the Bonga. 'As we found no other way out, we were forced to perform a voluptuous dance on your sacred streets. It was neither a hideous act committed by one of us nor an unintentional slip; neither was it intended to endanger nor insult anyone. Forgive us by accepting our penalty and the sacrifice we offer, and thus remain satisfied.'

The chieftain then held the sacrificial bird close to his member and slit its throat open, wetting the soil with its blood.

'Today we stripped ourselves naked and exhibited our parts, each penis with its foreskin pulled back. We did it meticulously, vigorously and splendidly. Now each penis should shrink back into its cover. Bongas on guard, please accept this sacrifice and stay satisfied.'

The mob dispersed. A silence, entirely unfamiliar, spread across the area. People bathed in the river and changed their clothes. Grief, dense and similar to the mourning at the death of a departed, shrouded the village. The last torch died down, unleashing darkness upon the place.

But on the miserable streets, piles of embers were still burning here and there. Chotroi walked along the edge of the road sobbing endlessly.

*

Darkness, denser than poison! Silence! Suddenly, rising from the edge of her forefinger, fear crept its way into her heart. 'Yo . . .' Drawing on her inner strength, she called out to her mother and cried. The woods brought back her cries in many waves. Where was her mother? Why didn't she inquire after her daughter who had gone through such miseries? Budhini had done no harm. Ma knew that. It was Ma who had dressed her up in panchi and parhan, put flowers in her hair. 'Yo . . . yo . . . Where are you, yo?' Crying loudly, she came out of the bushes. By then, her eyes had got accustomed to the darkness. She slithered into the stream whose water now looked black.

'Budhini Mei,' she heard a voice behind her. Budhini recognized the voice of Ramdhuni, which chilled her to the bone. What on earth was Ramdhuni doing here, by the stream, at this strange hour? Budhini ran without turning back. She felt something coiling around her ankle and tugging her down into the water. She shook her leg firmly. The thing that splashed into the water was a child. A child that was alarmingly white in colour. Its eyes were as large as its head; its face crinkled like that of a senile, old man. It started shrieking in an awful voice that belonged neither to a child nor a bird. And then, stretching her arms forward, it walked towards her through the water. The whiteness of its form was repulsively horrible, making her blood freeze. Its eyes were rolling ceaselessly. *Sima Bonga!* Terrified, she went blank. She wanted to run or cry, but her legs remained rooted to the ground. Her voice didn't come out. For a second, she called out to Marang Buru and Haram Bonga.

Bending down, with her hands supporting her knees, she called her mother. 'Yo . . . yo!' She screamed at the top of her voice so that her mother would hear her wherever she was. This gave her strength, and in a single leap, she crossed the stream. She could still hear the mournful wailings of that white monster behind her. She could listen to Ramdhuni calling her name. Without turning back, she ran to her village. She didn't think of the bitlaha. She was running away from Ramdhuni and Sima Bonga. Somehow, she wanted to reach her mother.

Marang and his friends were waiting, as if they had expected her return. They were armed with slings, stones and bamboo poles. They recognized the girl who was running towards them in tears. She should not enter their village. The wrath of Manji Haram should not befall them again. Stones were hurled at her, and the angry young men raced forward. They flung rocks at her as if they were chasing away a rabid dog.

'Baba,' she called out and ran back for her life. But they hunted her down and attacked her with stones. They warned her that they would stone her to death if they spotted her anywhere near the village.

'Water,' Budhini said, stretching her hands out.

17

Blood flowed. It ran down her thighs. Budhini tried to wipe it away with leaves and grass, but that didn't help much. She was hungry. She could feel her throat parched with thirst. However, more than food and water, she needed some old pieces of cloth. She thought of the bag that contained the used fabrics she had stored secretly, kept away from the eyes of the men at home. Ma always directed her not to let Baba, Shopon or Mani see those pieces. If they happened to see them, her bleeding would not stop. It would continue until the next year.

She needed that bag. She would go to the village to take it. No one needed that stuff there. They need not give her a glass of water or a gulp of gruel from her own home. But she needed the bag. What would the village do with it?

The previous night, when Marang and his friends had chased her with stones, she had felt a spurt of warm blood flowing out. She did not notice it as she ran for her life. Each time a stone hit her head or back, her body shuddered. She fell flat on her face. Then, somehow, she managed to escape. They drove her into the fields that lay bare and vast, extending as far as the edges of the sky. She could hear shouts of 'kill her, kill her', along with the vibration of stones and the advancing footsteps that seemed to be worryingly close. Running scared, she could not make out what was happening or where she was running to. She remembered she had cried out loud when they had hit her with stones. Crying thus, she had fallen asleep and woken up with her teeth chattering in the relentless cold. Bolts of lightning ran through her head; her body was writhing in pain. The stones might have broken her back. But as she sat up, she felt the jetting flow of warm blood down her thighs. Her head spun; her body swayed. Fearing blood had stained her clothes, she struggled to her feet. Ma had asked her to never let that happen. But now, a blood moon in all its fullness might have risen at the back of her milk-white panchi. She felt it with her hand, grasped the sogginess of the moon.

A cruel desolateness spread across the surroundings. Apart from the lonely black palm that stood on the narrow path that snaked through the fields, there was no plant, goat, sheep or man in the vicinity. There was a fearful stillness in the mist and moonlight of the early hours before dawn. Budhini noticed how the crown of the single palm moved strangely, though there was no wind at all. The Bonga that dwelled on the palm was alerting her about its presence. Holding her breath, she stared at the palm. 'Budhini Mei, don't ever go in front of a Bonga when you have your flow. If you do, you will never go back to your old self again. Lecherously, the randy Bonga will get inside you,' Phulmone had reminded her. This was when they went to the pond outside their village to wash the used pieces of cloths. Now, Budhini was on her monthly flow. She stood in a barren field at night with no one to support her, unable to stop the blood. The wind bowed with a strength that could uproot the black palm. Only the spathes that swayed indulged in a constant rustle of dead leaves. There was no wind anywhere else. Not a strand of her hair moved; there was no hint of a mild breeze on the fields.

In the moments when one fears for one's life, the body becomes irrelevant. Running would be the only thing it has to do then. Running not by muscle but by will. Budhini ran. However, as fast as she ran, she couldn't find an end to the fields. She stumbled upon the ridges; her feet were hurt because of stepping on the stubbles of stalks and the edges of the parched earth. She wanted to escape the eyes of the Bonga on the lonely palm. 'I am dying,' she said, 'I can do nothing more. I will fall now. A Bonga as tall as the palm is running after me, the Bonga who wants to enter a woman who is on her rag.'

However, she was running in the wrong direction. She had raced to where she was not supposed to go. She collapsed under the lush canopy of a sal tree near the jaher outside the village. Her body was throbbing with pain; her hair, face and clothes were smudged with dirt. The feel of the sal tree consoled her. Sal was a sacred tree that left no room for fear. Now that the terror had quit her heart, a sense of forlornness crept in. Bereft of all hope, she cried with long sobs. She hugged the sal tree securely. *Now, you are my Ma, Ba and Marang Buru.*

A bird that woke up first in the morning heard her cry. In the desolateness of the never-ending fields, it saw a child weeping, her arms around the base of a tree, trying to clasp it tightly. It laid eyes on her like a mother bird watching her hatchling, even while hovering above.

The enemy Bongas could not enter the jaher. It was a place radiating the power of Marang Buru. What Budhini was doing now was equally wrong. She was sitting near the jaher during her monthly flow. By sitting close to the sal tree, she had violated the rules of Marang Buru. Down on her knees, she touched the ground with her palms spread out and begged for mercy. Marang Buru was the Bonga of the magnificent mountains who guarded the village by guarding the mountains. How could he forsake a tender life from there? She told Haram Bonga, the Five and Six, Jaher Era and Gosae Era: 'I am entering the village; I need to take my pieces of old cloth.'

The village had not woken up yet. The streets of Haram Bonga were forbidden to her. She knew she would scare no one as long as she was innocent. This was what she wanted to tell Marang and his friends; even if it was mud, she would live by eating it. She stealthily walked through the backyards of the homes. Later in the morning, the villagers might see the bloodstains on the fallen leaves. Every step she took, she felt a lightning pain inside her head. With each move, her limbs contorted in pain.

'Yo,' Budhini said when she reached the back of her own house. She neither cried nor faltered.

'Yo, open the door.'

Someone moved inside. The crack in the door revealed nothing except darkness. It was Phulmone who opened the door. She shuddered as if she had seen a Bonga. The next second, she closed the door.

'Bavuji,' Budhini knocked on the door. This time, Phulmone didn't open the door. No more sound was heard from inside. The pigs squealed inside the pigsty, for they could smell her. There was great excitement inside the chicken coop as well. The goats bleated. Wagging its tail, Fatak ran towards her and stood by her.

'Budhini Mei,' Phulmone called out to her in a hushed voice, showing her face through the tiny window. 'Go away; if someone sees you, they will beat you to death.'

'Where is Ma? Call Ma.'

'Your ma and baba are not here. They have gone to your Ma's house because of the shame.'

'I . . .' But before Budhini could complete the sentence, Phulmone withdrew her face from the tiny window. 'Go, go,' she whispered from inside. Her child, meanwhile, woke up and started crying.

It was Ma's panchi and parhan, white as milk. The blouse that went with it had stripes and dots of the same colour as the stripes in between. Ma wore this for the first time during the last Karam festival. Its texture was smooth, for it had been made with the best cotton threads. Budhini tore apart the end of the parhan. A square piece of cloth that she folded from corner to corner. Again and again. Stringing the piece of fabric through the thread, she tied it around her waist and then pulled it firmly to the back to make it fit tightly. Suddenly, she grew more courageous.

There was no food, no water and no clothes to change. No place to sleep. The nights would be deserted and horrible. No one was with her. Anytime, she may fall, anywhere. This awareness made her angry, angry enough to vandalize anything that came her way. *Even if my home has abandoned me, I haven't decided to die.* Budhini walked back. Through the tiny window emerged the arms of Phulmone, adorned with silver bangles and holding two sweet potatoes. 'Budhini Mei, please go away from here, or else they will expel us also from the village.' Phulmone's throat croaked as she said this. Budhini took the sweet potatoes.

'Let Marang Buru save you.' Phulmone blew her nose.

I will live if I have decided to live. A Santal has to live, for that's her first duty. She chewed on one of the sweet potatoes, but she couldn't taste its sweetness. With the determination of one who has decided to live, she walked on, biting into the sweet potatoes.

Where the street ended, the fields began. The moment she stepped on to the field, someone hit her hard on the back. Shouting 'Setta, setta', Jog Manji Buhra started thrashing her with a long stick. Budhini ran. The jog manji couldn't run after her with his obese body and pot belly. Holding the sweet potatoes firmly in her hands, she got out of his reach.

Usually, the people of Karbona went to work at DVC well before daybreak. Budhini missed that early-dawn boat trip through the Damodar. Nothing excited her the way the sacred river in all its magnificence did. The sunrise would lure her and the oarsmen would sing:

We have seeded the crops in Ashad
We will have Bhadu in Bhadra-
The joyous fête.
Floods have boosted the Damodar
The sailors are stuck, they can't row.

O Damodar, we touch your feet.
Abate the surging power
The gala of Bhadu
Will be here but the next year.
O, let us row our boats in peace.

Hiding behind the bushes, Budhini watched the villagers boarding the boat, laughing aloud. She resolutely bit into the sweet potatoes she was still carrying with her. She, too, should've been there on that boat. The last ones to get on board were her ma and baba. Budhini quivered with anger. There was a way leading to the Panchet Dam through the forest as well. On the days they missed the boat, they went to work through the short cuts in the woods. She ran through the forest. Her stride was firm. She ran till she reached the front of Lekshmi Narayan Jha's tea shop. She didn't mean to stop there, but then she also didn't have the energy to continue. She simply caved in. This occurred seconds after Narayan Jha's wife, Suparna, had finished drawing an *alpona* with rice powder, after swabbing the small area in front of their shop with cow dung. Budhini collapsed into the centre of the alpona.

'*Mughpudi, ayile ki hobek.* Damn! Get up, you bitch, you have spoiled my alpona. Ruined everything! Dirtied it all! Pig! Chantala!' Suparna cried out as if something bad had befallen. With incense sticks burning in hand, her husband came running from the prayer room. Though he was initially taken aback by Budhini lying on the ground, he ran inside and came back with a cane used for beating snakes. His wife joined him with a broom dipped in cow dung. 'Go, run, you swine.'

People crowded around. They couldn't bear the offence Budhini has committed. 'What nerve! You low-class person! She deliberately came in the morning to defile everything by touching it. Say, Panditji, what should be done?' Narayan Jha asked Pandit Radharam who was shivering with hatred and bitterness.

Suparna said, 'What's there to ask? Thrash her to death. Look at the work I have to do now to ensure things are clean again.' She hit Budhini on the head with the broom and splattered cow dung water around.

'What are you staring at? Beat her brains out,' Pandit Radharam told the mob. 'The people, maddened by fury and bitter excitement, came running, grabbing whatever they could get a hold of. Lying prone on her knees, Budhini reached for the soil in prayer, her palms spread wide. Packing around her, the mob kicked on her back. They tried to strip her, but it was not easy. Someone fastened a stick-broom around her neck, while someone hung a pair of worn-out sandals. Pandit Radharam came near her, reached for her breasts and squeezed her nipples. From the other side of the street, the Santals and Chamars who were on their way to work witnessed everything silently. Some of them fled in fear. Though some of the young men were boiling with rage, they stood blanched with fear, unable to say a word. No one had the strength to resist the mob or pull them away from her. Like a little creature striving to crawl on its four legs, Budhini lay on the ground, flailing helplessly. They dragged her to the bridge across the Damodar. Tying her to one of the pillars of the bridge, they dispersed. Though she shivered ceaselessly, she didn't cry, not a drop.

The sun was marching up. Budhini's legs were getting burnt because of the scorching heat from the concrete posts. She tried shaking her body to try and break away. After a long time, she stopped trying to get away and stood with her head bent down to her chest. Two people came walking from the other end of the bridge. One of them spat at her. Then they walked off. A group of women came close, but when they noticed someone coming, they ran away in fright. After some time, a lanky figure—he was probably not more than forty—came pedalling on a bicycle. He was on his way to work in the small coal mine near Sanctoria.

'How cruel!' he said and untied her. 'How can people be so cruel to a child? How sad, how demeaning!' As he threw the broom

and slippers away, he grew more depressed as he saw the wounds
and bruises on her body. He helped the shivering girl whose hair,
face and clothes were repulsively stained with blood and dirt. He
helped her sit against the wall of the bridge. One of her cheeks was
swollen, her eyes were puffed up and her body was covered in fresh
bruises and abrasions. But she seemed quite deprived of sensations,
for there were no signs of fear or sorrow on her face. He took out a
mud bottle from the bamboo basket tied to the carrier of his cycle.
It had cold water.

'Drink,' he said. She downed the water greedily.

'What happened?' he asked.

She didn't answer.

'Well, I can make a guess,' he said. 'Where are you going?'

'To the DVC.'

'Do you have work there?'

'Yes.'

'Can you go to work today?'

'I can.'

'Have you eaten anything?'

She didn't answer. He might have guessed that as well. 'Come,'
he called and helped her to her feet. He helped her sit on the
crossbar of his cycle. Budhini felt scared. He was neither a Santal
nor a tribesman; he was someone who belonged to the high class.
Yet, he had touched her and lifted her gently. Pedalling slowly,
he reached the road to the DVC. People were having breakfast at
Lekshmi Narayan Jha's tea shop as if nothing unusual had happened.
Suparna had swabbed the floor with cow dung again and decorated
it with a fresh alpona in a new design. Parking his cycle under
the kadam tree, on the turn in the road to the DVC, he went to
Jha's tea shop, asking her to wait. The tree was in full bloom. The
blossoms were in the shape of flower-balls, of a golden hue, with
bees and butterflies hovering around. Budhini wanted to take a
bath and change her clothes. The cloth underneath was drenched.
She needed to reach the women's toilet at the DVC at the earliest.

He came back carrying two large pieces of bread on a sal leaf and some *tarkari* on a leaf plate.

'Eat.'

Breaking the bread with her dirtied hands, she chewed slowly.

'Go home today. You can come to work tomorrow. Where is your house?'

'Karbona. My village is far away from here.'

'Oh!'

He dropped her at the gates of the DVC.

18

The disdainful fib about Budhini being Pandit Nehru's wife had become the gossip at DVC. How strange is the force of intuitive power! A story takes too many turns in the hands of others. Some are close to the truth; some show no justice at all; some carry no affinity to the original. Budhini's case was no different. The cruel actions of the people of Karbona became known—believers of primitive superstitions, practitioners of barbarous customs!

While shovelling soil from the canal, Subodh Ray asked, 'We have justice and courts in this country, don't we? Who gave their gram sabha the power of the Supreme Court?'

'Has your Supreme Court ever given us any justice?' Karbona's Parinik Kisan Kisku said as if he was answering no one.

The Santals knew it was not possible to have a face-to-face dialogue with the dikus, particularly the Brahmins. They wiped out anger with acts of barbarities; Santals wiped out anger by singing songs, dancing till the end of the night or by playing on their flutes.

'Justice! Why the heck do you go after justice, Kisan. Don't you have a law of your own? Ashamed at having thrashed a child like this, aren't you? And then you ousted her from the village without giving her a drop of water! Shame on you!' Subodh Ray taunted him.

Both of them were engaged in shovelling mud, cleaning the ditch that was masked with soil and rocks deposited during the flood last year. Covered from head to toe in gritty muck, it was hard to tell Ray from Kisan.

'We can't violate the laws of the gram sabha,' Kisan said.

'Law? Is this what you call law? This is a crime. We will report it to the police. Good for you if you call that girl back to the village soon.' Subodh Ray's voice was threatening. From the ditch, he recklessly tossed a basket of mud to the ground above. Half of it landed on Kisan's head.

Was it for the sake of justice that they had humiliated Budhini in Lekshmi Narayan Jha's tea shop, almost killed her and then left her to die under the scorching sun? Can't we file a complaint with the police? Kisan Kisku wanted to ask. Instead, he moved away to resume his work after wiping off the dirt from his face and head. However, he couldn't contain his anger for long. He grumbled, 'They do it in the name of caste.'

How strange are the laws of the dikus! They divided themselves into distinct castes. Moreover, it was decided that some of them would be very high in the hierarchy and others very low. The beliefs of the Hindus were in stark contrast with the belief system of the Santals. *Sarana* won't buy the concept of divisions amongst human beings, for it believes in no hierarchy between people, no hierarchy between men and trees. A tree is pure and serene. Santals are people who bow in front of the supreme energy and the ubiquitous serenity of a tree. They do not know how to treat people, trees and animals—all animals, including birds, snakes, other reptiles, fish, crocodiles and all those that dwell under the deep water—in different ways. Budhini was punished not because she belonged to a lower class, but because she had defiled a Santal law.

'Don't expect anything more from dikus; they won't change. Dikus get married to our women just to dump them,' Kisan continued whispering. It seemed like he was talking to the shovel, to the muck, to himself.

'Here comes nonsense on horseback! Garlanding someone doesn't mean marriage, does it? Is marriage such a silly thing?'

Subodh Ray said and stepped towards Kisan. Obviously, he was in
the mood to start a row. Before Kisan could answer him, Marang's
friends got there, panting. They said Marang was being attacked at
the worksite in the name of Budhini. Kisan ran to the spot with
them.

The bickering had started during lunchtime. It was between
Marang and Suman Goshal, the one who faked the role of a
supervisor. They had been digging out dirt on the other side of
the canal. The dispute broke out in the area where the workers
washed their hands after lunch. Suman complained that Marang had
deliberately splattered water all over him. There was a gap of ten
feet between them. Suman, who never wasted an opportunity to
insult the Santals and the other tribes, was not ready to give up. For
the sake of Bengali bhadralok, he proclaimed that he was willing to
cut anyone's throat or end his own life. Marang's salubrious body
and carefree attitude had always affected Suman.

He vowed that the Santals were created by God as the slaves
of the bhadralok.

'That pig, the whore! Is she a wife! How dare she call herself
the wife of Pandit Jawaharlal Nehru! Phew! Who does she think
Nehru is? If I get my hands on that pig that feeds on crap, she will
get screwed,' Suman Goshal shouted and threw a vulgar gesture at
Marang. Budhini's ma and baba were there too. Usually, Marang
ignored such provocations. But he couldn't bear it any longer. He
raced towards Suman in such anger that he didn't even wash his
hands after eating. They pushed and pulled each other into a fight.
Suman's men circled Marang. As he fell, they kicked him hard.
The Santals stood aside, too afraid to come anywhere near. Blows
and boots rained on Marang for spreading fabricated scandals that
linked a high-class Brahmin like Nehru to a pork-eating Santal.

'Motherfucker, who do you think you are!' Suman and his men
took a leak on Marang's head as he lay on the ground, defeated.
Suman then resumed hitting Marang, bristling with rage, until the
DVC officers came and parted them. Seeing the officers, the Santals

withdrew in fear and peeped out from a distance. They were afraid
that they would be beaten in the name of Budhini. Under the tree,
their food, half-eaten on the leaves of the sal trees, lay scattered.
The crows were pecking at it by this time.

The DVC officials couldn't get Suman Goshal to calm down.
He yelled that he would rape Marang's wife. There were two of
them now—Suman and Kumar Sanyal. Both of them were ready
to lose their lives for the cause of Bengali bhadralok. They said they
would gather more people to rape his wife. 'Anyone can come, it
doesn't matter how many,' they shouted.

Fear got the better of the Santals. Both Suman and Kumar
Sanyal were capable of going to any extent. Neither Marang nor
any other worker from Karbona responded.

'Where is that pig? We will not let her work here in the name
of Nehru, not again.' With this, they ran amok hunting for Budhini.

*

Budhini's duty was in the DVC guest house that day. She had
swept the rooms and washed the restrooms. Dogged by her will,
she competed with pain as if it was the enemy she wanted to defeat.
As she started mopping the verandah, she heard a din approaching
the guest house. She saw Kalicharan Chowdari, the watchman,
running towards her. He dragged her by the arm and pushed her
into the storeroom. He warned her not to cry or try to talk. 'Stay
calm; don't speak until I open the door,' he said and locked the
storeroom from outside. Though he had asked her not to worry,
she kept wondering what was taking place outside. Soon after that,
she heard the mob yell and stampede through the verandah like
wild elephants rocking forest. She heard things being broken and
pulled down. Doors were being forced open. In one of the rooms,
not too far away from where she was, a mirror was shattered to
pieces. After a while, the din drifted away. She hunched into a
corner of that dark room with a long-drawn sigh.

By the time the watchman opened the door, it was dark
outside. He touched her with the cane that he was carrying.
Budhini jumped up in fright.

'Shush, you! You should leave this place immediately. If they
see you here, they will kill you,' he said.

She didn't ask who. She just stared at the darkness outside.

'I am telling the truth, girl. They are looking for you. Those
men left from here only after turning everything upside down.
They said they were carrying petrol with them. The moment they
spot you, they will set you on fire. Didn't you hear them bolting
through the verandah?'

Budhini had been sleeping. Her intellect had long ago quit
responding to dangers, just like her body had stopped registering
pain. Her tears had dried up. Sitting thus, she simply listened to
what the watchman had to say.

'I am worried. How can I send you out in the night? My
daughter is the same age as you. But if I let you stay here, I seriously
don't know what will become of me. Anyway, you have to wait
here for some more time. I will come back when the situation
is okay. Then you run far away from here. Do you understand?
These men are crazy. Make sure you don't run into them. Now
lie down and keep quiet. Remember, if they catch you, they
will burn both of us,' he said. Locking the storeroom once again,
Kalicharan Chowdari went outside. There were not many guests
that night. Only two or three rooms were occupied on the upper
level. Budhini knew that the storeroom near the kitchen, where
she was locked up, had two doors. It was not long ago that she had
left both the doors open to clean the floor.

There was a lofty mud wall, approximately twelve feet, just
outside the kitchen door. And in between the kitchen door and the
wall was a close verandah leading to the backyard. Budhini planned
to open the kitchen door and escape through that narrow strip just
in case someone showed up. She wondered who was after her.
Marang? Or Narayan Jha?

For a while she couldn't hear any sound from outside. She was feeling suffocated because of the darkness and the strong smell of dried chillies and other spices stacked up in the room. It was hard not to sneeze or cough. The thought of doing so frightened her. She covered her mouth and nose in an attempt to silence a likely cough. When something scampered between her feet, she shook her legs. From the sound and smell of it, she understood it was nothing but a rat. She longed to see its eyes in the dark. She sighed, thinking that there was one more life in that darkness to give her companionship.

Kalicharan came back almost after an hour. This time, he brought with him some roti and dal for her. The bread was stale and cold. Lowering his voice, he told her, 'They are drinking in the front yard garden. I have a feeling that they may not go tonight. Someone said to them that you are around here. They pushed me, stopped me on my way and questioned me for a while. But I didn't say a thing. They kicked me saying that the rat can't wait in hiding for long, that they would kill it the moment it jumps out. If needed, they bragged, they were not afraid to set fire to the guest house to kill the rat.

'"There's no one hiding in here. You can come and check any time you want," I extended my bunch of keys to them. They didn't accept the keys but forced me to drink. You should forgive me; I didn't do it on purpose. Hopefully, they will go after some time, or sleep in the garden itself. But you need not worry about anything, I will take care of things.'

Budhini found it hard to swallow the bread. She drank the dal in one gulp. 'Take rest, I will go on my rounds once again,' said Kalicharan.

He was about to lock the room when they heard a commotion from the front parlour of the guest house. The mob was coming closer, shouting like an extended thunderclap.

'Run, *Beta*, the kitchen door is open,' Kalicharan Chowdari said. Budhini ran.

'That hog is in there. Catch her!' They kicked the doors of the rooms open, pulled apart the wooden furniture and tossed chairs

around. Kalicharan couldn't stop them. When he tried, he was
beaten up.

Like any animal that would run in fear, Budhini ran for her
life. She didn't see the rocks or pits on her way. In fact, nothing
bothered her. Racing through the darkness, she ran down the steps
to the river. Through the treacherous shores of the Damodar, she
continued stampeding over thorns, bogs and wild bushes.

For the first time in her life, the forest frightened her. The
woods and the mountains belonged to Marang Buru. She need not
be afraid of them. However, the woods of the night, she thought,
were the manifestation of the wrath of Marang Buru. He seemed to
block her in his rage, not letting her enter the forest. She stumbled
over a log.

She looked back at the guest house, which was still visible.
Now that the lights were all lit, the silhouette of the building
became sharper, the shadows more explicit. She could also see the
men still running around. Maybe they would come after her. It was
not so far away after all. Folding her hands, she prayed to Marang
Buru.

The forest was never quiet. Yet, its nocturnal sounds seemed
rather strange and scary to Budhini. The trees blocked her way; nor
did they allow the faint village light oozed by the kind skies to enter.
Tripping and stumbling, she floundered ahead. Sometimes she
ran; sometimes she walked. There were probably reptiles crawling
around, hungry wolves taking rounds, and maybe even elephants
or tigers roaming around. Budhini was defenceless and unarmed—a
child with not even a sling in her hand. She remembered how
people had once brought to the village the young man who had
died in the forest. They had cried calling his name. Though she had
no idea who he was, she had also joined the dirge.

Baba . . . my son,
Came to gather honey.
Baba . . . my girl,

Began to pluck leaves.
Baba . . . my son,
Sleeps on the lap of Marang Buru.
Baba . . . my girl,
does not answer.
My peacock flapped away,
My parrot flew away.

Budhini climbed up the hills. Crying aloud, calling out to Marang Buru, she made her way ahead. Under the slowly rising sun, she saw unending rows of black mountains in front of her. Coal everywhere! To her surprise, she found herself standing inside a coalfield, all alone with no one close by. She could not walk a step further. Forest with its thorns, stubs of stalks and boughs had scratched her face, neck and limbs. Blood continued to seep out of the cuts. Budhini felt exhausted. Fatigued, she lay down between two large mounds of coals.

She woke up only when the warm sun hit her face. She saw four or five men standing around her.

'Oye, get up. How did you come inside?' the men asked her. 'Where are you from?'

She pointed towards the hills of Marang Buru. The next second, she heard a melodious voice like the music of salvation. He came ringing his bicycle bell.

'Look at her, Dattaji! She says she climbed down the mountains.'

Leaving his bicycle leaning against a tree, Datta came nearer.

'Come,' he extended his hand and held her hand in his. After that, he didn't withdraw it until the day he died.

He walked her to a tea shop near the coal mine, where he sat beside her and watched her eat. She was a hungry, gluttonous load of dirt and stench. As she ate, tears rushed out of her eyes and ran down her coal-smudged cheeks in two furrows.

'The wife of Pandit Jawaharlal Nehru!' he sighed.

19

It was a narrow lane. The roads paved with concrete blocks gave the street a greyish white look. On either side, drainage channels carrying waste water ran at length. There were rows of houses facing each other on both sides. The entrance to each home from the road was bridged by concrete slabs placed over ditches. Remnants of alponas drawn in the morning still lingered on the street. As it was evening, lamps were lit in the facades of each house. There were sounds of children studying and singing. Rabindra music could be heard from somewhere down the road. A novice was playing on his sitar. There was a mixed smell of fumigating incenses and drainage water.

With alarming fear, Budhini set her feet on the street, holding on to the back of Datta's cycle. That street belonged to the Kayasthas and other minor Brahmins, a place forbidden to the likes of her. Why did Datta bring her to a place where death lay sprawled under each step?

'O, Dattaji, who the hell is with you at this hour of twilight?' a woman from the other side of the street asked him in contempt.

'I brought her to work at home, Babiji,' Datta replied and continued pedalling without giving her further attention.

'For your household chores! Why don't you get married, Datta? Why drag such crap to this street?'

'Will think of it, Babiji.'

'Think, think well. Don't you know we can't allow such practices here? You may be modern, and you may do what pleases you. But that's no excuse for this kind of behaviour. I warn you, this won't be tolerated here.' A loud bang followed as she struck together the two metal plates she was holding.

Budhini was shocked by the unannounced clank and deafening vibration. Her grip on the back of the cycle grew tighter.

Datta rolled the cycle into the front of a small house painted in light blue. 'Come,' he called her. Budhini was not sure where to put her feet on the concrete slab. Lacking courage, she stood on the street, bemused. Datta parked the cycle on the verandah and opened the door of the house. 'Come through the back door,' he gestured her to go to the right side of the house that led to the backyard.

It was dark in the backyard. The verandah, closed off with wooden bars, was three or four steps above the ground level. Lighting a lamp, Datta came to her. 'There wasn't any other way but to bring you here. I don't think this place is safe for you. Let me try to get a job for you at the coalfield in the morning,' he said.

In one end of the verandah, was a small wooden cot lying amidst old wooden stuff, baskets, mats and broom. Datta dragged the junk to the other end of the verandah and made room on the cot.

'You may sit there,' he pointed towards the empty cot. Budhini did as he said. Now she moved as per his words. If she acted on her own, she would invite trouble. Datta said he would find a safe place for her.

He came back to the verandah after a considerable amount of time. Until then, Budhini sat on the cot, lost, not knowing her next move. He gave her a white sari with a blue border and a blue blouse. Judging by the anxiety on her face, he said, 'Budhini, this belongs to my *maji*. You should change, or you may get an infection. Here, carry this lamp. There is a bathing shed near the

well over there. Take a bath and change your clothes. You will feel
better. Meanwhile, I will prepare something for us to eat.'

Two trees stood on the east and west side of the lovely lake
on their farm in the village—a kadam tree in the east and a sal
tree in the west. When the kadam tree bloomed, flowers that
resembled golden balls glided over the ripples in the lake. When
the sal tree bloomed, the water in the lake carried its secret scent.
Both Budhini and Phulmone engaged themselves in a swimming
race while taking a bath. Touching the branch of the kadam tree
that bent over the lake, they swam back to reach the sal tree that
almost touched the surface of the water at the other end. It was
always Phulmone who gave up. 'Budhini Mei, are you planning
to be in the water till some crocodile gobbles you up?' a defeated
Phulmone would say. By crocodiles, she was hinting at the young
men hiding behind the bushes.

When a bucket of water fell over her, Budhini writhed in pain.
With a start, the wounds on her body opened their mouths to
devour her. Fear took hold of her and kept her from touching
Datta's mother's sari that had a strange and intimidating scent about
it. The whiteness of it was more than that was needed.

For how many days had she been wearing the same panchi and
parhan Ma had given her? When was it that she had dressed up as a
traditional Santal woman for the DVC? She wondered what colour
the blood stain would be on the back of her milk-white panchi.
She had to tear apart the end of Ma's parhan. Ma had worn it only
once, and now she could wear it never again. She plunged it deep
into the bucket of water.

Datta's mother's blouse was too large for her. She must be a full
woman, a huge woman with abundant, well-rounded breasts. But
the long cloth called sari confused her. Looking at the never-ending
fabric lying in front of her on the floor, she sighed, having no idea
what to do with it. Somehow, she wrapped it around her body.
But neither the blouse nor the sari held. She had a strong urge to lie
down, sleep or cry. However, Datta had asked her to sit. She waited.

By the time Datta came to the verandah again, Budhini was dozing off, still sitting. 'Eat this and sleep,' Datta served her rice, dal and fish curry prepared in mustard paste, on a big dish. 'Leave the plate here after washing it,' he said.

Budhini was not hungry. She felt sick just smelling the smell of food. A burning sensation ran through her body, and her head dropped down as if unable to bear the weight any longer.

'Do you know any housework?'

Budhini didn't answer. He understood that she was sleeping.

'Okay, you lie down now. If you need anything, don't hesitate to knock on this door.' He closed the door from inside.

Gusts of cold wind flurried through the wooden bars. That corner of the verandah had retained the smell of withered moringa leaves. Budhini slept covering herself in fear. Fear formed her pillows. It was fear that she breathed in.

Hearing a commotion mingled with radio songs from the adjacent houses, Budhini woke up, tired and panic-stricken. The voices came from the front of Datta's house. She could hear both women and men. Budhini tried to get up, but like a dog that has been stabbed in the back, she sat down, unable to lift herself up. Yet, she stretched out one hand with great effort and grabbed the wooden bar of the long window. Though her head was spinning and her movements were faltered, she tried to stand up straight by clinging on to the rails. It seemed as if her feet were too fragile to carry her body. Maybe she could crawl like a reptile. All the while, Datta's mother's big blouse kept falling down, baring her shoulders. She couldn't fasten the sari properly on to her body even though it was six metres in length.

'Get that pork-eating slut out here,' Budhini heard the harsh voice of a man very distinctly.

'I will send her away, Jagnath Ray. I have no intention of keeping her here.' She identified Datta's voice.

'You have no intentions! Look at the way he talks. You think there's no one to question you in this village? Do you want our children to see this as an example?' a woman asked in anger.

'It's not what you think, Babiji. That child has been wounded severely, and she has nowhere else to go.'

'Oho! You call that dipshit a child now? After all, aren't you a Brahmin wearing the sacred thread? I am going to call your mother and sister here. Let them know how their godly son has defiled their home.'

'Aye, Dattaji, would you be driving all the lost pigs to the *agrahara*?'

'Why do we even fight over this? Get her out this instance. We can handle things.' Budhini could hear the voices of the youngsters over everyone else's. They grew more and more monstrous, rising above the other noises from the street. Cutting through the uproar, they raced inside. They dragged the girl who was clinging on to the wooden bars, shivering like a wet kitten, out. They pulled her down the steps, through the slush near the well and towards the ditch on its right side. Then they threw her to the mob on the street.

'Thrash this pig to death, this slut who has come to stay in the agrahara.'

The young men slapped her on her face and kicked her into the ditch. Before they could finish her off there, Datta lifted her up.

'Enough! Enough of this. I will take this child to the place from where I brought her. You need not become murderers.'

He helped her get on to the crossbar of his bicycle. The youngsters were angry they couldn't do more. Roaring, they came back to attack her. Datta raised his hand and stopped them. Howling, they followed his bicycle through the street.

A street in greyish white. Open drains carrying waste water. Lovely alponas. A fusion of incense and slush. Rabindra music and the Gayatri Mantra . . .

Leaving it all behind, Datta pedalled vigorously to cross the village borders.

*

A black dust storm raged; the sky and the earth grew darker. All remains of light went out. A scary groan was heard, as if it was coming from the pith of absolute darkness: 'Kill, kill, throw, throw!' The coalfield wallowed. Footsteps approached like thunder that turns louder, harder and stronger. In the dark obscurity extending up to the horizons, Budhini sat alone listening to the heavy panting of the mob. She wanted to run away, but her limbs were numb. The burden of her head was more than what her neck could bear. If only she could open her eyes, she could escape. But her eyes had been closed forever. 'Kill, kill!' the drone of the stones drew nearer. Sharp-edged metal weapons clanged against each other. She could also hear the buzzing echoes of canes being whipped. If only she could cry out loud, she could escape. Unfortunately, she couldn't even open her mouth. She lay on the ground writhing in pain.

'Budhini,' someone touched her forehead. She opened her eyes. 'Baba,' she said and held on to the hand. 'Baba,' she cried aloud.

'You might have had some lousy dream. Don't worry. It is nothing more than a nightmare. Try to sleep now,' Datta touched her shoulders gently. He sat down beside her, pondering over the incidents and coincidences that had meddled with her life. How brutally they had changed her life! A little later, he realized that he was wrong, for life itself was a constant parade of accidents. Those who chased Budhini with murderous roars were the men who were a part of these series of mishaps that had destroyed her life. They were men who had taken the law into their hands; they had passed a judgement according to their whims; they were executing it in their own way.

Budhini didn't let go of his hand even after she drifted into a blackout. 'Baba, baba,' she continued sobbing.

The next day, throughout, she carried coal. He saw nothing except fear in her eyes. She was scared of the desolate enormity of the coalfields, of the black winds that stormed like the wail of the earth, of the people who came across her as she carried heavy loads on her head, of everything that she happened to see. As he placed a load of coal over her head, he noticed her neck crushing under the thirty to thirty-five kilograms. It was not as easy as carrying a bundle of firewood or a roll of rice straw. Every step she took, he saw her shambling. He thought she would fall or drop the load. Though he felt no love or affection for this child, the injustice done to her had stung his heart. And for that, he believed, she should be defended.

'Let her stay with me. You need not worry about her, Dattaji,' said Janbhari who had been working in the coalfield for the past forty years. Now sixty, she had been widowed at twenty. She began carrying coal loads to provide for her two daughters, and now she and coal had become inseparable. Her lungs were severely damaged because of the constant inhaling of fuel smoke, and these days she walked with an unsteady shuffle, spat out blood and coughed drastically as she carried the load. Her children had their own lives. She lived all alone in a small, rented room.

'I am glad there will be someone to give me water at the time of my death,' she said, holding Budhini's hand. She respected Dattaji, for it was he who always talked to the company for her cause. Janbhari, who could not carry five kilos, let alone thirty-five, was a loss to the company. But Datta had told them: 'She has been a worker with the company since its beginning. The company should sympathize with her. I am willing to work on her behalf too.'

Budhini couldn't spend a moment in happiness with Janbhari. The minute they went to sleep, the old woman would start tossing and squirming in bed, struggling for air. Leaning against the wall, she would wheeze in squeaky, demonic moans. Her eyes would roll back, and she would beat her chest violently in her strife to catch some air. It was an unbearable sight to watch—an old woman gasping. Budhini helped her take in steam using a cloth soaked in boiled water. She would rub the old woman's chest and her back till she got some relief. It was good if she got some sleep at least

towards daybreak, for otherwise she would sit drained and beaten
at the coalfield.

'Janbhari, clear off! You need not come to work again,' the
officials would scold her as usual.

'How on earth do you expect me to live then?' she would ask.
'I have spent my whole life in your coalfield, haven't I? This illness
is my price for that. Where else can I go now? I will work here
until my last breath.'

The company officials didn't wait to argue. They cut Janbhari's
wages by one-fourth. Beating her chest, the old woman cried.
'You are cheating me. I had carried thirty-five to forty kilos when
I was able to.'

Budhini asked her, 'Why do you suffer like this, Janbudhi? I
am working, am I not?'

This phase of peace didn't last long. Rumours and queries about
Budhini abounded in the nearby communities. Hearing that the
woman who lived with Janbhari was the wife of Pandit Jawaharlal
Nehru, people flocked to visit her. There were a lot of Muslim
families in the neighbourhood. The women surrounded Budhini in
great excitement. 'What! Jawaharlal Nehru didn't take his bride home
even for a single day?' They were surprised. 'The prime minister's
wife makes a living carrying coal!' They couldn't believe it.

Hearings took place in Munawar Ali's tea shop, where men
gathered in the morning to read the newspaper and listen to the
radio.

'Nehru abandoned his wife because he was a Brahmin, isn't it?'
asked Mirza Ali.

'Never, Mirza Saheb,' Firoz Khan, an ardent reader of
newspapers, corrected him. 'Nehru is a socialist. He is beyond caste
and religion. He wants the people of India to be free of chains of
caste and religion. He says you and I should be known as citizens
of India first and then as Muslims.'

'What does that mean? Is he trying to say that religion and caste
are no longer important?' Sohanlal Misra, who had been reading a

newspaper in one corner of the tea shop, asked with a loud thump on the table. The others fell silent for a while.

'No matter what Nehru says, Muslims will remain Muslims and Hindus will remain Hindus. The Indian citizen comes after that. No one should try to change that, or dream of Brahmins and Chantalas becoming one. Indians are Indians, and Pakistanis are Pakistanis,' Sohanlal's eyes reddened.

'This is not what I have said, Sohanlalji,' Firoz Khan explained. 'This is what the Constitution signed by Nehru says.'

'Constitution!' Sohanlal stormed out. The tea shop was eerily quiet. Though all talk about Budhini ended abruptly there, it continued in other places.

20

Datta's mother, who had been at her daughter's house, came home the following week. She seemed diminished and entirely broken, as if some emergency had befallen her. She cried without a break.

'Why do you end up in such disasters, Mani?' she asked Datta. 'You are forty-one now. You denounced a married life, and look, what did you drag yourself into? How on earth do you expect me to face people?'

'What disaster do you think I have got into, Maji?'

'Didn't you do anything? The whole village says you brought a low-class woman home while I was not around. How could you do this, Mani?'

'Haven't I explained it to you, Maji? Why do you believe what others say?'

His mother pretended not to hear that. 'How dare you take her inside our house, Mani? Did you let her enter the prayer room? Has she been to our kitchen? Tell me the truth, Mani. I don't want to hear lies.'

'She slept on the cot in the kitchen verandah, Maji.'

He felt humiliated that he had to answer her like this.

'How can I believe your words? Look at these plates; don't we eat from the same plates? She had her food from this, didn't she?

157

Ma Durga! What can I do now?' With this, his mother threw the plates into the backyard. They hit the walls of the well and fell with a loud clang. The neighbours peeped in. Humiliated, Datta went inside silently.

Shortly after that, he heard his mother screaming hysterically. He ran towards her. When she saw him, she shrieked as if she had seen a demon. She was looking at the panchi and parhan Budhini had dipped in the brass bucket in the bathing shed a week back. It gave out a foul smell. Datta dug a hole and buried the clothes and the bucket. Through her loud sobs, his mother said that they needed to take a decision on that 'gross' situation once his sisters came home that evening. She then chanted, blowing off steam at Budhini.

'They say she went out in my sari and blouse. How dare you, Mani? Giving that low-class woman my dress? Or did she open my cupboard and take it herself? If it is so, Ma Durga, I will burn everything once my daughters come home.'

Datta's sisters came home crying like their mother. *Why had their brother indulged in fornication without getting married? Why such a grave mistake?* They regretted letting him live a life of his own for so long. When his sisters and mother refused to quiet down, Datta lost patience. He cycled to Janbhari's house.

He sensed upheaval in the area around the coalfield. The people who had gathered there were murmuring. They stopped him. 'Who are you? What are you doing here?'

Datta told them his name. Before he could say more, they attacked him. 'You are Sohanlal's man, aren't you?' They kicked his cycle until it broke and then threw it into the fire. Someone hurled a long metal blade, scraping Datta's left shoulder. Blood spurted and Datta fell flat on his face.

Munawar's tea shop had been ransacked. Both the Hindus and the Muslims had started a riot. The pathways had piles of fire, smoke and ashes throughout. Datta had to crawl and find his way to Janbhari's house. Though he knocked on her door many times, neither Budhini nor Janbhari opened it. It was but minutes ago that a mob had invaded Janbhari's house and beaten the women most cruelly. They had tried to strip Budhini and hauled her along the street. She would have been killed had some young men from Munawar's tea shop not reached in time and rescued her. Before leaving, the attackers had threatened to burn her if she did not move out of Janbhari's house.

The situation worsened by the time it was eight. The opposition groups attacked each other's houses; shops were vandalised and set on fire. Obviously, the mob had gone mad. Rioters ran from street to street, grabbing whatever weapons came in sight. Havoc continued with the shouts of invaders and the cries of women and children filling the air with fear. Dogs barked and howled unendingly. Janbhari saw a group of people running towards her house with burning torches. She cried, 'Run, run away. Save this daughter.'

Holding Budhini's hand, Datta ran to the coalfields. They discreetly boarded a truck that was carrying coal to Purulia.

'Don't be afraid,' he said.

Budhini was not afraid.

21

28 May, 1964

'Budhini Mejhan, come sit by my side.'

Datta had called her to the entrance of their little hut, which was as humble as the earth itself. Budhini was breastfeeding Ratni. Carrying her daughter, she sat beside him even though there was not enough place for two people to sit comfortably.

'I want to talk to you about someone who is connected to your life,' he said and then paused to survey the expression on her face. 'Listen, there's nothing to be afraid of.'

Nothing to be afraid of? Again! Budhini looked at him anxiously. *Were the good days of her life, when she had slept without nightmares, coming to an end? Would she have to run away from her own life again?*

Datta showed her the front page of the day's newspaper, where there was a picture of a man with a calm face, sitting with his chin resting on his hand. A bolt of lightning flashed through her as memories flooded back. He read out the headlines to her:

Jawaharlal Nehru Is Dead
Sudden End Follows a Heart Attack
The Light Is Out!

Instantly, she remembered the simple, smiling figure of the gormen bowing before her so that she could garland him, and how the light of her life went out that very second.

'I heard the news yesterday, but I had a feeling that it would not be right if you didn't know about it. And above all, I want you to hear it from me, not from anyone else,' Datta said. He was sorry about reminding her of things past.

'I don't want to remember it,' Budhini said and put the child in the cloth crib.

When the world outside their dilapidated hut focused on the news of Nehru's death, she served the leftover gruel from the previous night on two mud plates. 'Please have this. Maybe they will pay me today. And if it happens, I will make rice and dal for dinner,' she told Datta.

Budhini smoothed out her clothes, fixed her hair, rubbed her face down with both her hands and set out. Thinking of something for a second or two, she went back inside. Holding on to the rope of the cloth crib, Datta was admiring his daughter. Budhini caressed his back. It seemed that he was expecting it.

'The yesterdays belonged to them, Budhini. Tomorrow will be for Ratni,' he patted her on her back.

Sometimes Budhini went to Purulia to work at the house of an officer from a coal mine in Ranipur. She was paid one rupee a day. A knoll of dirty dishes, a hummock of filthy clothes, smelly toilets and dirt-water ditches waited for her.

In the town, dirges streamed out from within the houses and shops. The air was desperate with people walking on the pathways. They had black ribbon badges pinned to their chests. Their prime minister had passed away.

'Budhini, I know you are scared of this. I am taking it off,' Datta had told her while looking into her eyes and removing the sacred thread from his body. Budhini wondered why she had remembered that incident all of a sudden.

The coal mining officer's wife, who had a small transistor radio by her side, said mournfully, 'Today is a tragic day.' Sad music continued to pour out of her instrument. Looking at her maids, she said, 'There will be no cooking today. I don't want anyone to talk to me either. I am going to sit by my radio and fast. I will not even have water.' Her eyes were misty. It was clear that she was holding back her tears.

Scraping off the leftover food from the previous day's plates, Budhini cleaned them with mud and ash. Falling down the edges of the plates that were laid out to dry, the sun shone brightly. By noon, Budhini was drenched in soap water, thanks to the laundry on the washing stone. It was then that the woman who cooked came to announce, 'Don't you know we are observing a fast today? Go home after finishing your work.' On her way to the kitchen, she asked Budhini, 'You might have heard of Nehru's death, haven't you? Radio reports nothing else today. By the way, do you know who Nehru is?'

Shaking off the bleaching powder into the waste-water ditches, sweeping away the dirt and smell with a hard stick broom, Budhini chased it all down with fresh water. When Datta and she got down from the truck, she remembered, they looked like two dark demons. The driver had said, 'Now what, Dattaji? Can you take her wherever you go? You are asking for trouble.' Datta had no idea what else to do. It was the truck driver himself who took them to a small coal mine in Ranipur. They worked there for two years until the company shut down. They lived in a small, rented house.

In bundles, Budhini carried the washed, dried and folded clothes and the polished plates inside. Clean toilets, clean yards, clean sinks, clean ditches. She left everything speckless so that it could all get dirty again by the time she returned the following day.

Washing her hands and face, fixing her hair, smoothing the folds in her dress, Budhini went to the kitchen and called the maid. Placing her forefinger on her lips, the maid came out, gesturing to her to not make any noise.

'Wage,' Budhini said.

'Don't you know it is not possible today? No one has come out of the room so far.'

Budhini walked back. From the houses and shops, mournful music crawled on to the street. From here and there rose pictures of Pandit Jawaharlal Nehru. People had placed flowers in front of it.

Home! In a land that belonged to no one, they, like two tiny birds, had gathered everything they thought would come to be of use and strived to make a hut under an old tamarind tree. It was in those days that they realized the waste materials they found on the way could be used to build a house. Branches, thick paper, cardboard boxes, brick pieces, palm fronds, sacks, waste cloths, mud . . .

Datta had asked her, 'Is this house secure, Budhini? Will the wind blow it away? Or will the rain wash it away?'

Budhini smiled. She sang:

O sweet tamarind,
Limbs far-reaching.
Blooms in red and white,
Fruit hung down in bunches.

No one ever made a living by eating tamarinds, even though people might have relished its juices. Datta joined the road workers. His lungs, already weak, became more vulnerable because of the tar, fire, coal and smoke. Budhini went to carry coal in the mines of Ranipur on the days Datta took ill. It was illegal, she could have been caught anytime. But they had to live, and Datta needed to be taken care of with proper treatment. She continued stealing, till the company got her to run away.

A group of schoolchildren stopped Budhini on her way. They gave her a piece of black cloth and a pin. 'Didi, wear this. India has lost her beloved prime minister,' they said and pinned it on to her left shoulder. All were sad, including the sky and the earth.

The same sadness, however, could not be found poking its head in the huts of the people where hungry children cried. Ratni cried ceaselessly. There was only water in their shelter, but the child was not willing to have it. Carrying her, Datta stood under the tamarind tree, waiting for Budhini. From afar, Budhini saw him wearing a black ribbon on his chest.

Lying sleepless with a rumbling stomach, Datta said, 'Budhini Mejhan, I have prepared a written application. We should go to Panchet and demand before the DVC to take you back. They dismissed you without any grounds.'

He thought he heard her hum.

22

'Where's your ma? Where's your baba? Call them. Come out. All of you get out.' Those who came to demolish the houses on the land that belonged to none rushed in. They threw out everything they saw, clothes on the line, pots in which rice was cooked, the broom, Ratni's mud horse. The child ran outside in fear and hid behind the banana grove. Ma and Baba were not around. Petrified, she watched the men who came to dismantle the house and were climbing on to the roof. By the time her baba came running, they had pulled the ceiling down.

Frantic with worry, Datta asked, 'Where's my child?' The men didn't seem to be listening. Ratni had not seen her baba worried like this before. When he came out of the house in search of her, she ran towards him and clasped him tightly. Carrying her, Datta crossed the tar road in a jiffy and ran towards the field where Budhini had gone to get water. He had absolutely no idea why he ran, for he couldn't quite pull it off with the child in his hands. Datta kept going, breathless and coughing and wheezing. Putting the child on the ground, he sat down, fatigued, on the edge of the field. Leaning back on his arms, he opened his mouth to breathe in. It was high noon and the sun blazed, showering fire over their heads. 'Baba,' the child rubbed his back. She knew her baba needed some water. To her dismay, she looked around to see only endless fields with no person in sight. There was no sign of water.

'Ma will come now. Come sit here with me,' Datta said to his daughter. The veins on his neck had become visibly prominent. His lungs, he knew, were blocked with coal and dust and would lead to the ultimate end of a miner. He clasped his daughter's delicate hand. Though he was sure that the house would be dismantled, truth be told, he was shocked beyond repair by the sight of it. On the day the tamarind tree was cut down, he had said, 'Budhini Mejhan, if we don't vacate immediately, they will demolish everything. The felling of the tree is a clear sign.'

'Can't we live here till they come?'

'Who is coming, Baba? Why will they pull our house down?' Ratni asked.

Datta told her about the lives of the poor in the land of the gormen. 'These lands are public property. Gormen's people will come to capture it.'

'Who is gormen, Baba?'

Ratni's baba laughed aloud. 'It is heard that we are ourselves the gormen.'

The child did not catch the meaning of either the laughter or the words.

During the five years they stayed on that land, Budhini had planted and raised banana groves, papaya, moringa and even a sal tree around their hut.

'All your own,' Datta would tease her. Budhini had continued tilling the land, sowing spinach and green chillies and building a trellis for the cucumbers. In front of the hut, genda flowers bloomed in abundance. Crossing the tar road, she would walk a long distance to get water from the pond in the faraway field. Watered thus, she had built a robust green wall that flowered and bore fruits around their fragile little hut.

Five years back, when they had built this hut on the land that belonged to none, there were no other houses in view.

Their shelter rose like a pathfinder for the homeless and landless. But within no time, huts started sprouting on both sides of the tamarind tree. The officials who noticed this encroachment gave them continuous warnings to evacuate. In between all this, Budhini's banana tree produced fruits, the moringa blossomed, the papaya ripened, the genda flowers diffused fragrance. The last warning they received was to evacuate within seven days. Datta had written many applications to stop the dismantling of the huts. We have no property, no house. Where can we go if you don't give us some other land instead? All the applications went unconsidered. But soon afterwards, the woodcutters came to chop down the tamarind.

At the first cut, the tamarind tree had shuddered from root to crown, shedding all ripened leaves in unison, colouring the earth yellow. After that, each time the axe fell, it rained green leaves, maroon shoots, red and yellow flowers, tiny fruits . . .

Budhini begged the woodcutters to be careful and not let the branches fall over the house. They became angry, for their bodies were wilting from the exertion of felling an enormous tree, the heartwood of which kept challenging their strength.

'We can't promise you that,' they said.

Though the hut was not even six feet high and a person like Datta could enter only by bowing his head and body, they had developed it into a one-room home with four mud walls and two tiny windows. For Budhini, it was the safest place on earth. With each branch that fell, she sat down with her wings spread like a mama hen hatching. When the trunk of the tamarind tree fell across the tarmac road with a loud roar, her house waved. Datta clung tightly to Budhini. She felt the branches of the heartwood encircling her. At that time, Ratni was lying on the floor that was swabbed with cow dung, playing with her mud horse. The horse was about to gallop with her to the land of the Kabuli-wallah. 'Please wait a while longer. Let me put on my bangles and necklaces and take sweets for the Kabuli-wallah,' she said, turning her back to the horse and pretending to wear her imaginary bangles and necklaces and wrapping up non-existent sweets. Then, hearing the roaring thunder caused by the tamarind tree falling, she ran to hug her ma and baba.

The long sounds made by Datta as he struggled for air terrified Ratni. She stared into the boiling sunlight pouring over the ground. When she saw her mother coming from far away, carrying water on her head and hips, she ran towards her with her hands up in the air, crying.

Water! He felt the comfort on his dried lips, throat, face, forehead . . . and the comfort of Budhini's hands. She supported Datta on her shoulder and scolded both father and daughter for roaming around. She was upset over why they couldn't just sit at home.

That night they slept in a roofless house, watching the sky. It was a full moon night. The moonlight was generous, and thousands of stars twinkled. A cold, soothing wind blew, urging them to forget the morning heat. It was like a deliberate push to say that the world was beautiful again.

'Let us leave Purulia, Budhini,' Datta said. 'We've been fighting here for six or seven years. It is time to wind up.'

'But . . .'

'Life will be hard wherever it is. Let it be in one's own land then.'

Even though Datta consoled her saying that the old hatred and anger would have subsided, Budhini couldn't think of going back to her homeland without fear.

'Do you feel like going back to your village?' Budhini asked, 'To your home, to your ma?'

After thinking for a minute, Datta said, 'No. Ratni should not be hungry. She should go to school and you should get back your job at the DVC. Then only . . .' A prolonged cough interrupted his words.

23

After the incident at the Panchet Dam, of a woman and her daughter committing suicide, Jauna Marandi had not heard any more about them. Someone said they had set out from his sister Hisi's house. Hearing this, Jauna had straight away gone to meet his sister in a state of panic.

'Where are they?'

'Gone.'

'Where?'

'How do I know?'

Jauna became angry. Hisi's arrogance and ungratefulness were apparent in each answer she gave. Besides, she was drunk. He called Hisi's children Thimbu and Numku. The children pointed in the direction they went out.

'Why didn't you stop them, Hisi?'

'Why should I do that, Bhaiya? Can't they guess? How can six people live in a place where there is not room for even two? They said they would go. I didn't feel like stopping them.'

'You have no gratitude. That woman worked hard, cleaned the waste-water ditches and holes with her own hands to look after your children. Don't you know that?'

'What of it? Can't she consider it as house rent?'

Jauna Marandi didn't have the patience to listen to more.

'Do you know, you stupid woman, that the woman committed suicide by jumping into the dam. I came to tell you this.'

Hisi floundered a little but then shouted at her brother again. 'Oho! So you are telling me that I am the cause?'

Seeing that Jauna was about to leave, Hisi called him from behind and said, 'Oye, Jauna, when I had to face bad times, why did you leave your nephews at the mercy of strangers without taking them straight to your house?'

Bad times! How dare she call them bad times! She was arrested for picking pockets, and she called it bad times! How could this situation be included in the list of trying times? Is it just a matter of picking someone's pocket? Or who knows what! Jauna thought to himself.

'Oye, Thimbu, Numku, don't you like your mami? Doesn't she serve you rice every day with freshwater fish? Then why the hell did your mamo leave you in charge of that reckless woman?' Hisi extended her insults.

Sick of it all, Jauna left the scene without saying another word. He knew that his wife hated to see Hisi or her children enter her house. This hostility developed soon after Hisi headed for a heedless lifestyle. It was the cannabis dealer, who called himself her husband, who had brought her down to this state of ruin. Jauna had seen him many times, walking stealthily around the bus stand with small packs of cannabis hidden safely in the folds of the *bagwaan* he was wearing. The money he earned was spent on the women who caught his fancy.

Hunger was such a devil! And poverty was the sole reason that justified Hisi's present circumstances. Whenever he gave it some thought, it would prick his conscience.

What did he do to help his sister and her children overcome their hunger? Hisi put the blame on Jauna's wife. Was it the wife alone? Even Jauna avoided Hisi when he happened to meet her. She was never not drunk.

Moreover, she insulted Jauna in public, called him whatever names that came to her mind. He tried hard not to let the traces of sentiments he felt towards his sister dry out entirely. And that explained why he visited her whenever he made some quick cash. He was concerned about Thimbu and Numku, both of whom grew up in dirt, mud and puddles. Hisi had no particular interest in her children who loved their dog more than their mother.

Jauna took sweetmeats whenever he visited them. Invariably, it broke his heart to see his sister and children devouring it. Sometimes he would think of his childhood. He would think of the suckling Hisi in their mother's lap and the way she would stop sucking just to give him a smile. These thoughts were more than enough to crush his heart.

However, Jauna was not willing to run after the police once he heard the news of his sister being arrested. Jail, he thought, would be good for her. At the least, she would not get knocked out like a regular drunkard. Jauna could raise Thimbu and Numku. But when he took the children home, Jauna's wife stormed at him, 'It is either the children of the pickpocket or me. You can decide who you want.'

He had no option but to take the children back to their home, where their dog was lying huddled, waiting for their return. 'Be here, Mamo will come back after work. The road outside is busy. Can't you see how vehicles race? Don't step outside.' A hundred worries would trouble him as he would leave his two and four-year-old nephews alone. Even though hatred for his wife filled his heart sometimes, he tried to think from her perspective as well. She complained that Thimbu and Numku were gluttonous, that they won't be appeased even if she gave them her share of food. Whenever the children were around, she had to sleep on an empty stomach. But Jauna knew that it was a lie. She was not the kind of person who tolerated hunger. Like a fool, he consoled himself thinking that at least his nephews had their dog by their side.

His profound sadness came to an end the day he chanced to meet Datta and his family for the first time. They boarded his jeep from Dhanbad. They were looking for a place to live in, and work that would earn them at least a meal a day. The likes of them were everywhere, the people of a poor country, without a job, no salary and who couldn't afford even rice. Cities spat the likes of them out; villages were in misery. Even those who worked till sundown went to bed on an empty stomach.

'Could you live with two little children in their house? It cannot be called a home though; it's just a hovel,' Jauna Marandi had asked Datta.

'With two kids?'

'Yes, Bhaiya, two boys. One is two and the other one four,' Jauna's throat rasped in pain. He cried, 'You could stay there and search for work. I could also help you find a job.'

That was how Budhini took on the responsibility of filling the bellies of three children instead of one. Apart from the fact that they got a place to sleep in, Asansol gave no comfort to Budhini or Datta, not even a bit. Budhini realized it was not a wise idea to think of returning to Panchet. She had approached the DVC many times, travelling in Jauna Marandi's jeep that plied from Asansol to Panchet early in the morning, but in vain.

'Put your application in that box,' the officers would say. 'We'll let you know.'

'I was asked to give the application directly and explain my situation,' Budhini would say.

'Who told you?' the sepoy at the door would ask.

'My husband.'

'Your husband? Who is he? Is he the prime minister? Whoever he is, you cannot go inside. Leave your application here.'

Datta and their daughter, meanwhile, would be waiting for Budhini outside the office.

'Did you give it?' Datta would ask.

'Yes.'

'What did they say?'

'Nothing.'

However, contrary to their hopes, neither had the hatred of the villagers subsided nor had their animosity lessened. The moment they recognized Budhini at the DVC, they gave her the same old dirty look. The contempt they harboured towards her darkened their faces.

'Look, Ratni's baba. How strange it is! My clan hates me. They turn their faces away when they see me. And here I am, striving hard to feed two Santal children.'

Datta consoled her. 'If only I could find some work, we could raise them better.'

Every day, Datta went out in search of work. Some days he found a job, but on most days he returned home desperate. Besides, he couldn't do labour that demanded severe physical exertion. Jauna Marandi found a job for Budhini in a small hotel near the Asansol bus stand, where her work was to clean dirty dishes. There was no pay for the task. Food for two was the reward!

Not only hunger but poverty too plagued them! Sometimes it was replacing torn clothes or a broken kanda, kerosene for the lamp, medicine for the children and a hundred other needs that demanded money. After six months, Budhini gave up the work at the hotel after a contractor who oversaw the cleaning of the ditches took pity on her.

Stinking, sluggish black water stagnated in the waste-water ditches of the town, with human faeces floating over it. People passed by it with their noses covered. Budhini had secured a job there for ten rupees per day. Dealing with dirt, she was forced to abandon her memories of crystal waters from a distant past.

Hisi returned on the last day that Budhini and her daughter went to the DVC office. She shouted, saying that strangers had occupied her house. She was so drunk that she could barely stand.

'Please sit here. Jauna told me that his sister would be coming,' Datta said gently.

'I know that crazy Jauna let you stay here. He might have received rent from you as well. But, now I tell you, this is my house and you should leave at once.'

'Please have some food. Aren't you tired after the long journey?' Datta tried to reassure her again.

'I don't eat with strange men,' she said and took out a bottle of booze from the folds of her dress. 'But I don't really mind drinking with a stranger. I will give you what's left.' Shaking the bottle, she walked towards him. He got up from there and went outside. Budhini followed him.

'Are you both going already? Take this girl also. This is my house, the house of Thimbu and Numku. I don't even let their father inside this, let alone a stranger. Go, go away.'

Hisi forcefully held her children back as they started to follow Ratni. When Thimbu and Numku began crying, their dog barked at Hisi. She reacted by kicking it. Budhini, her daughter and Datta sat outside the house listening to the commotion inside. Budhini wanted to go somewhere that very instant. Datta said, 'We will go in the morning after saying goodbye to the children, Budhini Mejhan. Or they will worry or wait for us. We have to inform Jauna as well. He has helped us in times of difficulty.'

Later, they said goodbye to the children, though Hisi was not fully awake. They couldn't meet Jauna. After that, Jauna hadn't seen them again.

24

Suchitra bought sanitary pads from 'Somnath Hembrom's Ladies' Choice', a shop for knick-knacks. Somnath, who was wearing a rust-coloured jacket on top of his faded clothes, looked like an older man with a face that reminded one of Lal Bahadur Shastri, who had prominent, rounded cheeks, a depressed nose, sunken mouth and serene eyes. He was busy reassuring himself time and again by looking through his thick glasses and counting money.

The store, which was part of a building with many stores adjacent to it, was tiny in size. The road in front, marked by two easily removable hoardings, advertised a beauty parlour and a CD shop on the top floor of the same building. Gold-plated ornaments were the prime goods in Somnath Hembrom's store. Golden bangles and necklaces were displayed in the front to make it look like a real jewellery shop. But inside the shop, there were many other things that ranged from beauty products to steel dishes. Next door was a printer-cum-courier service centre. Next to that was a cool bar that saw a lot of activity. It sold a variety of paans with cool drinks. Any person who climbed the steps up to the bar went away chewing on a paan. Suchitra bought the day's newspaper. Rupi Murmu had gone to a mobile shop near Chirkunda to get a new charger for her iPhone, to replace the one she had lost.

Sitting on a stool in front of Somnath Hembrom's shop, Suchitra opened the newspaper. 'Godda Burning', the headline announced.

'Watch out! The stool has a broken leg,' looking through his thick glasses, Somnath warned her. Inside the goggles, Suchitra thought, his eyes were as large as chicken eggs. She remembered Bottle-Bottom-Kitchu (BBK), her uncle's son, Krishnan, who got the sobriquet because of his funny-looking glasses. Nevertheless, the lenses gave the brilliant BBK the look of a country jerk.

Smiling at Somnath Hembrom with gratitude, she shifted the stool to a different position. From there, she watched the older man polish the stone-studded rings with a piece of muslin cloth, trying on each ring before putting it back in the case. She couldn't concentrate on the newspaper. A Santal of his age, she thought, would definitely have something to say about Budhini Mejhan. Somnath Hembrom's next question allowed her to open up.

'Are you a tourist?' asked Hembrom.

'No, I am a research scholar.'

'Oh! What are you researching?'

'The dams on the Damodar.'

Hembrom's eyebrows shot up. He looked at her from over his glasses.

'There are two of us. My friend is a Santal, Rupi Murmu.'

Somnath continued to polish a ring that looked like an imitation of blue sapphire.

'We are on our way to Karbona today. How far is it from here?'

'Karbona! That sounds interesting. It was my village once. What's there to research?'

'We are after a story, a strange kind of a story that has got something to do with Jawaharlal Nehru's connection with a Santal girl. Her name is Budhini Mejhan. We would like to know more about it.'

'Hmm,' Hembrom who appeared totally uninterested went back to polishing the rings.

'Do you know where Budhini is now?'

'No, I don't know,' Hembrom answered without taking his eyes away from the ring. It was apparent that he was not interested in talking about that topic. But Suchitra continued, 'We have met a tiriao player from Karbona. His name is Chotroi Soren. We got some intriguing information from him, especially about bitlaha.'

'There's no bitlaha these days. Maybe it is still happening in some nook and corner, secretly.'

'This is about 1959. Budhini was ousted from the village by bitlaha.'

Hembrom said he didn't know anything about it as he was not in Karbona at that time. He was admitted to a government hospital in Asansol due to a high fever. He claimed to be unaware about the visit of Pandit Jawaharlal Nehru. And even if he had known about it, he was too naive to understand its significance. 'Somu, the wretched! Everyone thought he would die a premature death, but he didn't. There were many occasions in life when he could have died, but he survived. There would be such occasions in the future too,' Somnath Hembrom smiled. It had the tenderness of that of a child.

'You are of the same age as Budhini, aren't you?'

'I don't know about it. Chotroi is the person for you. He spends his life in the village, and so he must know better.'

'And you?'

'It may sound funny, but the land I had there was wiped off the map a long way back. Now it lies under the water, like slush,' he said polishing the stone-studded rings. And with that he began the story of the evolution of his piece of land. His family used to own five acres of land near the river. Each year, the riverbank would erode a part of it. Nani, Ma and his aunts would pray in tears:

O Damodar,
We fall at your feet . . .

But there was no use, for the river had its ways. 'As we went to sleep, we listened to the gurgling sound of the river gnawing at the banks, eating away everything that was ours. Bdhum, bdhum.' There was nothing to be done. 'What can we do now, Somu's baba?' Somu's ma would ask his baba mournfully. Though his baba himself had no idea, he consoled her without giving up on hope. 'We will work hard on the leftover land. What else can we do?' With that, Somnath's ma would regain her energy and let go of her insecurities. Somu's baba was a man of his word. Both his mind and body were healthy, and he knew how to take care of his family. But was it right to let him carry all the burden? Everyone had his or her responsibility. She would call her children, turn the house upside down with her anxieties, pay the neighbours a visit and flaunt a show of enthusiasm.

'Listen, Damini's ma, this sowing season we will double the spinach seeds. Somu's baba says there's nothing to get worried about. Spinach abounds in silt-like blades of grass in the woods. I can't wait to see those leaves! If you have seeds of sweet corn, please do give us some. Somu's baba has started tilling the soil. I am also not going to waste a minute more. Somu is a grown-up boy now, isn't he? So let him do his share as well. Thanks to Marang Buru, Somu is not a lazy chap. I tell him, "Somu, you are the eldest one. You should help your baba in the fields." He nods with a smile in return. And my girls? I take care of them very well. I will not let them sit idle for a minute. Oye, Jugita, did you see this bundle? These are the most exceptional seeds of okra. You have to grow them. Your sister is busy tending to the cows and milking them and preparing buttermilk and curd. This year, Baba is trying basmati. Such a wise decision! There's nothing to be afraid of, Somu. Let the land that has gone to water go. Luckily, whatever is left is the most solid. The river will not fail us. We will be busy once we start draining the water from the fields. Think of all the fish we will gather just by stirring up mud and puddles. My mouth waters thinking of the yummy smell of fish roasted over a fire. We could make a profit for sure.

'Chunki, ask your baba for some land for a banana farm. I will also help. Don't we have two lean pigs in the sty at present? I don't think that's enough. We should have more of them, and also a loafing shed full of goats. We need a lot more . . .'

'Ma would go on and on. She would get up before everyone else in the house and go on prattling even if there was no one to listen to her. She would talk to the walls or broom and never get tired of it.

'By the time I was ten, the last patch of land had disappeared, bitten away by the river. People sympathized with my baba. "What are you going to do, Raghunath?" "How sad, your area has fallen into the water. How will you farm in the water?" they asked him. Others said, "Misfortunes never come alone. Look at your children, aren't they still young? How will you provide for them, for the three children and their mother? We wonder what kind of bad luck is after you." My baba didn't want to leave Karbona. Leaving a village was like a banana falling out of its cluster. What if we don't have land of our own? Couldn't we work on other people's property? However, Baba left Karbona after the first row that happened during shared farming.

'I grew up with my sister Jugita in an orphanage run by Christians. Ma, Baba and Chunki worked in their farms. They had offered us a job and a house if we agreed to a religious conversion. Ma found it to be a great sin to convert from the Sarana faith. "Keep your belief in your heart, Chunki's ma. It is more important to have a meal a day," Baba advised her.'

Here, Somnath Hembrom stopped and thought for a while before saying, 'I haven't retained detailed memories of my village. However, I long to go back one day.' Keeping the box of rings back in the showcase, he took a crate of bangles out. 'This should be rubbed at least three times a day. All gold-plated. It takes but a second to show off its real colour,' he said with a smile.

'We heard that Budhini is in a critical condition these days. We would like to see her before she passes away,' Suchitra once again opened the case of Budhini. Somnath Hembrom gave her a scrutinizing look. A customer came asking for some insecticide to kill roaches. Hembrom went inside the shop.

Later that day, Rupi Murmu told Suchitra that Somnath Hembrom was not someone they could dismiss easily in their search for Budhini. His name was on the list Madhumita Tiwari had given her. Headmaster Dayananda Tudu and Robon Manjhi were the other two. Hembrom, who was Headmaster Tudu's right-hand man in the strike against the *jathedars*, had spent considerable time with Dayananda in Kolkata. Madhumita, Rupi Murmu's dance teacher and a theatre person who guided her throughout her study of the magnificent temples, knew both of them very well.

'Let him polish as many rings as he wants to. We need to dig something up too,' Rupi said.

*

There was a gathering near Panchet that evening, commemorating the late Viswanath Hasda. The programme was conducted by an organization called Johar Ol-Chiki. During her search for majestic temples, Viswanath Hasda's name was one Rupi had come across repeatedly. Most of the stories were unbelievable, blown up with lies and knitted together so tightly that it was hard to tell them apart.

The first *asthi visarjan* ritual that followed soon after the devastating flood of 1943 was alarmingly disquieting. With intense grief, tens of thousands of people who lost their relatives and friends in the flood had reached the Damodar to immerse the ashes of their dear departed. 'Most probably this will be the last asthi visarjan,' the people had said to each other.

'Why do they say so, Baba?' Narayan Tudu's family, who came for asthi visarjan every year without fail, asked their chieftain. This time, they had lost seven members of their family. The Damodar had washed them all away. Narayan Tudu and his two brothers were the only ones who came from his family for the asthi visarjan.

'People talk about a lot of things, Narayan. I don't know if it is true. It is heard that the British government is going to build a dam on the river to curb its flow. In that case, they will not allow asthi visarjan in the coming years.'

'Where else could we go?' the Tudu family asked uncertainly. 'Where else could our dear departed find the refreshing coolness if not in the fathomless depths of the sacred Damodar?'

Viswanath Hasda was the Santal leader who had come forward against the British government's plans to build dams. Hasda's clan was connected to water. Their motif was a waterbird. It was not the only reason. Hasda started the revolt as a protest against the encroachment by the British people. He was apprehensive of the consequences of dams. Besides, he had an idea of the terrifying breadth of the land the British would appropriate. Even before this, white men had captured the soil. And all those times, there had been trouble.

He took the villagers to the highest hill. From there, they could view the thickets, rivers, fields and villages. The people of Karbona believed in the prophetic powers of Hasda. His prophecies, they thought, were warnings from the Bongas.

'All this you see now will sink under the experiment of the white folk,' Hasda prophesied. 'The river is not the cause of floods; it is the rain. But how can they stop the rain? The storm that pours down now will pour down again; the raindrops that fall on the mountains will fall on the river too; the rain that would pelt down over the river will pelt down on the dams as well. Then, how on earth will they tame the river? Don't believe their words. The river should flow on its course.'

The villagers had had grievances against the white men well before that. It was in the name of logs and timber and forests, which were the pacific dwellings of the Bongas, and the mountains that belonged to Marang Buru. Their life lay in worshipping the Bongas of the woods. Sometimes, there would be a Bonga under the rock you stepped on; sometimes, a branch that had been chopped off a tree would be the residence of another Bonga; sometimes, there would be a Bonga living in a handful of water that one may take from the river to drink. The white men came, galloping on their horses, taking into account none of this, ravaging the residences of the Bongas.

The woods, they realized, excited the white men in a different way. They did not appreciate the enticing smells of the leaves, the roots or the animals, or the cryptic darkness as one went deeper into the woods. They did not care about the purity and rush of the wild streams; even when enclosed inside the forests, their eyes longed to see the world outside. They traversed the woods resolutely, dug the earth, excavated, made tunnels, cut wood, sized them to lumbers and stacked them. They measured and divided the forests on the basis of these stacked treasures that could be carried quickly out of the premises. Whoever came to demur, man or animal, was shot down.

Sitting discreetly on the branches of trees, or in the ridges of the mountains, the young men of the village observed them. The white men captured those they saw and thrashed them inhumanly. They finished some of them within the forest. The youths vowed to take revenge on the white men.

'White man is gormen. We can do nothing against the gormen,' the villagers expressed their fear.

'Who said? Can't we do what Baba Tilka Manjhi and Sidhu Murmu have done?' The youth grew angry.

'Do you think you can scare the white man out of the forest if ten of you go carrying your bow and arrow? Don't you know you are going to face guns? Will it be challenging for those who shoot elephants down to kill a few mosquitoes?'

'Killing mosquitoes is the real challenge, Manji. It is easy to finish off elephants. Mosquitoes can lead a guerrilla war.'

'Don't beg for trouble, you pawns. Sidhu Murmu and Tilka Manjhi fought against the white men with tens of thousands of men backing them.'

The young men seemed to know it all. Maybe, they knew history better than the older men of the village. They did not believe in fabricated tales. The armed war Baba Tilka Manjhi had led against Lord Cornwallis was history; it happened more than a century ago. Sidhu Murmu, on the other hand, secured tens of thousands of men and created a parallel government against the British. They declared the white men could not make their lands permanent residence. The youth of today could also organize tens of thousands of people, spark their thoughts and give them weapons to practice with.

The women of the village attacked the loggers in unison on the day they felled rows of sacred karam trees and cleared the land. Girls carried boughs of the divine trees to the village during the Karma festival they observed every year. The villagers were blessed with children for worshipping the karam trees. Each year, maidens waited for the celebrations, to carry their propitious boughs from the forest.

The woodcutters were from the neighbourhood, the coolies of the white men. The women of the village surrounded them with sticks, burning firewood, hoes, knives and whatnot. The woodcutters cried and pleaded that they were only working for daily wages. Those who axed the karam trees for the white men were deadlier than the white men themselves. The women didn't show them any mercy. Most of the coolies were brutally wounded. Though the police rushed to the scene, they couldn't arrest anyone.

The women, who had assumed that there would be an advance from the police, took cover in the forest. To give vent to their anger, the police demolished nearly everything, setting each house on fire. The village became a heap of ashes where Viswanath Hasda remained like an ember that didn't burn out.

Viswanath Hasda—it was the name of self-respect that kept burning high in the memory of his people. In the stories of the villagers, he was taller than mountains and stronger than rivers. Even the children who hadn't seen him in person sang eulogies, praising his encounters with the police.

25

Viswanath Hasda, the chief mentor of Karbona, invariably looked forward to its future.

'We know how to live in the present moment. But the life we live today will alter us tomorrow. We should be aware of how these changes affect us,' Viswanath Hasda advised the gram sabha. When he came to know how the white men's gormen had connived with the officials to prepare a treaty for building dams, he counselled the manji to call the gram sabha into a session at the earliest. Not just the people of Karbona, the people of the entire neighbourhood were asked to be present there. He needed them all. The white men were writing a treaty that could end their future generations.

A huge number of people flocked to Karbona. Most of them were from the villages situated on the banks of the Damodar. People from the seven main clans—Hasda, Murmu, Kisku, Marandi, Tudu, Soren and Basku—were present along with those from the other minor tribes.

'Nothing else but man interferes with the affairs of the sky and earth,' Viswanath Hasda told the people. 'The sky is unknown to man. They know something about the earth. Apparently, they don't know anything about the Bonga world that exists in between the heaven and the earth. We, Santals, we live with the Bonga world. The white men are preparing to hinder the course of the aadi bhoota. We are her children. We are born from the aadi bhoota, the one who carries the driving force of life within her abdomen. The river is deadly and graceful, and its beginning and ending were not decided by us mortals. Even her course is not in our control. The Damodar was here long before we came. She was born before us, much before the many, many generations that lived here. She will go on living even when all of us are buried under the earth; even when our future generations rot away. Her life is her course. White men say they have the sense and capacity to harness her. Knowledge is of many kinds. Some are blunders, and blunders should be corrected. The world of mistakes should be history. It should never be allowed to intervene with our tomorrows. We are well aware of the wrath of aadi bhoota; we know how it is going to affect us. The creator dwelling inside some foreign chambers of the sky will call the earthworms back. The worms that move in keeping with the words of the creator will start eating our shores away. Within seven nights and seven days, they will finish off all the borders, banks, beaches, strands and shingles of the world. And in the seven nights and seven days that follow, they will drop it all back into the sea. Whatever is taken from the water must be returned to it. Only the amphibians will remain. What about people? Though their generations have lived through centuries, they couldn't become water-breathing animals. What I am trying to tell you is that everything is on its way back, on an incredible return voyage. The future looks scary. We need to be more careful. Do not step into the sacred river with arrogance. Ask the river politely, or beg. That's what you are supposed to do. Isn't it disheartening to see criminals and innocent trees getting penalized alike? It hurts to see breastfeeding-animals and egg-laying birds going extinct. The world of the tiny ants will come to an end too. What will the bees and butterflies do? I can see a condition where the entire earth will be under the water. Sadly, crocodiles and eels will glide over the surface of the water. Even the frogs will not be happy. The earthworms and tortoises will lament, thinking of the human beings for whom they worked hard and laboured non-stop to build a shore. Feeling dejected, the tired crabs will lie prostrate on the shells of tortoises. No more will they be able to cling on to anything with their harpoon-like claws. Sadness alone will prevail upon the earth. And so, the whirligig of sorrow will go on whirling around the fingertip of the creator. The creator, on the other hand, will remain idle.'

Hasda was depressed because of his special gift to foresee the future. If man was not engaged in a continuous discourse with nature and the Bongas, he would end up in misery and perdition. And that was what was happening now.

'Is game meat private property?' he asked.

'No,' the people said, 'the entire village has a claim to it.'

'Who will have the first portion?'

'The Bongas will.'

'Should the river go on flowing, precisely as it is now?'

'Like how Marang Buru remains the god of the mountains, forever.'

'Before the ropes are cast off, we seek the permission of the river, don't we?'

'Like how we catch fish.'

'The river gives us a pot of gold. And carries it away just like that!'

'Oye . . . River Damodar, mitigate your inner force a little bit.'

Closing his eyes, Viswanath Hasda ruminated for a long time until the gates of the future opened before him, until the blistering winds of a moistureless time heaved within.

'Viswanath Hasda, you are the mentor, and I am the manji of this village. Our people are panicking. Tell us what to do.'

Hasda, who had already arrived at his resolution after due consideration, told him, 'We need to talk to the gormen, convince them about the situation. We should inform them about the villages and woods that are likely to sink under the water. We should take count of the communities that will get submerged along with the houses, people, the length and width of the fields, woods, birds, and the animals in the woods, our trees, flora and fauna. By my calculation, more than a hundred villages will go under the water. Seventy-five thousand families will lose their land and homes. Apart from that, our conscious mind will not be able to contain or count the cost of destruction of movable and immovable things other than human beings.'

The estimates seemed implausible. But since it was Viswanath Hasda who presented it, the people believed it, even though it made them all the more indecisive and frightful. Hasda continued, 'The gormen has no form of its own. A conversation is not possible with something formless. The police are one of the many forms of the gormen we get to see. Hence, let us talk to them.'

The villagers lived in constant fear of the police. Most of them had not even seen a police station before. Their disputes were always settled within their village. For them, no other court was more significant than their gram sabha; no other judge more eminent than their manji. Nevertheless, the white men's police had forayed into their villages many times on different pretexts. The community had its own law and jurisdiction, where penalties were decided entirely by the gram sabha. The police stormed through the villages to execute their punishments. Often, their language was one of whipping, thrashing, setting fire and killing.

'How can we talk to them? They will beat us for sure. Doesn't matter if we are innocent or not,' said Sivlal Tudu, who had been attacked by the police when he was a child. His right leg, below the knee, now hung lifeless. Though the village physician had fastened bamboo sticks to his leg and sought to cure him with herbal medicines, his leg had remained semi-paralysed.

'Facing beatings from the police is nothing compared to drowning, is it?' a woman called Dhiru Soren asked scornfully. She was one who had faced life's hardest blows. Her husband, Bikram Soren, was taken away by the white men's police one night. Shouting, they had kicked him awake and dragged him away.

'Do you know Jangal Santal?' the police had asked Bikram.

'How are you related to him?' They had asked when they received no reply.

When he said that they were related since they were both Santals, a deadly blow fell across his face. Crying out in pain, he fell flat on his face. The police asked Dhiru where Bikram was going out of the village, that too so often. They jabbed at her ribs with their canes. She said she didn't know who Jangal was. They were too cruel to spare even their children. They threatened them and asked whether Jangal Santal came to their home. Terrified, the children started crying.

'What business do you have with the estate workers of Darjeeling? Are you one among them?'

Claiming his answers to be contradictory, the police assaulted Bikram once again. 'Even if a bullet hits us . . .' the police mocked the first part of their revolutionary slogan. 'Now you tell me the rest of it,' they said, compelling Bikram Soren to sing the rest of it. When Bikram Soren refused to open his mouth, they used their canes to force it open. After the police dragged him away, Dhiru Soren sat dumbfounded for a while. Then, addressing the darkness outside, she completed the rest of the slogan, 'We will not die of hunger.'

The next week, Bikram Soren's body was seen floating over the Damodar. The police said that he had committed suicide. 'A Santal would never take his own life,' said the villagers. No further inquiries were made.

Bikram Soren's eldest son, Massi Soren, was a follower of his baba. The police arrested Massi for writing slogans that proclaimed the upcoming victory of Tebhaga on the public walls in some of the main centres of the village. Later, it was heard that the police had set him free and that he was working with the estate workers of Darjeeling. Dhiru Soren was anxious about her son, thinking he too would have to face the fate of his father. She was not ready to lose him as well. When Parinik told her that Massi had been to Purulia once and escaped the police only by pure luck, she took her grievance to the gram sabha. 'I have already lost Bikram. What will I do if I lose my son as well? Why do the police chase Massi? Why should they punish him? Can't the gram sabha put him on trial and make him pay the penalty?'

'There are laws superior to the gram sabha. We cannot save Dhiru's son,' she was told. 'Good for him to remain incognito,' was the advice she got.

Dhiru Soren found it hard to accept that the police were more potent than the gram sabha. That was quite insulting!

'All of us are going to drown, sooner or later. The police may use batons. But that's no excuse for us to keep quiet, Juhi's ma,' Dhiru Soren said.

If needed, she added that she was willing to go and talk to the police all by herself.

'Why should you go alone, Massi's ma, when we are there for you?' the women, especially the young women, aficionados of Massi Soren, told Dhiru.

A group of people set out for the police station under the leadership of Viswanath Hasda. On their way, they kept singing an old song: 'My heart burns in sorrow . . .' There were about three hundred people, including the chieftains of twelve clans and sub-clans, the manjis of villages, advisers, naikes, ojas, village physicians, other leaders, women, men and children. They were people armed with bows and arrows, sticks and drums and tiriaos.

Munni,
You agreed to meet me at the beach,
I waited.
Night fell,
River Damodar drifted off.
The lantern in my boat waited,
Her eyes wide open.
Munni,
My heart burns in sorrow.

They sang, banging on their drums, playing on their tiriao and banam, dancing on the open ground outside the police station. Sudhansu Biswas, the sub-inspector, bellowed, 'Shut your mouths, you brutes.' He stomped on the floor with his heavy boots.

Viswanath Hasda was in the lead. Sudhansu yelled at him, 'What the hell is this, you wild boar? How dare you do this dirty dance in front of the police station?'

At first, Hasda was taken aback at this unexpected profanity. He felt his self-respect wounded. But dismissing it, he said calmly, 'We came here to discuss some decisions made by the gormen.'

'Excuse me!'

'Their decision to build a dam.'

'Oh ho! So that's how it is. You are against the government, aren't you?'

Sudhansu Biswas looked at each and every person, up to down. With a pointed baton, one of the policemen lifted Ravilal's chin. His brazen face, daring and youthful, reflected pride, anger and frustration.

'Now, you dork, you tell me? What's your problem with the dams? Will the dam starve you out? You don't really look forward to the good of the country, do you?'

As they all stood dumbfounded, Dhiru Soren called out from the mob, 'Leave him. How do you expect him to talk by pressing his mouth shut? You want to know the consequences of the dams, don't you? Very well, let our manji explain it to you.'

With those words, a murmur spread across the premises. 'Let Manji explain,' all of them said.

Karbona's manji came forward.

'Now, you tell me, what's wrong in building dams?' Sudhansu Biswas asked him contemptuously.

'Aadi bhoota will become furious. Everything will sink.'

'Listen!' the sub-inspector clapped his hands and looked at the other policemen. 'Aadi bhoota! The government is working hard to save the country from floods and this blockhead tells us that some bhoota will catch them! Ram Singh, mark my words, what we need in the first place in our country is the eradication of superstitions and evil rituals. Who is going to teach them that dams will eliminate their poverty?'

Constable Ram Singh nodded in agreement. The sub-inspector was a learned man, hailing from a family of freedom fighters. Besides, he had scientific knowledge. As a young man, he had jumped into the freedom struggle. But his father, who was a Gandhian, had stopped him, 'Look, Sudhu, now it is your time to study. That is your duty because what your country needs now is the service of hundreds of thousands of educated young men. Sudhu, soon our country will be free. What else do we have apart from a country that the white men have transformed into an empty gourd shell after looting it? How many people will there be who will be unable to afford two meals a day? Sudhu, what else can we do but die, in case an epidemic breaks out? We will have to work, day and night, if our spines need to be upright. We need an army of young men who are willing to work towards that. And you should be in the front. Listen, my son, the country needs scientists, doctors, teachers, lawyers and economists. Choose one and try to become one. Learning is also a part of the freedom struggle.'

Sudhansu couldn't become a freedom fighter, but he did become a part of the British police force. Within the khaki, the dreams of freedom continued to writhe and burn.

'On the one hand, it is deplorable, Ram Singh. Nehru and Ambedkar are beating their brains out, thinking about how to save our country. Even after the British looted us, our reserves had not dried out entirely: coal, iron, manganese, mica and all. But where do we go for scientists, engineers and technology? If white people can do it, why can't we utilize these resources to develop our own industries? Agriculture alone won't save us. We need industries. And for that, we need electricity. But from where do we get power? There lies intelligence, Ram Singh, there lies technology. Our rivers will give us power. Can the British take away our rivers?

I will say, Ram Singh, I will say it aloud. I will speak like a devoted citizen for the fear of the British is over. Will I lose my head? Let it go. Why do I need my head, after all? To bow in front of some foreigner? Maybe I will lose my job. Let it go as well. Bharat will soon be a free country. All of us will be employed. We will live with our money. You don't really think of all this, Ram Singh, do you? Every month, you stretch your arms before the white men and go home satisfied with your monthly salary, thinking of nothing. You buy your wife a new sari and sweets for your children. The heads of those who really don't care about others won't blow off. Their heads will always be safe above their shoulders, won't they, Syamcharan? Isn't it so, Mangol? Even you don't think, do you? Then why on earth should I find fault with these wild tribes?'

Sudhansu Biswas plunged into his chair desperately. 'Ma Durga, how will this country escape its fate? How long will it take? Will India live a life of freedom during our children's time at least?'

He gestured to disperse Viswanath Hasda and his followers. Then he leaned back on his chair, sadly closing his eyes. *Why scare them, the miserable people. Let them go.*

'Call everyone and clear off,' Ram Singh told Viswanath Hasda.

'How is that possible? We need assurance that the gormen will amend the mistakes and give up the idea of building a dam on the Damodar,' Hasda said.

'What the heck will you do if we don't give up?' Sudhansu jumped up from his seat. Obviously, he was outraged.

The sub-inspector, with all his scorn and patriotism throbbing under his uniform, pushed Hasda back. In an instant, ten or twenty of Hasda's supporters, armed with bows and arrows, encircled Sudhansu. They shot their arrows without warning; no one had expected such a move. The next moment the place had transformed into a chaotic battleground. The Santals ran amok in different directions. Some of them lay prone, wounded in the fracas. Though most of those who returned to the villages were maimed only slightly, the children were seriously injured. They had almost been trampled. It was the police themselves who took the injured people to the hospital in Chirkunda. They were recorded as being wounded in the mass unrest at the police station. The police had filed a case against all of them, charging them with rioting in the station premises.

Karbona's manji had arranged for a prosecutor called Jyothi Ram Misra to bail them out. But many young men were denied bail. They never came back to the village.

Jyothi Ram was a worker in an organization called Azadi Jagaran Manch. It was run by some young men to instil scientific perception and reasoning capacity in the minds of people. 'Dams offer no harm but gains,' they said. According to them, dams were the golden gateways to the future. The prosecutor tried to convince the villagers, but he couldn't influence Viswanath Hasda, who with his followers, crisscrossed through the villages spreading awareness about the dangers of the dams. 'Dams will devour us,' Hasda predicted. But Jyothi argued that it would affect only those who lived within the precincts of the dam. It would not affect Karbona. And the gormen would give ample compensation for those who stood to lose their land. He tried to teach them that the path to freedom lay in eliminating ignorance. But the villagers didn't believe him for he was a diku, an outsider, and Viswanath Hasda, a Santal. A Santal would never cheat another Santal. Dikus, anyway, were different.

The villagers who believed in Hasda were reluctant to follow an outsider.

They held meetings under the title 'The natives who are going to get drowned'. They urged the gormen to abolish all plans for the dam. Songs, dance and drumbeats were their methods of protest. The police said Hasda was a rebel standing against the interests of the country. The natives who were going to drown were the enemies of the nation.

'White men should go back. Natives are not willing to drown,' Hasda declared. 'A free country will not sink its people to death.

Such things happen in the land of slaves. Once we get freedom, we will decide whether we need dams or not.'

Viswanath Hasda, however, didn't live long enough to see what happened in a free India. With a deep cut on the back of his neck, the Damodar returned him to the villagers.

Hasda's murder didn't get much attention. As per police records, he was attacked by a leopard. The villages pulsated with tumultuous uproars. The protest of the natives who were going to drown hyped up enough to trigger a raging riot.

Shortly after, the country became free, and the people, forgetting the loud uproars, rushed to join the revelries.

The long outer wall of Hasda's house was decorated with a beautiful picture of water that seemed to be in perpetual motion. White swans swam in it; water flowers were in bloom; fish popped their heads out; frogs slept peacefully on the leaves of the water lilies. It was a fantastic work of art.

Concealing this serene beauty, Hasda's wife plastered the walls with new mud. Instead of the old picture, she drew the image of a young Santal killing a leopard. She said she was carrying out the instructions of her husband. Hasda, who was now a Bonga, lived on the top of her roof. From there, he guarded the family, watched over his children and wife and lived with them. Hereafter, people saw Hasda in the young Santal killing the leopard.

Among the stories Rupi Murmu had collected for 'The Other Side of the Great Indian Temples', the story of Viswanath Hasda occupied a prime position. Hasda remained as a saviour and ardent warrior in the memory of the people who were above sixty.

*

There were not many people at the memorial meeting. However, Somnath Hembrom was there from the beginning to the end. He devoted himself to each speech with the same devotion with which he polished the stones on the rings.

26

All day, Rupi and Suchitra wandered around Kumardubi railway station. They had received information about Budhini being there. Kumardubi was only ten kilometres away from Panchet. Though they got there with a lot of confidence, they were soon disappointed. They didn't get any concrete information that would help them find Budhini. Each person they spoke to detailed her life the way they wanted to. Some said she died a long time ago; others said she begged on the streets of Kolkata; some others reported scornfully that Budhini was well off with all the money that she had amassed through the years; others accused her of setting out with a diku, defiling the traditions of a Santal woman. However, none of them had any idea about where Budhini was.

The rented house where she had arguably lived once was now occupied by a Muslim family. They hadn't even heard of Budhini.

'When we moved in here, this house belonged to Mr Navin Gupta, a railway clerk. The owner rented this to us only when he shifted to the railway quarters,' they said.

It disappointed Rupi and Suchitra to see their investigation flounder. If the information they got from the local sources was so vague, then the news that she was alive could very well be a scam.

Though they still clung on to Madhumita Tiwari's words, their trip to the house of Headmaster Tudu was somewhat dispirited.

'He knows Budhini. He was one of them who helped her meet Rajiv Gandhi. I know that very clearly,' Rupi said.

Headmaster Tudu lived in Maithon. Taxis ran through the middle of a road lined by massive trees on both sides; they called it the street of ancient trees. They noticed the posters stuck on each of the trunks: 'The Memorial Day of Kanu Da'. The image displayed was familiar to Rupi and Suchitra—it was a picture of Kanu Sanyal's calm and childlike face, with a round collar T-shirt and thick glasses. Following his suicide, this was the image that had repeatedly appeared in the newspapers.

'Seems hard to think of such a man committing suicide,' Suchitra said.

'Maybe he was going through depression and pain,' Rupi said and remembered her colleague Badri.

Badri, who roasted the revolutionaries with pointed criticism, had erupted in outrage at the news of Kanu Sanyal's alleged suicide. 'Why the hell had he raised it if it was to be abandoned halfway,' he said. Throughout the day, he rebuked revolutionaries, revolutionary movements and ordinary communists. He called them names. 'But he ended up writing the most persuasive piece on Kanu Da for the following day's papers. Badri says Kanu Da had become an introvert, almost a brooder, during the last days of his life. He had slipped into depression,' said Rupi.

An age-old sal tree stood behind the rickety gates of Headmaster Tudu's house. The tree, too, bore a poster of Kanu Sanyal on its blistery bark. Interestingly, that was not the only painting there. There were images of young Santal warriors armed with bows and arrows pasted on either side of the poster. A spread of terracotta figurines was set beautifully in between the protruded roots of the old tree. Elephants, horses, birds, mud pots, and a lot more. A mud bowl filled with water, some flowers and lanterns were also on display.

'I went to Sephtulajoth a few days after Kanu Sanyal committed suicide. I was with Vinayan. In fact, it was for him that I went there, to give him company,' Suchitra said. 'We spent some time in that small house where Kanu Sanyal lived. There we met a middle-aged man who still cherishes his time with Kanu Da. He showed us the place where Kanu Da had hung himself. The man soon became friends with us. Vinayan asked him about the paralysing stroke from which Kanu Da had suffered. He wanted to know whether that was the reason for his depression. 'He suffered a lot, didn't he?' Vinayan asked him. 'He stayed out of Sephtulajoth for his treatment for a while. But he came back earlier than we expected. Apart from that, he never left us. Not even now. Now the question of paralysis! Is there room for doubt? Even the Testaments are vulnerable to paralysis,' the man answered him. 'Kanu Da's words still count in many ways in our lives,' Suchitra said.

The headmaster's house, which was an extension of the shade and coolness of the trail leading up to it, was comparatively large. The high outer walls on either side of the main entrance resembled large canvases painted with gorgeous images of dancing girls and percussionists. At the threshold, two mud peacocks, facing each other, stood on vigil. Flowering vines and long tendrils decorated the upper side of the door that led to an enormous courtyard with broad verandahs that had doors opening into different rooms. With great curiosity, they read the English lesson written in neat calligraphy on a blackboard in the centre of the courtyard.

A for Adivasi
B for Bidesi

Children's pictures, books, slates, pencils and colouring boxes were lying carelessly on the verandah. There was a variety of musical instruments on one side. Clothes, mainly dhotis and shirts of white colour, hung from the tightly fastened clotheslines. Spinach, papaya and other vegetables rested on a winnowing sieve that lay next to the mud stove in the courtyard.

Hearing footsteps, an old man dressed in a white dhoti and sleeveless khadi top came out of one of the rooms. His long, grey hair had been braided at the back like a woman's. Maybe he was in his late seventies. Though he had a slight hunch, he seemed tall. His face was rather calm. The moment they noticed the lifeless right arm hanging from its joint, they were sure that the man in front of them was none other than Headmaster Tudu.

'Headmaster?'

'Yes, may I know who you are?'

They felt that his face had lost colour, and he seemed slightly taken aback when they said they were there to see him as per the directions of Madhumita Tiwari.

'Madhumita?'

'In Delhi . . .'

'Oh! Please sit down.' He pointed to the charpoy in the courtyard and went inside. 'Sephali,' he called out.

Carrying a tray with a brass pot of water, a young woman, slim and dark, came out. *She must be Sephali*, Rupi and Suchitra thought. Placing the pot at their feet, kneeling down on her knees, she bowed to them with her hands spread out on the floor. When she went inside, Rupi Murmu asked in a whisper, 'Didn't his face fall when we mentioned Madhumita's name?'

Suchitra agreed. 'Wasn't it Madhumita who asked us to come here?'

'But . . .'

Rupi Murmu knew the stories, including how the headmaster was arrested from Madhumita's house. It was her father who had informed the police. Paramjit Tiwari failed to accept Dayananda Tudu. Caste was the only reason why he couldn't appreciate him. The thought of his one and only daughter roaming around with Dayananda's theatre group didn't let him sleep a wink.

Moreover, he found it awfully offensive. He was sure that he could not convince his daughter out of it. She acted only according to her free will. He, however, was a Gandhian whose life revolved around principles. But come what may, he could not convince himself about the need to abolish the caste system. Caste, he thought, was never a barrier in obtaining freedom from the British. How could it be even a temporary barricade?

He didn't trust Ambedkar. His arguments against him were vehement; he had disagreements with Nehru as well. Each caste, he thought, had a separate duty to perform; people should live accordingly. A Brahmin cannot live the life of a Chantala. It was time for Nehru to keep the caste system out of his socialism.

Since her fifth birthday, Madhumita had worn only khadi clothes. She spun the cotton at home and travelled through the villages holding her father's hand. She hated the British, dreamed of freedom and never ate meat. Her youth was simple and unornamented. She too observed the rites of the caste system without fail. Paramjit thought it was Dayananda, the one who rose in the west, who had set her mind on fire.

'What freedom? Who got freedom, Baba? Did Boysakh Marandi get freedom? What about Tapan Kisku and Sivprasad Hembrom? All of them carry an invisible leather collar around their neck even today. The air around them still hums with the sound of a whip. Why do their debts remain unpaid? Boysakh's son was born a slave. The sons he is going to have sooner or later will be no different. Slaves born out of slaves, more slaves. Why do they always have to be slaves, even in a free country? Why are their fields, where they farm three times a year, captured even today, like it was yesterday? It was always the greed for this or that. There's coal underneath that field, and there's iron beneath this soil. Iron is needed to run trains; coal is needed to melt iron. Slaves do not know what lies beneath the earth, Baba. They only know how to till the soil thoroughly. They are not just one or two, but hundreds of thousands of people. Stop prattling lies for the sake of it. Who became free here?'

The way Dayananda and his characters stingingly ridiculed the hard-earned freedom of the country was beyond Paramjit Tiwari.

Hundreds of thousands of people like him had fought hard and suffered much to attain this freedom. How could one tolerate someone mocking it? Only a traitorous anti-nationalist could think or act this way. And his daughter, as pure as a flame, was keeping such a man company!

Dayananda said he had transformed the story of Boysakh Marandi, who had borrowed thirty rupees from Jathedar Subratho Sarma, on 15 August 1947, into a drama. 'It's not me, but "they" who are asking questions,' Dayananda told Paramjit Tiwari. 'My characters are real. You doubt that, don't you? Come with me, let me introduce them to you. Even after twenty years, Boysakh couldn't repay that loan. The jathedar says it is because his debts have multiplied beyond the recovery with interest, recurring interest and the additional interest of that interest with the money borrowed again to pay it off with its new interest, and so on. He won't possibly be able to repay it in the next thirty births.' It was no tittle-tattle; the jathedar was giving a blow-by-blow account of his calculations. And counts, sharp as crystals, are always valid on paper.

'Tell me, Baba, what has Boysakh got to do with papers? Since his birth, he hasn't known a smudge of ink on his fingertips. Ask him to total up his expenses of sowing and planting. He may need no pen and paper. He calculates with his mind, with the fingers on his hands, and always precisely. After each harvest, the jathedar talks to him based on numbers. "What can be done, Boysakh? You are still borrowing money. Why don't you ever try to repay it completely? I have only one thing to tell you. Work hard and try to repay your debts by at least the next year, and make sure you don't ask for more."

'Will there be an end to this? Ever? Look, Baba, this is 1967, isn't it? It's been twenty years of freedom! Yet, Subratho Sarma sold Boysakh's eighteen-year-old son, Fatik, to Kalicharan Misra. And all this happened in the name of money, the interest Boysakh couldn't pay. Do you think this is becoming of a free and democratic country? Even now, Boysakh earns just two rupees and his wife a rupee. That, too, is not paid rightly. How could he not borrow then? How could they live? Listen to what Boysakh has to say: "The gruel we make at home has no rice in it, Babu, just water. Yet, we talk of it as the milk of the black cow. Rice water is sacred, Babu. How hard we work to get a handful of rice?"'

The first scene of Dayananda's play opened with the two sugar-sanded lemon drops—one yellow and the other orange—the jathedars give Boysakh after hoisting the national flag and singing the national anthem. The moment he puts the candy in his mouth, he spits it out with loud barfing noise. He thought he had tasted the extreme sourness of a vomiting nut. To get rid of the last suggestion of sourness, he put his finger in his mouth and threw up.

'Are the lemon drops bitter?'

Boysakh said yes.

The jathedars disagreed.

Many people tried the candies. Police, ministers, judges and jathedars. They all said in unison, 'Lemon drops are sweet! They have the tantalizing smell of fresh lime and oranges, and the classic shape of an orange's sac carpel. Boysakh lies. Sweet is not sour, milk is not curd; he must be put on trial.'

'Is he the only one intelligent here, Madhu?' Paramjit asked his daughter, who got carried away watching Dayananda's play. 'Can a person who loves his country write and enact such a mean scene? Those who should be singing praises of their flag with pride are talking about how bitter their freedom tastes. How horrible! What kind of a generation is this! Bapu, you fell to a bullet shot for these hooligans! I know, Madhu, the rate of poverty is very high in our country. Still, do you consider these acts of defiance a remedy? Denying the jathedars! If the jathedars are not kind enough, where else would they go for work? How could they live? Such people were there in the freedom struggle as well. Freedom was won by fighting alongside them also. You know that, Madhumita, don't you?'

'First, we should fight with our own self and attain freedom, Baba.'

'What do you mean, Madhu?'

'We have got freedom from the British, but our minds are still in chains. For whom did we gain independence? Was it exclusively for you, Baba? You are not willing to share a meal with Dayananda. What freedom are you boasting about?'

'How is that possible? We should keep away those who are meant to be held at a distance. How can I make friends with a Harijan, flout my tradition, rituals and manners? Madhu, are you talking about negating the practices of casteism? Only you could welcome an untouchable home. Even if Gandhi and Nehru asked me in unison, I don't think I could do that.'

'But remember, Dayananda has the same rights as you.'

'What rights?'

'To consider you an untouchable and keep you at a distance.'

'You call me an untouchable! I am a Brahmin, Madhu! Don't you know that, Madhu?'

'A person becomes an untouchable not by his birth but by his acts, Baba. In a sense, you are untouchable.'

Paramjit Tiwari was shocked to hear this. It made his blood boil; his eyes reddened. *What happened to my daughter Madhumita!* How well Dayananda had manipulated her!

After that incident, the father and daughter didn't talk any more. Sometimes, they had a row at home. Most of the time, their house pulsated in an unpleasant silence. The day Madhumita announced that she was joining Dayananda's theatre group, Paramjit Tiwari caved in, literally. He argued, coaxed, threatened and pleaded.

'If the theatre is what you want, Madhumita, why don't you join the groups of Supriya Zen or Deb Misra? I will not stand in your way. They have top-rated plays that people always queue up to see. "Mrinalini" is running full house even now. You know, people value art and its aesthetics. Who's going to watch some street plays by Boysakh and Dayananda? Or why don't you pursue your dance classes? Let's start a dance school and train children. I will invest money if you wish. Rich people are crazy these days about sending their children to dance and music classes. I can influence them. You will not have to worry about anything. Tell me, Madhu, I would like to open a dance school and name it after your mother. Padmalaya? What do you say? How happy her soul will be? She was your first dance teacher, wasn't she? Tell me, child, isn't it more appropriate to open a school in her name?'

Madhumita said she was not interested in opening a dance school. It was not easy to take her mind off Dayananda's theatre, or to change her views.

Dayananda had a roaming theatre that travelled from village to village. Madhumita set out from home, slept in Santal villages and partook in its hunger and hardship. She felt she was on a more righteous path. 'Tell a slave he is one and tell him there's no need to remain so.'

It was a turbulent time. Great storms were seen rising from somewhere around the margins. Dayananda taught her to look into it, into the mirror that reflected the winds. He didn't give her a role in his plays. Her character and looks did not match with his characters, he said. 'The stain of caste still lurks on your face, Madhumita, no matter how much make-up you put on,' he said. Thus, she ended up doing roles behind the curtains—the make-up woman, the stitching woman, the cook, the janitor, and sometimes, the backup singer.

The night-time classes where the children and youth of the village were taught Ol-Chiki, was something Madhumita savoured. She joined the Santal children. It was only recently that Santali language had developed alphabet just like Bangla, Devanagari, Hindi and English. Pandit Raghunath Murmu was the brain behind the script. However, there were not many people who had practiced Ol-Chiki. When Dayananda began giving them free classes to learn their alphabet, they called him 'headmaster'. He hung a board with the words 'Pandit Raghunath Murmu

Ol-Chiki School' in front of his house. Authoritatively, he was neither a headmaster nor a schoolteacher. Yet, he taught them to take pride in Ol-Chiki, which he said was not just a tool for reading and writing. 'Now, we need not borrow alphabets; like the woods, like the Damodar, we have our own alphabets,' he said. They enjoyed the rhythm of the alphabets on their tiriao, banam, dhams and tumduk; the figures of alphabets on the tree trunks; the tunes of the alphabets in the streams; the taste of the alphabets in the damaadi.

Relentlessly, the jathedars hounded the wandering theatre of Dayananda Tudu. From many places, the theatre group was driven away. With canes whipping in the air, police flared across some areas following the instructions of the jathedars. The police visited the premises of the Ol-Chiki classes. There was a reason behind it. The jathedars had started hearing some discordant notes recently, some sharp voices that they hadn't experienced before. Hands that hadn't been raised so far were rising. Slavery was departing; the threat was spreading fast. Soon, there would be no more slavery.

The jathedars took a tough decision. Until and unless each debt was repaid, the villagers would not be given a coin or a grain of rice. The villages plunged into famine. The decision of the jathedars, the execution of which lasted more than a week, incensed the villagers. It triggered bickering, unrest and uncertainty. The police suspected that the villagers were conniving with one another to break into the grain stores of the jathedars. They warned the jathedars, who then informed the police that Dayananda was the man behind the plan and that the Ol-Chiki classes were a ground for conspiracy. The woman who was with Dayananda was not a Santal. Even the villagers didn't know who she was. Why was she here? The peasant women, who had fanned out across the fields to confiscate the grain harvests, had attacked the jathedars and appropriated their stores in other parts of the country. Maybe this woman had come to conspire with them and make plans to attack the jathedars.

The police couldn't capture either Madhumita or Dayananda. They went into exile much before that. But after a gap of two months, the police arrested Dayananda from Madhumita's house. It was Paramjit Tiwari who had helped the police.

27

Dayananda walked out of prison a free man four years later, after the jury found no evidence worthy of convicting him. But the figure that came out of prison was but a shadow of Dayananda. His right arm was paralysed, and it took him a great effort to speak. Mostly, in between the tremors of facial tics, he stammered, and at times, he babbled a confusion of sounds. He had become an old man of thirty-one!

The village physician prescribed a long-term treatment. On the third day after his release, Madhumita visited him. The villagers didn't like her coming there; they felt that she had betrayed their headmaster. She said she had come to apologize for her father's mistakes. Dayananda listened to her story unemotionally. And at last, he asked, 'Then what was your role in it?'

She had no idea how to convince him of her innocence. He, on the other hand, didn't say anything after that. For the first time, Madhumita sensed storms being triggered inside her in his presence. She asked him timidly, 'Will you let me live with you?'

An awkward smile brightened his face. He turned over in his bed, facing the wall. Lifting his left hand, he gestured her to leave.

After that, Madhumita didn't hear much about him. Once, she heard that the one-armed leader who got arrested from Andhra with a man called Somnath Hembrom was him. There were stories that they were carrying weapons in large quantities in their vehicles; some denied it saying they were transporting cannabis. Following this, there was news that the police had found him among the estate workers of Darjeeling. Each story was far from the truth.

Repentant, Madhumita fell into the clutches of depression, turning Paramjit Tiwari's last days into a series of miseries. Madhu locked herself up in her room for days without talking to anyone or having food, and not even taking a bath. Paramjit closed his eyes, desperate and tired. After his death, Madhumita moved to Delhi. It was her maternal uncles who took her there. Joseph Jobon Murmu brought his children to Madhumita's 'Padmalaya' for learning Rabindra music and Kathak. Rupi was fifteen then and Anandi thirteen.

*

On a brass plate, Sephali brought out glasses of cold ginger and honey lemonade. The headmaster said, 'Now, tell me, what I can do for you?'

Rupi Murmu talked about Budhini Mejhan.

'Budhini?'

'Yes, the woman who inaugurated the Panchet Dam.'

'I understood.'

'Do you know where she is now?'

The headmaster sat silent for a while. 'Maybe Robon Manjhi will know. Don't you know him? The DVC had selected him and Budhini to receive Nehru. Whenever there's any talk on Budhini, he gets very disturbed. He says he doesn't want to remember anything.'

'We heard that you took the lead in helping Budhini meet Rajiv Gandhi,' said Suchitra.

'Actually, it was a group of young journalists who took the initiative. My friend, Somnath Hembrom, was also with them. During that period, we were actively associated with an organization called "Swatantra Adivasi State". What we needed then was not a state called Jharkhand, as we have today.'

It was at Hembrom's house, in the year 1985, the headmaster said, that he saw Budhini for the first time. She was with her husband, Datta. Both of them looked like incarnations of infirmities and sufferings, her husband in particular. Then there were his friends, Avinash and Udaysankar, two young journalists in the lead.

Budhini had said, 'If I ever get a chance to meet the prime minister, I will tell him. I am a woman who lost her life because of your grandfather. I have been wandering for the past twenty-seven years without a place of my own. I had a house and a family, but unfortunately, I lost everything when I was fifteen. I also had a job and a small salary. That, too, was lost in the name of your grandfather. The DVC dismissed me from my job with no apparent reason. My village punished me, and my family abandoned me in the name of your grandfather. Can you imagine how cruel is the gram sabha? Where can I go, how can I live, where do I sleep? Now, I wonder why I didn't die! It was the people of DVC who had asked me to put the garland around your grandfather's neck. I did what they had asked me to do. When the village punished me, they could have convinced the gram sabha about the truth. Paying whatever penalty the gram sabha would pronounce, they could have taken me back. My family could also have done the same thing. But they didn't do it either. They might have thought that their peaceful life in the village was more important than the life of a mere girl. I don't believe that your grandfather was not aware of all this. Maybe he took it as a joke. The government and the DVC were playing a practical joke with my life, weren't they? It was no joke for me or my village. Why didn't your grandfather or the DVC convince my people that it was not a marriage? What did they do instead? They dismissed me from my job. When they had recruited me, they had told me that it was a permanent job. No one had really thought about how a girl who was forsaken by her village and family would survive if she was going to be expelled from her work as well. How many times I climbed up and down the stairs of the DVC office. How many applications I submitted! If only I had my salary, I could have afforded a meal a day. How many years have passed after that? Still, I don't discern any change in the villagers or the DVC. They have stopped throwing stones at me, yes. But I am here in front of you. I am tired of starving. We don't have a house. We don't know where to go the next day. Please ask them to give me my job back. I haven't done any wrong. My life was lost because of your grandfather.'

Wiping her face with the end of her sari, she sat down with her eyes downcast. It was apparent that she didn't like to cry in front of others. Datta placed his hand on her shoulder.

'Rajiv Gandhi understood the situation, Budhini Ma. We have worked hard to ensure that happened,' Avinash said.

'The moment Avinash came to know about Dattaji's letter, he was solely working on it. We were resolute that the message should not go unnoticed by Rajiv Gandhi. He is a very sensible person,' Udaysankar added.

'Budhini Ma should get a chance to talk to Rajiv Gandhi in person. That's what I wish for,' Avinash said.

*

'Truth be told, I was only a witness there. Somnath and the journalists were those who worked towards it,' the headmaster said, opening an almirah that was in the corner of the verandah. He fished out an old file, a folder made of natural jute. 'But who intrigued me the most that day was Datta, Budhini's husband. He said Jawaharlal Nehru was worried about the future of our country. That he was apprehensive about India's freedom, which he thought would not last like that for long. And he was right. We are walking backwards,' he said and from the file took out a photograph a little bigger than a postcard. 'Take a look at this.'

At first glance, it was the picture of a woman with a strong identity of her own. A slim figure clothed in a white floral-printed sari with a green border and a sleeveless blouse, light pink or violet, with the end carelessly hanging down the front of her left shoulder, the way the Bengali women carry it. She wore glasses and her hair was probably in a bun. She had two small earrings in her ears and a thin chain around her neck. Each arm was adorned with a thick, round bangle—it could have been brass or silver—and a *baju* made of black thread on the right arm, above the elbow. She stood tenderly caressing the crown of a plant next to her, whose leaves were on her palm. She was looking at the leaves, at the greenness of it. There was a twinkle in her eyes and a soft smile on her lips. Her expression was serene and warm.

'Budhini,' the headmaster said.

'Really?' Rupi and Suchitra asked in unison. They wondered what resemblance the fifteen-year-old Santal girl they had seen in a picture of the inauguration of the Panchet Dam bore with this woman.

'Sephali, prepare food for them too,' the headmaster said when Sephali came in from the yard with a bundle of moringa leaves in her hand.

By lunchtime, people who performed musical dramas started coming in to greet the headmaster. That evening, they were to stage a performance in the nearby village on the life of 'Baba Tilka Manjhi Murmu', the text of which was inspired by a poem written by Dayananda Tudu when he was barely nineteen. Dayananda used to be part of the drama at one point, with his clear voice, striking on his drums. He played on his banam during the melodramatic scenes and the tiriao for the sad moments. He was an artist who rocked the streets. Those who saw him perform spread the word that Dayananda could quickly jump up to the height of a sal tree.

The Santals listened to the story of Tilka Manjhi with awe and reverence for the hero. From the peaceful villages that lay amidst the hills, farms and water bodies, people came to the place of performance as if they were on a pilgrimage. Tilka Manjhi was their hero, the symbol of freedom. He was the wild horse, the rooster, the male peacock, the flying arrow, the fig tree and the fall of rivers. Who else but Dayananda could play the role of Tilka Manjhi?

Dayananda entered on a horse, screaming 'Tilka Manjhi!' The excited background musicians struck their drums in a frenzy to produce the sound of a hundred hoofs pounding the dirt.

> *Sidho,*
> *You graze the buffaloes*
> *Behind the white bush.*
> *And I*
> *Drive the white men away.*
> *Sidho,*
> *You pluck flowers*
> *From the sal tree that grazes the sky.*
> *And I*
> *Drive the white men away.*
> *Sidho,*
> *You stand on vigil for the fig tree.*
> *And I*
> *For the abandoned house.*
> *Our milk tree, uprooted*
> *Janamdada flew away.*
> *If those who enter our doors are robbers,*
> *Sidho,*
> *My arrows will grow wings.*

Dayananda was a poet who wrote in the spur of the moment. He wrote his best poems when he was on stage, improvising on something. They were always better than the ones he composed and tuned painstakingly at home. However, he didn't perform after his incarceration. Instead, he trained a lot of young men. The Santals decided to present the story of Tilka Manjhi at least once every year. On that day, they adorned Manjhi's statue with a garland of red flowers.

Ramay Kisku, the clerk of the village office, essayed the role these days. He was a tall man with a robust body, a square, flat face and deep red eyes. He was well-versed both in Hindustani and Rabindra music. His voice was sturdy, his steps were adorable. Above all, the sharpness of his looks, like blazing fire, was becoming of Tilka Manjhi. According to the headmaster, 'This is precisely how Baba Tilka Manjhi's eyes were. Dead, yet living, his bloodshot eyes continued to haunt the white men.'

The white men, too, feared ghosts and demons and superstitions. They believed that Tilka Manjhi practiced black magic, and that was why their ammunition couldn't conquer him and their army had failed them. He slipped out of their hands like a fish; dashed out of their clutches like a cheetah. And then, when they least expected it, he would pounce on them. The white men strongly believed that Tilka Manjhi did all this with the help of some evil forces. To cut a long story short, some white officials even sought the advice of native sorcerers to capture him.

It was when Tilka Manjhi was twenty years old that the uncompromising drought and famine hit the villages. The abnormally dry period of starvation took several lives, both men and beasts. It was during that time that the East India Company took control of the lands of the farmers and made negotiations in favour of the jathedars. Tilka Manjhi then came forward, proclaiming to tear apart the laws and hate-filled manifestoes of the Company. 'The rule of East India Company should come to an end in our country. They seize our lands and assault us perpetually. They take our young people as slaves and assail those who react against them. They don't mind killing our people or setting fire to our villages,' Tilka Manjhi told the Santals.

The angry young man proved to be an open door for those who were desperately seeking an escape route from the perpetual violence of the white supremacists. 'For the blood that my people

have shed, I will make the white men drown in their own blood,'
Tilka Manjhi vowed. He talked to the youth daily, organized them,
trained them to use weapons and made them aware of the need for
an armed force to fight the white devils.

Tilka Manjhi attacked the white men and drove them away
from the forests whenever he got a chance. The guerrilla wars,
under his administration, always ended well. This annoyed the
East India Company. Its officials began their hunt to capture Tilka
Manjhi. But the military pawns of the white men were never able
to catch a glimpse of the warrior.

The white men had guns and cannons and well-trained
soldiers, but they were no match for the wild thickets and hidden
attackers. The Santals, meanwhile, needed more weapons and
people to lead a fight. Tilka Manjhi started sending messages to
every Santal family. He wrote his letters on the leaves of sal trees.
They would have the words 'we should unite'. The awe-stricken
Santals knew that they needed to stand together against the East
India Company and the jathedars. The quick and positive response
from the people resulted in the expansion of Tilka Manjhi's army.
Consequently, the unexpected attacks by the Santals disrupted the
East India Company's workings and it soon realized that an armed
uprising of the Adivasis was fast approaching. The white men
appointed a shrewd commissioner, Lieutenant Augustus Cleveland,
for Bhagalpur. Cleveland plied the Adivasi leaders with gifts and
favours and offers for huge tax relaxations, all in an effort to try and
manipulate them. He planned to dismember Tilka Manjhi's armies
making emotional appeals to some of the leaders. Tilka Manjhi
questioned this, but some of the self-centred Adivasi leaders didn't
approve of his demand for equal justice for all. Thus, the East India
Company wreaked havoc by splitting the army into two.

Finally, in 1784, Tilka Manjhi shot an arrow that killed
Lieutenant Cleveland.

Several versions of the story sprouted from far and wide. All
of them applauded Tilka Manjhi's gallantry and intrepidity. One

version spoke of how he sneaked to the top of a palm tree and shot the arrow from there; according to another, it was not an arrow but a shot from a sling that killed the lieutenant. In yet another version, the lieutenant was killed during pitched battle between the two.

After this incident, Tilka Manjhi moved to the more mysterious, innermost part of the forest that was entirely inaccessible to the white men. The white men's army set foot into the woods but couldn't trace even the shadow of Tilka Manjhi. They returned with their animosity doubled, with bull-headed mulishness for payback burning among them. The Santals, on the other hand, unleashed a series of ambush attacks. In January 1785, Tilka Manjhi was caught by the police. They resorted to drastic measures, flaunting the depths of the cruelty, hatred and hostility they harboured against him. Binding him to the tail of a horse, they dragged him with the galloping animal till Bhagalpur. Hitting rocks and thorns, sinking and rising with the ups and downs, his bruised body reached Bhagalpur in bloody form. But he was not dead. The spark of an eerie light darted out of his eyes as he looked at the officials, frightening them. There should never be another Tilka Manjhi, they decided. Those who had assembled needed to disperse, and there should be no more assemblies. The officials wanted to scare people, to set an example. They hung the battered Tilka Manjhi on a banyan tree by his arms. It was a horrible sight. The soil of Bhagalpur was soaked in the blood of the great warrior who didn't let a single cry escape despite the excruciating pain. Not a tear from his eyes touched the earth.

The headmaster became sentimental. 'The history of the freedom struggle should begin not with the First War of Independence but with Baba Tilka Manjhi Murmu. Not in 1857, but in 1771 itself, we, the Santals, started the strike against the white men, asking them to leave India. We attacked the East India Company. We had martyrs. But those who wrote the chronicle of freedom struggle conveniently ousted us from history. For the historians, the only strike is the one led by the jathedars and the Brahmins. But for us,

Baba Tilka Manjhi Murmu was the first freedom fighter. As
children, we heard stories about him and cried imagining him being
dragged by a horse. Our bodies ached feeling his pain; we felt as if
it was us being dragged. We felt the abuses and tortures Baba had to
go through, which insulted us, incensed us. Baba sacrificed his life
for our soil, woods and people. We exchanged sal leaves amongst
us, with messages asking everyone to stand together written over
them. Our main game was the war between the white men and the
Santals. Our goats joined us in our games. The white goats were
the army of the white men, and the black goats were us. That's
how, at eighteen years of age, I ended up writing a poem on the
life of Tilka Manjhi.

    Rhythm! Drums! Drums!
    Rhythm! Rhythm! Drums! Dance!
    All but the dancing ground!

Ramay Kisku started his performance. On the ground, sitting in a
semi-circle, the spectators watched spellbound. A vacant space was
left in the front row for Rupi and Suchitra, the guests that night.
Though they couldn't make it on time, it took them no effort at
all to fall into the enticing grip of the performance. The makeshift
stage, they noticed, was decorated with yellow and orange genda
flowers, the dark green leaves of the sal trees and crimson silk.
The incense burners on the corner continued to smoke. The
performance, which had started around 9 p.m., extended till 3 a.m.
    Though Suchitra couldn't grasp the performance fully, as she
had no command over the Santali language, her camera saw no
rest. Ramay Kisku surprised her.
    Rupi was in the same boat as her. She could talk in Santali, but
it could not be said that the lines of the song yielded to her entirely.
Yet, they stayed till the end of the show.
    'Baba . . .' a sing-song dirge began with a long cry. It lamented
the tragic death of Tilka Manjhi. The spectators, sorrow-stricken

as they always were when they watched the shows, partook in the mournful lament that was both tranquil and upsetting.

Gradually, the mist grew slightly thicker with the moonlight coming to an end. A cold wind kept blowing. Some of the spectators had gone home; some lingered; some slept covered in sheets. The wind carried the scent of the faded genda flowers.

There were people sleeping on the verandah and courtyard of the headmaster's house. Sephali was there with a lamp in her hand. She had made sleeping arrangements for them in a room that opened from the west side of the verandah. On the floor where they were to sleep, Sephali made her bed. They slept the moment they lay down. In the morning, when they sat down to have breakfast, the headmaster asked timidly, 'Will you be meeting Madhumita?'

'Yes, we will.'

'Convey my regards.'

Rupi and Suchitra couldn't begin to imagine the feelings he had for Madhumita then. Suchitra broke the silence.

'Thank you very much for showing us that picture, headmaster.'

'Which picture?'

'Budhini Mejhan's.'

'The Somnath Hembrom you were talking about yesterday— if he is the one who runs a stationery shop in Chirkunda—we have met him already. He said he knows nothing about Budhini.'

'Of late, his mind has been troubled. His eyes are weak. His family is not with him, which has left him heartbroken. You should meet him one more time. Tell him about your visit here. I am sure he will be of help.'

28

When Sita, Somnath Hembrom's third daughter, was just a year old, his wife, Dulari, left him to return to her own village. This happened the very day that she arrived with her children at the house where her husband had been living. Dulari's baba had no other way but support his daughter and her three children who came to share his poverty. Together, they worked hard on other people's farms whenever there was an opportunity, but most days they couldn't find any work at all. They shared an infinitesimal portion of a quarter at the edge of the village, where more than half of the land was occupied by iron founders who lived in groups with their families.

Though Dulari had crossed the age of thirty, her baba couldn't get her married. To carry on the tradition of *raybar bapla*, the entire village needed to be given a feast with ample food and liquor. Marriage was a big day in a person's life, the most significant event, perhaps. And hence it was inevitable to please the villagers and the Bongas on that day ordained by fate. But all these pushed the cost up massively, making it something beyond what Dulari's baba could imagine. The village accepted only those nuptials where the ceremony of sindur *daan* was witnessed by the entire community.

It didn't help that Dulari was neither beautiful nor intelligent; in fact, she was considered dull and miserable, thanks to her family's monetary condition. The young men of the village never pursued her with offers of love. When Somnath Hembrom, who came to work as a sepoy in the post office outside their town, asked for her hand in marriage, Dulari's parents and the rest of the villagers were speechless. How could a government employee like Somnath Hembrom fall in love with a woman like her! Moreover, he was a very young and handsome man, younger than Dulari. Many girls desired him as he hurried on his bicycle amid the admiring stares of the villagers, dressed in khaki, with the solemn look of a police officer. The girls, wherever they would be, would reach the street in a wild rush the moment they heard the bells of his bicycle chime which tantalized their feelings.

Letters were a rarity as far as the villagers were concerned. Usually, the sight of a postman knocking at someone's door would get the entire village excited. But the case of the village damsels was different. Whenever the postman would go on his cycle, the girls would shoot hidden glances his way. Often, letters arrived at the doors of blacksmiths, from their children who worked in the foundries of Hyderabad and Mumbai.

After their wedding, Somnath Hembrom admitted that he had first heard of Dulari as a story. He had not seen her before he had proposed to her. But he had said that he would marry her on one condition. Because he had no house or place of his own, he would stay at Dulari's home after the marriage. Dulari's baba informed the chieftain, the jog manji and the naike about this rather unusual request from the bridegroom.

'Though I would like to arrange a raybar bapla, I don't have money for that. Dulari is over thirty now. What can I do?'

'If you don't have money for the feast, postpone the wedding for a while,' the jog manji suggested.

'If both of them are willing, let them live together,' the chieftain advised. 'The wedding can be arranged once the money comes.'

'But don't you know that such a marriage, without the blessings of the villagers, won't have their consent as well. The children born of such marriages will also have no status or name in the village. Even if they live together, they should find the money for the feast at the earliest,' the naike said.

Dulari's baba agreed with them. How many people in the village lived together without getting married! Sometimes, they got married after the birth of their second or third child. And sometimes the eldest sons worked to find the money for the 'sindur daan' of their Ma and Ba. It was decided. Since Somnath Hembrom had no one or nowhere to go, he would stay at Dulari's house even though it was not usual practice. It was sad to see a girl unmarried in her thirties. And Dulari was a girl who had never wandered her whole life; she had never fallen into the trap of the rogues from the houses of the blacksmiths or dikus. Somnath Hembrom and Dulari could not opt for *tunki dipil bapla*. Even though her baba was confused, he let Somnath stay with them.

'Sometimes, I will be out for my tours of duty. I can't tell how long it may take and when exactly I may return. Dulari, you should not be cross with me or cry when I go,' Somnath Hembrom had said coaxingly. 'It doesn't matter where I go, or for how long, I will come home to you anyway.'

Dulari had no idea where a postman's duty would take him. Her baba also didn't know anything. But Dulari got worried that Somnath had cheated on her when he went on a tour after six months of their wedding and didn't come back for almost a year. She was three months pregnant at the time of his departure. The villagers, especially the brokenhearted damsels, began teasing her.

Dulari's daughter was almost a toddler when Somnath Hembrom appeared on the scene and then fled before the child could get to know him. Nothing could have prepared Dulari for the ridicule she faced from the villagers.

'Oye, Dulari, does your sepoy have a wife and children in some other village? Was he here during the previous Sohri festival? Isn't it time for the Badhu festival now? Each time he comes, you are pregnant with a child in your belly. What else does this relationship provide you with?' The women who came to fetch water or wash their clothes sympathized with Dulari.

Dulari named her second child 'Draupadi'. She didn't have any news about her husband till her daughter turned eight months. If he comes again, Dulari's baba thought, he would give him a piece of his mind. On a night after the first rain, when the earth was cool, Somnath Hembrom knocked at Dulari's door.

'Let me ask you one thing, son-in-law. Where were you all this time?' Dulari's baba asked. His sosuma gave him a dry towel to wipe his head and a bowl of warm rice water.

'I told you last time, Baba, I . . .'

'That you are working in a post office in Andhra?'

'Yes, Baba.'

'But when the jog manji inquired, he was told you were on a long leave.'

The son-in-law floundered. His face grew darker. 'Yes, that's true. I have some other business there. And that's the reason I went on leave.'

'Some other business! What is that?'

When there was no answer, the father-in-law's face fell.

The news that Dulari's husband had returned became a topic of discussion in the neighbouring households. Poor Dulari! He was going to present her with one more child before he left.

That time, Somnath stayed for two months. It was the month of Aagan, the season of tilling the land and sowing seeds. Until the sowing was complete, Dulari's baba depended on no other workers from the village.

'Take rest, Sosur. I am here to help you,' the son-in-law said to his father-in-law. The very next day after sowing, he left the place as usual, not saying even a word to Dulari.

Dulari's energy died down; her body weakened. She remembered how tightly she had wrapped her arm around him as they slept, and how discreetly she had tied him to her body with the end of her parhan.

Well, it's time. He is gone. A reoccurring nightmare of hers was where he left home repeatedly. It haunted her even when he was at home. She would spend the dream wandering around looking for him. In her search, she would traverse the wildest of woods, mysterious towns, dilapidated dwellings and the blacksmiths' sheds.

Aagan passed by, as did the months of Magh and Fagun. Dulari was stressed by the time the month of Choth came around. She lost weight and fell sick. Boysakh, Jenth, Ashad passed by too, and then the rain pelted down. Dulari had exhausted herself waiting for Somnath, but he didn't return. To her surprise, she received a letter one day. It was the first time that a letter had come to the house. It was a postcard written in Bangla. Dulari approached the naike's son, Devan, who studied in a government school, to read it out to her. It was from Somnath. He had asked her to tell her baba to send their eldest daughter, Santhi, to the government school outside the village. The letter ended saying that he would be home soon.

Dulari waited with growing abhorrence. At the end of each day, when men and beasts, the trees and mountains of Marang Buru slipped into blissful sleep, Dulari would open her tiny window. She would stare into the night, or the moonlight, outside.

'What can we do if our son-in-law stops coming?' Dulari's ma would ask her baba under the secrecy of the night, thinking that Dulari was fast asleep. This conversation would start a fire in Dulari's heart, one that would never burn out. Maybe what she heard about her husband was real. Perhaps there was a woman younger and more beautiful than her, with the colour and smoothness of tamarind seeds, fluttering like a bunch of mango flowers in his life. Maybe he lived with her and their children in a comfortable little house. What he had said about having no home or a village of his own would then be a lie. Dulari was not good at talking, especially to her husband. Whenever she ventured to say something to him, she would stammer and withhold half of what she intended to say. Perhaps, like the other young men of the village, Somnath

Hembrom too felt nothing for her. But she found this idea hard to believe. Whenever he was at home, he would shower affections upon her as if some flood gates had opened. It frustrated her that she couldn't hate him. Otherwise, why would her body and soul writhe in titillating pain at the mere touch of his hand? Like the other girls, she too had tattooed green images on her left arm and chest before her wedding. Responsive to his touch, Dulari lost her balance when he wrestled with her tattooed breasts, saying he would make the green peacocks tattooed on them fly away. Goosebumps would line her skin the moment he would grab her by the waist. She would imagine him devouring the green snake she had tattooed on her right breast after the wedding. He would swallow it inch by inch. She would scream when he would gently glide over her inner thighs. How could she even think of living without him?

When Dulari became pregnant for the third time, her parents got annoyed. 'Do you really think we can look after all the children you give birth to? Why did you open the door for him?'

Dulari was startled by the way her parents questioned her. Through her stammer, she pillow-talked her husband to take her to where he worked. 'I will stay wherever you are.' Somnath Hembrom didn't answer. He was thinking of something else. Tears ran down her eyes, even though she had promised him that she would not cry. Seeing her break down, he said, 'My life is not like you imagine, Dulari.'

'What kind of life is it? What's so special?'

She didn't get an answer for that as well. However, the odour of her husband's sweat got her mind ticking. Nowadays, his sweat carried a different smell. The smell of boiled rice, which she craved, which hung strongly on his hair, neck, armpits, chest and in the folds of his thighs had been replaced by a salty and unfamiliar odour. His breath was caustic and his tongue bitter. He might have gone astray. Perhaps, this was the smell of that woman with the colour of tamarind seeds, the intense, speedy, persistent scent of her.

Dulari herself smelled like grass, like a goat's mouth—calm and serene. Somnath Hembrom used to say, 'My heart becomes peaceful the moment I smell you.' But her friends had told her something different. 'Women should have the sort of smell that makes men go crazy, not the smell that lulls them to sleep,' they said.

'He takes aim and gets ready to shoot his arrow, but Dulari, how will he shoot if your smell calms him down?' they would say and burst into peals of laughter, singing songs about a charpoy with broken ropes.

Braided ropes broke,
Charpoy sagged in the middle,
If you are a man, come close to me,
If you are a Bonga, just go away.
By your hips,
I may open and close mine.

Maybe Somnath's tamarind girl was like someone in the song. Dulari became all the more discouraged. She worked hard in her baba's field, went to collect firewood from the woods and sold them in the market.

'Oye, Dulari, where are you dragging your big belly?' The women asked, looking at a pregnant Dulari carrying wood, walking over the slippery rocks of the river. She gave them a smile in return.

Much before harvest time, Dulari took to swabbing the floor with cow dung. 'Dulari, can't you sit and take rest for a while? Aren't we here to work?' said the wife of the naike. Dulari smiled. Taking a handful of cow dung blended with coal, she swabbed the tall mud walls. When she pulled a rainbow with her right palm from the left corner of the wall to the right, her eyes were wet. She drew a black rainbow with the cow dung mixed with coal and a green rainbow with plain cow dung. She followed this pattern of black, green, black, green.

River Damodar,
In the month of Ashad,
Overflows at both ends.
You, on the other end of the river,
And I, here.
I cry thinking of you,
The more I think, the more my eyes surge.

When Sita was one year old, Somnath Hembrom returned. Standing in front of the manjithan, Dulari told him, 'Hereafter, I will not stay anywhere without my children's baba.' She stammered as usual, but said what she wanted to say. That was how Somnath Hembrom was forced to take Dulari with him.

29

After having commenced their journey on a train from Kumardubi railway station, they covered some miles by road on a bus and then got into a rickety jeep. By the time they got to a hillside country lane in Andhra, it was almost sundown with gloomy skies looming above. An intense dust storm blew past them. Engulfed by the soaring red sand, Dulari couldn't see anything for a while. Gradually, the modest junction with four or five shops, a tea shop, a post office and a panchayat water-well became visible. The moment the people in the tea shop saw Somnath Hembrom, they stood up.

From there, they continued their journey on a bullock cart that was returning from the market. Dulari and her children sat in the cart while Somnath Hembrom walked alongside, holding the wooden rail. Some people, two or three of them who were sitting inside the tea shop, accompanied them. Dulari could understand that they were talking in Telugu as her neighbours, from the houses of the blacksmiths, mostly talked in Telugu or Odia. Those who walked with Somnath Hembrom spoke about a certain Thimma who was attacked on his way back home late at night. They said that the attackers were Muddy's men. Somnath didn't respond. Dulari sat nonchalantly in the cart, as she had no idea who Thimma or Muddy was. She thought about what kind of house Somnath had. Maybe it would be the house where his wife and children also lived. If that was the case, how could she live with him in that house?

The bullock cart bounced and rattled down the track. Slowly, the darkness began spreading over the fields on either side of the road. The moon was rising, and Dulari realized how sombre the moonlight was. After half an hour's travel through the fields, they reached a small house. From the road, the house seemed to be in a pit. Walking down the steps to the house, Somnath Hembrom called out, 'Bollamma, Bollamma.'

An older woman came out of the house with a lamp in her hand. 'Who? Somu?' she asked. She was slim and tall, and in her seventies.

Bringing the lantern to his face, she nodded. 'Come, Somu, come inside. How long I have been waiting for you to bring your wife and children.'

Somnath Hembrom asked the others to wait outside. Then he looked at Dulari and said, 'I have to go with them urgently. You stay here with Bollamma.' He went out into the darkness. Dulari stood dumbfounded. Bollamma brought out a plate full of sliced mangoes and placed it in front of the children. 'Have it. They are delicious and home-grown. Your nana likes it very much. Eat, Dulari.'

Dulari grew more restless. She had trouble believing that the woman knew her name already. It made her upset and angered her. Somnath Hembrom had told that woman about her. But what had he said? Had he told her that they were living together without getting married? That her children were illegitimate?

Leaving them in the custody of some bollamma in a strange land, he had disappeared. Whose house was this? Who was this Bollamma? The more she looked at her, the more she assumed that she was some kind of a sorceress. She turned her eyes away.

There was a photograph of a woman on the wall opposite where Dulari was sitting. A garland of braided red threads was hanging on its frame. In the light of the lantern, the face of the woman in the photograph glowed like fire. Dulari, who had kept silent until then, asked without stammering, 'Who is she?'

'Nirmala!' Bollamma said, expressing astonishment at the fact that Dulari didn't know about her.

'Is she your daughter?'

'Yes, she is . . . everybody's daughter.'

Bollamma sliced more mangoes for the children. Dulari didn't take her eyes off Nirmala. Who was she? Why did Somnath come to this particular house? Did he stay here? Had Nirmala also stayed here?

Bollamma, meanwhile, was watching Dulari closely. Dulari's unpleasant face perturbed her.

'How did she die?' Dulari finally asked.

'She was shot by the police.'

Why hadn't Somu said anything to his wife? Why was she pulling a long face?

'When will Sita's baba return?' Dulari asked.

'Oh, how could he possibly come back today? It is heard that Thimmappa is going to die. If something like that happens, how will Somu return? We can't let the murderers go free, can we?'

Dulari felt her head spin. What was this old hag saying? She felt trapped.

Bollamma spoke just then, as if she had smelled her fear, 'What's there to worry about? It's just one night. He will come back in the morning. May I serve dinner now? The children are already falling asleep.'

Bollamma insisted, but Dulari was reluctant to eat.

'Have some rice and fish curry. Try this spinach and dal, and the tender mangoes pickled in mustard oil. Please have some.'

Dulari didn't eat even though she was hungry. Bollamma fed the children rice and fish curry. Santhi and Draupadi started crying because the spicy curry burnt their tongues. Bollamma gave them a piece of jaggery each. Dulari, meanwhile, was indifferent to everything around her.

'Murders have occurred in the village of Maripad, before this too,' Bollamma said. 'Muddy's men slaughtered Malli and her husband who were on their way home from work. It was an act of vengeance for not handing Malli's fields over to Muddy. Muddy had confiscated almost everyone's lands. That day, we couldn't capture the murderers. But later we killed three of Muddy's people in the fields, as revenge for the two he had taken from us.'

Bollamma talked about the murder nonchalantly.

'Who . . . who killed them?' Dulari stammered.

'All of us were there. Somu, Krishna Raja, Manganna . . . The weapons were in the hands of the men. And a newly cast sickle was what Nirmala had. Somu and Nirmala went into exile before the police came. We ran in different directions.'

Bollamma sat with her legs stretched out on the floor, rocking Sita on her shoulder. For a second, Dulari wanted to grab her child. She couldn't believe a word of what that woman had told her. How could she think that Somnath Hembrom had killed a man? Suddenly, the image of Somnath Hembrom rising from the pond in their field, shaking his head, scattering droplets of water everywhere flashed in her mind. Each droplet had a sun of its own. Like a water sun, he emerged spilling blood instead of water! Dulari shuddered. The fact that Somu and Nirmala had gone into exile echoed in her ears like wild drumbeats. In exile? Where? For how long? With her secretly in a cave? Giving her the company that I never enjoyed? Dulari's imagination broke boundary after boundary, making her more vulnerable than ever. Like fire, coal and smoke, hatred accumulated within her.

Bollamma brought out a big pot of black tea.

'Please drink this, Dulari. You look very tired. I have boiled this with tea leaves, tulsi and guava leaves.'

Dulari didn't even look at her. Nirmala, Somu, Bollamma, they were the same. Only she and her children were the outsiders. Nirmala! What connection did Somnath have with her? Like her village people said, was this his wife's house? Dulari continued to stare at Nirmala's picture.

Spreading out a mat, Bollamma lay down on the floor with the children. She was humming a song to help the children drift off. Humming and buzzing, it seemed, she too had fallen asleep. Dulari couldn't sleep though. The night was crawling slowly. Suddenly, she thought bewilderingly, Somnath Hembrom had turned into a perfect stranger, alien to her. But still, with each noise she heard, she struggled to rise and look out of the tiny window.

'There is nothing to be worried about, Dulari. We have walked over fire, let alone a burnt piece of coal. Somu knows how to handle Muddy's men. We killed Muddy, and now what's the trouble in killing his ass-kissers?' Bollamma said, half asleep and half awake.

Dulari lashed out. 'Killing? Killing people?'

'What else can we do, if we can't stand them any more?' Bollamma sat upright. She tied her loose hair into a bun on the top of her head. Two nose pins glistened on either side of her nostrils. The sparks emitted from the stones on them, Dulari thought, were frightening.

'We need to live, don't we? All that we know is farming. No one owns an inch of land here. All the property in the neighbourhood belongs to Muddy and his men. Do you know how much we get if we work for them in their fields? A rupee! How can we live with that? Naturally, we have to borrow. From whom do we borrow? We have no other option but to turn to the murderers. They give cash at cut-throat interest rates. For a single rupee, we need to give our fingerprints on hundreds of papers. After the harvest, we are shown the expenditure on a piece of paper, according to which no grain comes to us. Our debts remain intact. But that doesn't mean we won't borrow more, will it? Our roofs will still leak; it'll be time for a daughter's birthing; kids will come down with ailments. All these stretch us and we have to take life as it comes. If it means more borrowing, so be it. Place your finger here. Put it there. One more over here. And this trap continues, my dear. Deliberately, we let ourselves be trapped as there is no other way.

'My grandson, Appanna, a boy of fifteen, died without getting medical care. How can the poor seek treatment? I still hear him cry, "Take me to the hospital, Nana, save my life." Even if I close both my ears, I can hear him crying. We couldn't take him to the hospital. His mother, Nana and I would be in Muddy's fields till sundown. If we finished our work and wound up a little earlier than usual, Muddy's men would thrash us in the name of the interest rates we owed him. Finishing with the fields, his mother and I would run home. His nana, however, had to wait at Muddy's place to get some money.

'On his way to bed after dinner, Muddy said, "Are you not ashamed to beg at night? Go, go away."

'His nana returned empty-handed. He cried out loud talking about how two days ago Appanna had sat down, fatigued on the dike, due to the fever and how Muddy's men had carried him back to the field.' Bollamma sat silent for a while and then sighed, 'They didn't have to take Appanna to the hospital anyway.'

Dulari heard Bollamma blowing her nose and wiping her face. She knew Bollamma was crying.

'After his funeral, Nirmala, along with Somu, Ganpati, Krishna Raja and some others who were not familiar, gathered in this house. Nirmala said, "It is Muddy who killed Appanna." Listening to her, I cried and beat my chest. Somu asked, "What's the use of crying, Bollamma. Will we be saved?" My daughter-in-law had not regained consciousness. My son had crumpled into a corner, not saying a word. "It is Muddy who decides whether we should live or die. Can't we decide that?" the person who had come with Somu asked. At first, I didn't understand what he was talking about. Then Somu explained calmly: "If we do not have money to provide medical care to our son when he falls sick, why on earth do we toil all year in Muddy's fields? Why do we continue as debtors?"

'We decided not to go to work the following day. As expected, Muddy's men came, lashed their whips and dragged the women out by their hair. Yet, we didn't go. The same scene repeated the next day and the day after that. Muddy, who had fixed a day for the harvest, lost his cool.

'At last, he had to yield. He said he would no longer charge us interest. But we were no fools to believe him. During our peaceful protest, Muddy had misbehaved with Ponnamma. There was not a single woman in the village who he hadn't touched. He kept a lot of pimps in his service, who hauled women to a deserted spot in the field or to his storehouse. They never missed an opportunity to please their master. Ponnamma was a child of eleven. Somehow, she escaped from Muddy's grip.

'"Muddy will not lay his hands on another woman again," Nirmala said assertively. "Such villains, who eat like pigs, prowl around licentiously, are a burden to the earth. They don't leave any woman alone, any worker unbeaten. The earth need not suffer such burdens any longer." We organized a group of around two hundred women, with Nirmala in the lead. Our men backed us. "We will finish Muddy. It is our right," Nirmala declared. In the middle of all this, we got information that Muddy was planning to bring the police during the measuring of the grain after the harvest.

'"The cheat! What's left to wait any more?" Nirmala asked. Together, we went to his fields, harvested the crop, attacked his storehouses, confiscated the grains, and burned the fake documents and records of loans and interest to ashes. We distributed the confiscated rice and grain amongst us. When the police came, we ran away. They took some of us with them. "Muddy should be killed," Nirmala said. And we did it. We were more than two hundred women, all of us carrying sickles.

'"Don't cry. Hold your sickles firmly. Reap, reap, reap," Nirmala directed. And we reaped! Not just Muddy, we killed the other landlords too, like Bhuchander Rao and Appala Swami. We had the support of Somu, Ganpati and other men. But we, the compassionate mothers, executed the plans. The men went into exile as the village was raided by the police and the military. We heard guns, the army galloping in, the dogs barking and our children crying. How many people had they killed! We thought Nirmala, Somu, Manganna and Krishna were safe, but there were spies among them. The police blockaded Nirmala and her friends and shot them. Somu and some others escaped. After that, we didn't hear about Somu for a long time.' Bollamma stood up. Taking the lamp in her hand, she descended the steps to the backyard.

'Want to take a leak?' she asked. Dulari followed her without answering.

'When is the first bus in the morning, Bollamma?' Dulari asked. 'Let Sita's baba come after finishing his work. I need to go back to the village.'

Without waiting for Somnath Hembrom, Dulari returned to her village with her children. After that, she never lived with him.

30

When Rupi Murmu began talking about Budhini, Somnath Hembrom spoke in a calm, cold and impersonal tone, 'Budhini! Isn't it an old wound that hasn't been cured yet? Some kind of senile gangrene?' His voice felt like he was running a sharp-edged weapon through fresh flesh.

'I wonder what more you will learn about it. You may hear a lot about how Budhini's life ended up in such misery due to the superstitious practices of her own clan. Sooner or later, you will reach your conclusion. You should go to Godda. You will see how Budhinis are made there,' he added.

This was another side of Somnath Hembrom, one they were not familiar with. This person bore no resemblance to the man who had the miserable, egg-like eyes they had seen behind the bottle-like glasses, or with the head that stooped low to concentrate only on polishing cheap stones stuck on metal rings, or with the older man who carefully reached out to his shelves to take out a few things, or with the soft voice that had told them his story.

Obviously, his mood was bitter. His behaviour seemed to be the opposite of what Dayananda Tudu had told them. Rupi and Suchitra found themselves at a loss, not knowing how to respond.

A lanky man came from inside with a brass pot of water in his hand. A strong stench of sweat, dirt and nicotine emitted from his body. He was wearing a white undervest and a white bagwaan with green stripes, soiled and faded.

'Doso, get the things from the shop,' Somnath Hembrom threw a bunch of keys at him. Though he stretched his arm out, he couldn't catch it. It fell down after hitting the wall with a chime.

'Try to be a little smarter, Doso,' Somnath Hembrom said bitterly.

'Yes, Baba,' Doso climbed down the steps and gathered the firewood that had been laid out to dry under the sun.

'Do you think it is challenging to seize land from people like him?' Somnath Hembrom murmured. 'Go. Get some wheat and dal from the shop. Leave the firewood there and hurry up, your bus arrives in fifteen minutes.'

'The logs will get soaked if it rains, won't it, Baba?'

'That doesn't mean you can miss the bus.'

Like an obedient child, Doso put the logs down. He crossed the courtyard and climbed to the verandah at the back of the shop.

Hembrom was not in the shop when Rupi and Suchitra came to see him. They met him at his house behind the shop. The headmaster had given them instructions to reach the backyard, as the house was hidden from view. A narrow, crooked route by the side of the shop led them to a tall gate of bamboo sticks and thorns, which opened into a broad courtyard.

A mango tree at the end of the yard had spread its boughs so lavishly that it provided shade to the entire area around the house, giving the air refreshing coolness and the fragrance of mango blossoms. Four rooms opened out from the verandah, and one of them was the shop. Under the tree, a dog bundled up on a charpoy was basking in the sun. The middle of the charpoy, where the dog lay, had sagged because of overuse and now looked like a cradle. Though the dog had seen them, it didn't make an attempt to move or bark. Raising an eye as if to observe the scene, it wagged its tail slightly and went back to sleep again.

'Please wait, I will walk him to the bus stop and come back,' Somnath Hembrom said.

Doso came out of the shop carrying a heavy load on his head.

'Shall we go, Baba?' he asked.

'Where's your shirt, Doso?'

Doso had forgotten to put on his shirt. He was embarrassed for a moment. Putting the sack on the floor, he went inside.

'Doso is my son-in-law, Sita's husband. They live in Mali in Godda. He came only last night. He said Godda was burning.'

'We know it, the . . . Company.'

'Company! Tell me no more about the Company. When are we going to be free of these companies? Companies are everywhere, always, all the time; it is one or the other. East India Company, DVC company, BCCL company, his company, their company! We live somewhere, happy with what we have and harbour no plans, no luxuries and no hopes. But the companies are not like that. They come after us. Haven't you seen their bulldozers? Those people are like that. Go away or we will crush you.'

Doso came out wearing a shirt that was dirtier than his undervest. Also, now he had a turban on his head.

'If they won't give us the land, let them bury us in it, Baba,' Doso said. Somnath Hembrom tapped him on his shoulder as if to console him.

'No, Beta, please don't talk like that. Presently, our lives are as turbulent as the Damodar during monsoon. We have no idea whether our canoe will see land again. But that won't stop us from paddling, will it? Sita and your children are waiting. Come, I will put you on the bus.'

Raising the end of the shirt he was wearing, Doso wiped his eyes. But he had no control over his tears.

'My palm trees, Baba. I had thirty of them. The Company uprooted the palms I had looked after like my own children. Holding their feet, I had cried, "Company Babu, please don't remove our palms. How will we live without them? Please go away from our land." But they ran their earthmovers over our saplings, Baba.'

'I know that, Doso. Please come with me now or you will miss your bus.' Holding one side of the sack each, the father-in-law and son-in-law lifted it. Stretching its body and limbs, the dog woke up as if to see Doso off. It nudged him with its nose and followed him wagging its tail.

'Go sleep, Joggu. I will come back soon. But how will I get a piece of jaggery the next time I see you? Your Sitaji will call me from behind. "Oye, have you taken the jaggery for Joggu?" She will think that I have a bad memory. But that's not the case, Joggu. I put a piece of jaggery in my pocket the moment I put on my shirt. But what can I do? Our palms have flown away, Joggu. Stop following me, or I will cry. I don't even know if I have a village to return to. Go, go sleep.'

'Please don't cry, Doso. Wipe your eyes and come with me. Let Joggu also come, poor thing, he is more than sad, just like you.'

Carrying the sack stuffed with rice and wheat, the two men walked to the bus stop. Joggu followed them, and at times ran ahead of them.

Somnath Hembrom said that Doso's bus came the second they reached the bus stop. He was back within ten minutes. 'Poor Doso, he was crying inside the bus as well. What can be done! This is the condition of all the villagers in Godda. Things are worse than what Doso said. I heard that there might be some firing.'

He called Sita on her mobile phone. It was Sita's five-year-old daughter, Durgi, who answered the call. 'Dadu, come fast . . .' The child was crying over the phone. She said her mother was about to throw her and her infant brother to the bulldozer. She had heard her ma shouting to the Company Babu: 'First you bury them here, and then you can come after our lands.' Her ma had tried to push her and her brother in front of the bulldozer. Frightened, the child had run away and hid inside a basket. It was good that she had her ma's phone with her. She cried to her grandpa, 'Dadu, please come fast. Ma might've thrown my little brother already.'

Somnath Hembrom consoled the child. 'It won't happen, my dear. Ma and Ba will be worried if they don't see you. Please come out of the basket and go to Ma.' The child cried louder than before. She was determined not to step out. Somnath Hembrom was visibly upset.

A little later, he told Rupi and Suchitra, 'I am off to Godda by the next bus. I have arranged for someone to help you out, a Mr Mangol Manjhi. He is a teacher here at the upper primary school. He is on his way already. And please don't worry about whatever I told you earlier. I just hinted at what was going to happen in the case of Budhini.'

Suchitra was unaware of the severe situation in Godda. Though she was embarrassed to admit it, she asked Rupi about it the minute Somnath Hembrom went inside to change. 'What's happening in Godda? What's the problem?'

'Problem? It is not as easy as it sounds. It's like those dark fairy tales where witches come on black nights and grab everything that was yours. The next morning you wake up and find yourself in rags, broken and begging on the street. In Godda, the government is confiscating farmers' land by force. Reality is worse than a Grimm's tale there.'

Her speech was interrupted by the squeak of the bamboo gates opening. Joggu entered, followed by a tall and thin middle-aged man.

'Come, Mangol Manjhi, please be seated,' Somnath Hembrom dusted the charpoy.

'When are you leaving for Godda, Bhaiya?' Mangol Manjhi asked.

'I made a mistake, Mangol. I should have gone with Doso. Sometimes I act without thinking. Maybe I am too old to think straight.'

'Our ideas and brain seem to be of no use at times, Bhaiya. Injustice is towering above everything else.'

'I don't think corruption can continue for long, Mangol.'

'I went to Godda some two years back. I knew exactly what was going to take place there. My calculations were right too.

Isn't it clear now why the prime minister who visited Bangladesh in 2015 brought this Company Babu with him? Was he merely accompanying the prime minister? Or was his purpose sightseeing? I am no fool. As soon as they came back, he started running for the sake of keeping the word the prime minister had given to Bangladesh. Only the target was not clear. Now that it has struck our eastern parts, especially Godda, it makes sense. A clear-cut decision, quite understandable as the area is rich in coal, water and land. The land is always the responsibility of the government, isn't it? The prime minister's word can be fulfilled only by creating a thermal power plant. The Company Babu was persistent that they should get a minimum of two thousand acres in Godda itself. But . . .'

After this abrupt pause, he continued, 'The land that they had found suitable had a lot of farms and fields. The government must remove such obstacles. The government is for the Company Babu and not us, isn't it? The day I went there, the Company had confiscated and fenced nine villages, including Nayabadh, Gankta, and the Mali village of your Sita Mei. There was nothing to be seen except panicked villagers running amok, crying their hearts out. There were more policemen than the villagers. Women cried beating their chests, older farmers rolled up and down the soil, wailing and bellowing like their animals, "Bhaiya, the Company Babu says our land is theirs, that the government has given our properties to the Company. But how could it be possible, Bhaiya? This is the place where my baba used to work. My baba's baba also made a living by toiling on this very land. How could this land belong to the Company, Bhaiya?" Throwing a handful of mud over their heads, they asked everyone who visited them. They cried. Some of us, with the workers of Swatantra Adivasi Samsthan, gathered the villagers and went to see the superintendent of police.

"Why do you come here? Go to your local police station and file a complaint there. It is they who should take action on this," he told us.

"Local police station?" the villagers were surprised. "The local police are in the pockets of Company Babu. They are the ones who beat us."

'The superintendent couldn't control his anger any longer, "How dare you speak rubbish? The police are only doing their duty."

'When the villagers, who were reluctant to leave, raised a hue and cry, the deputy commissioner intervened: "The money for your land is in the government office. Go, get it."

"What's the use of money? It will dwindle to nothing in no time. The land is not like that, is it? Is there any end to farming on the earth? We live the whole year tilling on our soil. What will we do if there's no earth? What will our children do?"

'Have the cries of villagers ever cracked the walls of any police station? Never, there's no chance.'

'Now they are expelling people by force. The earthmovers are getting rid of houses and the soil,' Somnath Hembrom said.

'The government should not be allowed to break rules. That is the cause of all these misfortunes,' Rupi Murmu added.

'Rupi Mei, they club law with a dirty word, *vikas*, which is worse than the bulldozers and earthmovers.'

Somnath Hembrom's bus to Godda was at 2 p.m. 'Oye, Joggu,' he called the dog to his side and gave him a plateful of boiled grains and steamed roots. 'Will you be here till I come back? Or will you wander? Here, eat this.'

The dog devoured the food and went to lie down on the floor of the shop. From there, it sent stolen looks at Somnath Hembrom and wagged its tail.

'I will take them to Robon Manjhi. What do you say, Bhaiya?' Mangol Manjhi asked Somnath Hembrom.

'Good, Mangol. Make sure you meet Vijaykumar. They should listen to what the DVC has to say, shouldn't they?'

'Of course, Bhaiya.'

Robon Manjhi's house was in Panchet, nine kilometres from Chirkunda. Rupi Murmu called a taxi. Three or four children who were picking coals from the mounds of mud lying on the sides of the road stood up on seeing the car and waved their hands. They were little girls whose faces, clothes, hair and hands had become black because of the coal. The woman who was carrying the coal collected by the children turned and scolded them.

'Robon Manjhi is Ravan Manjhi. He has lost his vigour though,' Mangol said.

Robon Manjhi's house was at the end of a narrow tarred road. It was different from the usual houses in Santal villages. There were tarred public roads for buses and cars, running in between the houses. The house was a sizeable two-storeyed building painted in green and white. Two or three young men looked down, leaning against the wall of the verandah on the top floor. Mangol Manjhi went inside the house while Rupi and Suchitra waited at the door. There were pictures of two bulls painted in blue on either side of the door. They had to enter the courtyard after crossing a small threshold and door on the left side of the house. Staring at the women clad in the clothes of the townsfolk, the children ran inside. An infant was lying on the charpoy in the courtyard, crying. A girl was singing at the top of her voice to calm the baby down. On one side of the yard was a drove of pigs. The goats, chickens and ducks sauntered around. It seemed as if the house was packed with people. Women, men and children walked about. The young men standing on the verandah said something and laughed looking at Rupi and Suchitra.

'Robon Manjhi barely walks these days. He may find it a little challenging to move around,' Mangol said. A woman in a red salwar-kameez rushed towards the charpoy and took the baby in her arms. She was probably the mother. She went inside, leaving them with the livestock in the courtyard. After some more time, the young men from the verandah brought out three plastic chairs. 'Sit,' they said. Their faces flushed as Rupi Murmu smiled at them. A minute or two later, two men came carrying a large wooden easy chair. They put it across from where Rupi and Suchitra were sitting. Without greeting them, they went inside and helped a

giant older man walk to the easy chair and helped him sit on it.
Robon Manjhi was wearing a white bagwaan with blue stripes
and a maroon sweater over a white vest. He didn't seem to notice
anyone in particular. He just sat there on the easy chair and looked
somewhere.

'These are the people who came with Mangol Manjhi, Baba.
They would like to know about Budhini. Don't you remember the
Panchet Dam . . . ?'

Robon Manjhi didn't seem to have heard anything. Even if he
had heard, he definitely didn't listen. He merely looked at Rupi
and Suchitra, nodded his head at Mangol Manjhi.

'Don't you remember how Budhini was ousted by bitlaha?
They wanted to know about it, Baba . . .'

Robon Manjhi didn't answer.

'Baba used to say that he didn't want to remember that,' his
son said.

Robon Manjhi's son brought a glass-framed picture from inside
and showed them. It was the picture of a tall and handsome Santal
youth posing for a photograph with Pandit Jawaharlal Nehru.

'This is Dadu in the picture,' a young man said. He closely
resembled the young man in the picture.

'Don't you have anything to say to them, Baba?' Robon
Manjhi's son asked him again. He looked at him closely. 'Nehru
had promised to give us a home and electricity for free. We haven't
got it yet. Please remind him.'

'No matter what you ask, Baba only says this much,' the son
said.

'I want to lie down,' Robon Manjhi said and tried to get up.
They helped him up. As he walked inside, dragging his legs swollen
because of oedema, Robon Manjhi told Rupi, 'Please remind
Nehru that it's all dark in here. He had promised us free electricity.
We got nothing.'

Laughing, his son said, 'The current supply went last night. It
isn't back yet.'

The two men came back and carried his easy chair inside. The infant had drifted off to sleep. The woman came back and put the baby back on the charpoy, as if it was the most peaceful place. Two children sat on either side of the charpoy to watch over the baby. Cackling, the chickens flew by, the goats bleated, the pigs moved to the shade under the charpoy on which the baby was lying. Seeing the pigs moving in unison, a dog barked, and a duck and its countless ducklings passed by them.

On their way back from Robon Manjhi's house, Mangol asked, 'You might be thinking what good it did to see Ravan?'

Rupi smiled.

'I wanted you to know that he is trapped in the memories of 1959. The word that was given then remains unkept to this date. In the first Five-Year Plan, the amount set aside for those who lost their lands was very meagre, just 4 per cent of the total amount. Even that amount didn't reach them. Robon Manjhi suffers not from memory loss but from the unremitting memories of things past.'

Suddenly, as if she has remembered something important, Suchitra said, 'Rupi Murmu has written a study titled "The Other Side of the Great Indian Temples". I would like you to read that book.'

'I will definitely read it if I get it,' Mangol Manjhi smiled.

Rupi said she would send it to him once they were back. She wanted all three of them to read her book: Headmaster Dayananda Tudu, Somnath Hembrom and Mangol Manjhi.

Vijaykumar, the PRO of DVC said he was not free that day to meet them.

'I will keep the whole day aside for you tomorrow,' he told Mangol Manjhi.

31

Beside the statue of Baba Tilka Manjhi Murmu, installed at the facade of the Bibliophile's Club building in Panchet, Rupi and Suchitra waited for Mangol Manjhi. It had been decided that he would come there from Maithon with Vijaykumar.

'I have a feeling that we may get some real news about Budhini from Vijaykumar,' Rupi Murmu said.

'Hopefully, he will tell us what the DVC knows,' Suchitra said, focussing her lenses on the massive banyan tree at the entrance of the building. With a luscious canopy and aerial roots spreading out on all four sides of the trunk, the bountiful banyan seemed marvellously ancient. With every step they took, the fallen leaves murmured.

'Forgive me, ladies,' said Vijaykumar, who had arrived half an hour later than expected. 'It's not my mistake. Mangolji couldn't make it as he had to go to Godda. There has been a deadly conflict between the Company's men and the villagers. A lot of them have been critically injured. The police have resorted to baton-charging. Mangol has some relatives in Godda. He has gone to inquire after them.'

Rupi's face fell; Suchitra also seemed equally disappointed. They were upset to see one more day go to waste. Already, they had spent more money and time on this research than planned.

'Why can't we consider a more frugal life?' Suchitra had asked Rupi the previous night. 'For instance, we can cut back on our taxi payments and turn to the bus instead, and take a train rather than a flight. Cut out a meal from the regular three times and consider a small, inexpensive dhaba instead of hotels. Some financial prudence is what we need now, some strategies. We can't cut back on our hotel room rent though. I need a clean toilet, or I will get pissed off with everything.'

'Don't fret about it now; I am sure I can borrow money from my baba,' Rupi Murmu had consoled her.

The DVC's PRO was a gentleman, calm and quiet. 'Please don't worry about Mangol's absence; you are my responsibility now. I will take care of everything. You are the guests of DVC. But there are some changes in the schedule I had planned with Mangol earlier. Is that okay with you?'

'Mangolji didn't tell us anything about the programme schedules.'

'That's nice.' Vijaykumar smiled. He had brought an older man named Chundu Soren from the canteen near the club. 'It's better to have someone from the village when we go there,' he said.

'Why so? Is the Pathalgadi rebellion active here?'

'No, not in these areas. It is active in the districts of Khunti, Gumla and Singhbhum, where outsiders can't enter many villages. The villagers, especially the young men, are always on vigil with bows, arrows and slings. Fortunately, we don't have such problems here. Chundu Soren will take us to the village where the girls are getting ready to perform a dance for you.'

Pale and unfit with persistent hunger, Chundu Soren looked like a tree that was about to fall. A haggard man!

'Don't take his looks into account, he is one of the finest musicians we have around here,' Vijaykumar placed an arm around his shoulder and drew him close. 'He has written and composed more than three hundred songs. He knows a lot of the traditional Santal songs. That's the reason why many outsiders come in search of him. Most of them are from universities. Some of them make him sing so that they can write down the words and make books out of it. For him, it's a pleasure to sing. His name won't be found on any pages though. They would probably have given him a little something for his songs, or maybe some food. He considers even that a big deal, isn't that so, Baba?'

The musician smiled in humility and nodded his head. Vijaykumar continued, 'But Chundu Soren has a son with a permanent, scornful look of someone who always keeps his teeth clenched. If anyone starts the Pathalgadi movement in Panchet, it will be him.'

Vijaykumar started the car. Rupi and Suchitra inspected Chundu Soren and imagined what his son would be like—a young man wearing a white bagwaan, white vest and a white pugree with a red tape tied around it. He would have a red garland around his neck, a quiver on his shoulder, a bow and arrow in hand and a dogged look in his eyes. And then he would declare, '*Jal*, jungle, *jameen* is ours. We will not let you lay your hands on them again. We don't need your law and your police; we don't need your Constitution either; we follow what our gram sabha says. Our rules are inscribed on a stone at the entrance of our village. Haven't you seen it? Pathalgadi is not just a tombstone to be placed over the head of those who have gone. It stands for the protection of the living. We don't need your vikas. For us, happiness counts. We need peace. It is not you, but us, who are the rightful people of India. The real India is a land of peace.'

The closer they looked, the more they found Chundu Soren transforming into his son. They found themselves folding their hands before him in awe.

'First, we will go to see the underground powerhouse at Maithon,' Vijaykumar said.

'What is the big deal?' Rupi and Suchitra communicated through exchanged looks. Maybe, it was part of his duty as the PRO to show it to the guests. Talking to them in simple English about the underground thermal plant of Maithon, he proved himself eligible for carrying out his mission not mechanically, but with the innate interest of someone who does his job with joy.

'This is a real wonder!' Rupi and Suchitra exclaimed.

No matter how many times in the past he had expressed astonishment at this, the expression seemed genuine, sincere and charged with passion. Vijaykumar talked about the River Barakar, the hill adjacent to it and the underground thermal power plant that tunnelled through the rocks under the mountain. He also elaborated upon Pandit Nehru's visits during the different stages of construction, and the jokes he used to crack while examining the project. Finally, he spoke about the inauguration of Maithon dam by Nehru in the year 1957, on 27 September, and how the workers experienced goosebumps when the dam was declared as the most extensive underground power station in Asia. He paused here for a while, as if remembering the grand, unending applauses, the compliments received by the DVC and the advantages the country stood to gain. He also talked at length about Nehru's vision of a new India. 'Technology was not so developed back then. Remember, it was manpower that helped to dig a tunnel through the rocks to build the underground powerplant that is 80 metres below the summit of the hill.'

Neither Rupi nor Suchitra had any knowledge about these technological details. Yet, they listened to him with the ardent expression of schoolchildren listening to stories. What they wanted to know about was Budhini. They were resilient enough to suppress any amount of yawns to keep the PRO satisfied.

When the car approached the bridge built over the River Barakar, Chundu Soren, who had been silent since the beginning of their journey and was just looking out of the window, said, 'This area was a wild forest once. It was difficult to cross the river here.'

The path that descended underground was broad and cold. There was a hill, they thought in astonishment, 80 feet above their heads. There would be a forest on the crest and a river flowing

through winding paths. It would most likely be breezy at the top
of the hill.

Though there were long rows of fully lit electric lights, a
wet and unpleasant kind of darkness lingered in nooks of the
station.

'What we have here are three horizontal shaft-generating
units,' Vijaykumar said. They nodded their heads.

Though the machines were gigantic, there was something
cute about them. They immediately liked the way the tools were
arranged, including the gigantic machines, and the neatness and
ample space surrounding them. The underground thermal power
plant was almost silent as none of the engines had been switched
on then. Anyhow, the noises from the external world didn't reach
down there. Suchitra captured several images of a bewildered
Chundu Soren staring at the super-enormous machines.

How, and through where, does the river flow in, how did they
operate the complicated switchyard, how was power generated,
how did it reach the transformers through different channels, and
how was it distributed again—whether they understood or not,
Vijaykumar went on explaining till they came out.

'When each unit works at its maximum power, 20 megawatts
of energy is created. Three groups together make 60 megawatts.
There are variations in the rates at times, depending on the
availability of water. Now, production is deficient. But what of it!
The DVC has thermal plants and gas turbines. It is not going to
affect the DVC if the water power plant stops working.'

Back outside, Rupi Murmu said laughing, 'My grades were
below average in the sciences. I just got through with the bare
minimum.'

'Me too,' Vijaykumar laughed with her.

'I was not that bad,' Suchitra said. She took a picture of Chundu
Soren sitting on his haunches, playing with a dog.

The village they visited had sprawling grasslands and frangipanis
that bore crimson flowers, though there were not many trees that

offered shade. A hot wind kept blowing. A Santal girl, wearing jeans and a top, brought them fresh lemonade.

'Santhimoyi Hasda,' Vijaykumar introduced her. 'She works as an engineer here. She will take you to the Maithon Dam site. I have a little office work to finish.'

Well, all the dams were the same, right? They were streams hindered or trapped within the walls of two mountains. A quasi-lake, pseudo in its essence.

'The water level is down in the dam. The rain was not heavy this year,' Santhimoyi said. Grass grew wildly on the banks of the reservoir, along with wild plants and creepers, where muddy ridges and pebble beds extended at length. In large groups, goats descended to the dam to drink water, their shepherds chasing them.

'Sometimes, wild beasts also come down. Deer are a usual sight. Would you care to go boating? What do you say? We will get to see a lot of animals as we move deeper into the forest. There are some rare birds as well,' Santhimoyi offered.

'We would love to do that, but we are running out of time. We need to return to Delhi in two or three days. And before that, we have to complete our assignments. I think Mr Vijaykumar is dealing with our programme here.'

'In that case, let us go to Kalyaneswari temple,' Vijaykumar said.

'What for?' Rupi and Suchitra exchanged looks one more time. Not missing the confusion on their faces, Vijaykumar told them, 'That is very important.'

It was a nine-kilometre drive on the national highway to reach Kalyaneswari temple, near the River Barakar. Trees crowded around on both sides of the road. When the car entered a small street lined with shops selling idols and puja articles, Chundu Soren said, 'I am not coming inside. I will wait here.' Vijaykumar didn't force him.

'This is a five-hundred-year-old temple. There's a connection between this temple and the Maithon Dam, which is a magnificent temple of modern India. Have you any idea about it?'

It was the first time Rupi and Suchitra had heard the name of the temple. They just smiled.

'They are related by name, Maithon came from Kalyaneswari. For the natives, this place is "mayi ki shtan". "Mayi" is mother and "sthan" means place. The word "sthan" was diminished to "than" by use, and thus we have Mayitan! Mayitan in turn was reduced to Maithon. Mayithan, the temple, is on the shores of River Barakar, and Maithon, the dam, is in the river itself.'

A tree in full bloom enhanced the beauty of the small temple which was a happy, safe haven for wild monkeys. The abundance of the bright, dazzling strips of silk, with tassels and bells dangling on colourful threads, tied to the branches of the tree by the devotees outnumbered the clusters of flowerets. Hundreds and thousands of temple bells chimed in the wind.

'There is a popular myth that couples will be endowed with an heir if they pray here,' Vijaykumar said and then launched into a story.

'Human sacrifice was widespread in the precincts of the Kalyaneswari temple once.' He showed them the sacrificial altar. 'Everyday, it was the priest who fed the deity. One day, he realized there was a shortage of food while feeding her. Panicking, the priest went to collect some food, leaving his daughter in charge of the goddess. The goddess, upon opening her eyes, saw the child sitting there. Thinking the child was her food, she killed the child and ate it. When the priest came back with food, he fell unconscious seeing his daughter brutally murdered. The deity saw how sad and affected the priest was and decided to do penance. She blessed all unfortunate, childless couples who visited her with heirs.'

Vijaykumar then gave them a pamphlet published by the information and public relations department of the DVC. There was a small description of Kalyaneswari temple. The cover page featured a solitary canoe moving on a river reflecting red and golden hues of sundown. The travellers and the boat appeared dim against the bright shades of the setting sun. Darkness had fallen on the banks of the river, too, making it look sombre.

The view behind the temple was more gorgeous given the presence of enormous trees, piles of boulders, little avalanches and narrow streams. Lost in the beauty, Suchitra went on clicking pictures.

'Don't you want to go?' Vijaykumar asked. 'We don't have much time here, we can only try to see it all. Let us move to the village with Chundu Soren. The Santal dancers are getting ready, only for you. The entire community is very excited. We need to head back to Panchet at four in the evening to see Budhini.'

'Budhini!' Rupi and Suchitra couldn't believe what they had just heard.

'Ah . . . Mangol told me that you wanted to meet Budhini. Don't you want to see her?'

They took time answering that. It was something beyond their expectations. Initially, they had hoped for some information from the PRO of the DVC, using which they planned to advance their investigation.

'Is Budhini Mejhan alive? Can we see her?'

'Why do you ask so?'

Vijaykumar found the wonder and excitement in their question rather strange. Tourists sometimes asked about Budhini. At times they saw the picture of Budhini and Pandit Jawaharlal Nehru inaugurating the Panchet Dam in the DVC's pamphlets. It was natural for people to ask about her out of curiosity. Some even insisted on seeing her. As the PRO of the DVC, it was Vijaykumar who took them to Budhini.

Bending down to the ground, spreading out her arms, Rupi Murmu saluted Marang Buru: 'Johar Marang Buru'. Suchitra noticed a twinkle in the eyes of Chundu Soren, one she hadn't seen before.

'The girls bought new panchi and parhan yesterday for their dance,' Vijaykumar said. 'They will dance singing the songs of

Chundu Soren. He has a group of singers and percussionists.'
Chundu Soren laughed wholeheartedly. But neither Rupi nor
Suchitra had any interest in the dance or the songs. Budhini! Their
only aim was to see Budhini.

However, they couldn't see the dance or reach Budhini. On the
way to the village, Vijaykumar received an unexpected phone call.
It was Mangol Manjhi. Many people had been injured in the police
shooting and baton-charge. Three people, including a woman, had
died on the spot. One of them was Somnath Hembrom.

32

S omnath Hembrom was to be buried in his daughter's field, near the pond in the ancestral graveyard of Doso's people. Even Doso kept no count of the ancestors who had been laid to rest there.

The bodies of Juri Besra, a thirty-six-year-old woman who was always in the lead during uprisings, and Shubho Lal, a young man, were to be buried in their own fields. This would undoubtedly lead to a more vital revolution; since the fields belonged to the Company now, they were guarded by armed policemen.

Things were not that simple though. After the post-mortem, the bodies were brought back to the village in a prolonged mournful procession, accompanied by drums. The beats of the drums planted fear in the streets of Mali. The banam players continued playing a sad dirge fit to break any heart. People from inside and outside the district of Godda were part of the procession. They flowed through the streets silently. Many of them held placards with slogan against the Company and the government.

Under no circumstances, the police said, would the bodies come on to the land of the Company. They put up barricades at different points.

'Please take these bodies somewhere else without creating further trouble,' Godda's commissioner of police said.

'This is our graveyard. Where else shall we take these bodies?' the villagers asked. They refused to move. Circling the bodies, they played on their drums, pipes and banam. The sun was scorching, but no one left. Moreover, more and more people reached the scene, hearing of the tragic deaths. The situation was getting tense.

'How can you bring the bodies to the Company's land without permission? It is trespassing; it is against the law. We are here trying to maintain law and order,' the police said. The villagers grew impatient with anger. Sita got up from her baba's side and walked towards the policemen.

'Now you are protecting the law, you are guarding the property. Where were you when it was time to preserve the law for us? Why didn't you guard us?'

'We execute only the decision of the government.'

'In that case, let the government decide what they should do with my baba's body.'

Presenting the corpses to the police, the mourners sat around it. There was a groundswell of discontent.

'Please disperse or we will have to take action,' the police commissioner warned them. But this only instigated the people and made the situation more turbulent.

'If you want to shoot down more of us, we are ready,' they said.

The villagers moved forward in unison, ready for an encounter. The police realized that things were not in their favour. The villagers started to tear down the barricades and the wire raised by the Company around the fields. At breakneck speed, they ran into their lands. Many of them were crying loudly. Women screamed, hugged and kissed the soil as if they had found their lost children.

The bodies remained under the sun for almost five hours. After hours of disputes and debates, the police agreed to let the villagers conduct the last rites, provided they left after the rituals.

The Company, without taking into account how precious Doso's pond was—it had fed many generations of his family, many generations of livestock and agriculture; it was on the banks of this pond that Doso's forefathers were put to rest, their children and he would be buried there too, and his children and their children—took barely fifteen minutes to bulldoze the ground and cover the pond. Splashing some water around with a loud 'plop', the pond had closed its eyes.

Why did the Company need little ponds? What they needed was the strong current of the river.

Doso's dead people rested in the coolness under the shade of the trees, plants and undergrowth near the banks of that little pond. The wind that carried the scent of the soil ploughed by Doso always blew over them. He knew the Bongas would be watching him toil, sitting on the branches, dikes, palms and rocks. Seeds sprouted and saplings grew healthy under their vigil. The Company had destroyed the dwellings of the Bongas, who were now wandering somewhere between the sky and the earth. Doso felt an intense burning within him thinking that he will have to bury Baba in such a place.

He had seen Baba's glasses falling from his face as the bullet hit him. He rushed to grab it, but it was crushed under several feet. With much difficulty, he picked up the pieces. Baba was calling out to him. 'Run, Doso, run . . .' He turned back. Baba had his hand on his chest. All of a sudden, Doso saw people carrying Baba away. How quickly the place seemed deserted! Holding the glasses in his hand, Doso stood bewildered. One of the legs of the glasses was missing, and both the lenses were broken. But still, it was Baba's glasses. Baba saw them through these glasses. How affectionately he used to admire his grandchildren! Baba had seen the fields through them; the world, deaths, sickness, everything, through those lenses.

Doso had also looked through Baba's glasses. 'Baba, can you see everything clearly with these?'

'I can, Doso.'

'Why can't I see anything?'

'Your eyes are healthy, Doso. That's why.'

With time, Baba had told him, he too would have to wear glasses. What one sees through the lenses, Baba had said, were magnified images and visions. Even the blind see things, Baba had explained. Some of it Doso understood, and some things didn't make sense.

'Try to see things without lenses, Doso,' Baba always reminded him.

It was Baba who had first warned them about the coming of the Company and the possibility of their lands getting confiscated. Back then, no one believed him.

'Doso, your father-in-law looks like he is a little off his rocker these days,' the farmers of Mali would say. They laughed and said that, according to them, it was the older man's way of creating discord wherever he saw harmony.

Doso turned the broken lenses upside down. Baba's body was in the centre of the mob. He had been trying to get there for a long time. In their panic, the people rushed to the front and pushed others back. Each time they drove Doso further away. If it was going to be like this, he won't be able to send Baba's lenses with his body.

Sita's mother didn't come to Godda. 'I don't want to see him,' Dulari had said. Sita was outraged. 'What is there to see, after all? The gun shot hole on his chest!'

Had a policeman not pushed Doso out of the crowd, he would have reached Baba much earlier.

Headmaster Dayananda Tudu shrouded Somnath Hembrom with a red shawl. Shocking the people of Mali, a flow of red wreaths streamed through the crowd. These people were not from Mali; there were men, women, villagers and townsfolk among them. Struggling, Doso somehow reached Baba. Or maybe the people pushed him towards the body. Over the red cloth, Doso placed the broken bits of his glasses. Tears welled up and he couldn't see anything, not even Baba. His eyes drowning in a surge of tears, he asked himself: Where was Baba's face, where were his arms, where was the chest that was riddled with a bullet hole?

'A death of a different kind would not have suited him,' Mangol Manjhi said. 'Time is crucial, Bhaiya. The clock's hands never run backwards. Even if such things happened, we couldn't live a different kind of life, or die a different death.' Taking off his watch, he placed it next to Somnath Hembrom's wrist.

*

Rupi and Suchitra reached Mali in Jauna Marandi's taxi. It was Vijaykumar who had arranged it for them. He knew the villages of Godda very well. Jauna said he had great respect for Somnath Hembrom. When they reached Mali, the mourners were carrying the bodies in a procession. They joined the funeral train. Rupi Murmu asked Suchitra to capture as many pictures as she could. While walking with the mourners, she kept sending messages to Delhi: 'Merciless usurping from the Company', 'The martyrdom of farmers', 'Old revolutionary Somnath Hembrom died of gunshot wound', 'Villagers struggling to bury the bodies in their own fields', 'Police strategies!' and 'Turbulent!'

On their way back, they were completely silent. Their hearts felt heavy; their words lay barred. It depressed Rupi Murmu to think how lonely each person was. What kind of loneliness had Somnath Hembrom? All his life he had lived alone in a house in Chirkunda. Had the old man ever regretted abandoning his secret pleasures? If things had not turned out like this, would he have lived the regular life of a sepoy, wedded to Dulari? Thinking of the four or five hours Somnath Hembrom's body—the body of a fervent abolitionist who had spent an entire lifetime in a state of denial, living in exile, living behind bars, living in pain and tears—lay under the searing heat charged Rupi's heart with a conflict she had not known before. His face had become a darkish blue, his cheeks were so swollen that it seemed they were going to burst. A bloody fluid oozed out of his nose, and his abdomen was swelling up. The body bore no resemblance to the Somnath Hembrom Rupi knew.

Holding her camera close, Suchitra leaned against the seat of the car and closed her eyes. She had got some good photographs of Somnath Hembrom. In the last picture, he was feeding Joggu before setting off to Godda. Maybe Joggu was still lying on his charpoy, waiting for Somnath to return.

Open fields on either side of the road were swimming in bountiful moonlight that was flowing down from some mysterious blue mountains, from a faraway land. The crowns of the trees swayed gently while the playful wind danced vigorously on the edges of the wayside grass. White moths bounced around the heads of the lamp posts. What was there for nature to get so excited about? The Grand Trunk Road extended unendingly. Except for the occasional vehicle that sped past them, the road was uncannily empty. Jauna Marandi turned on the radio. Maybe he was feeling a little drowsy. A male singer with a sonorous voice sang gloomily:

In this dreadful night of darkness and storm,
A lonely figure crosses the sea in a single canoe . . .
O, the one, who is not afraid of this fatal night or storming sea,
What intense passion drives your boat ahead?

*

'I don't think we can meet Budhini today as well,' Vijaykumar said. They were having breakfast at the canteen of the Bibliophile's Club. Rupi and Suchitra had not eaten anything since the previous day. They didn't even drink water before joining the funeral. On the way back, they hadn't felt like eating. They decided to have breakfast in Panchet, as they had to meet Vijaykumar, who was waiting for them at the club.

'Budhini hasn't returned yet.'

'Where has she gone?'

'She went to Godda the moment she heard about Somnath Hembrom.'

'She was in Mali!'

'Yes, she is still at Hembrom's daughter's place.'

Though there was no reason to not believe what he had said, they still couldn't accept the fact that they participated in the funeral procession of Somnath Hembrom with Budhini.

'We have heard that Budhini met Rajiv Gandhi with the help of Somnath Hembrom.'

'Budhini hasn't met Rajiv Gandhi.'

'What?'

'These are stories people tell.'

'But I have read articles on how Budhini met Rajiv Gandhi in Delhi in 1985. No one has negated these statements. In fact, many newspapers reported the same.'

'That's wrong. Nothing like that happened.'

'So, was Rajiv Gandhi not the reason the DVC took her back?'

'It's true, Rajiv Gandhi did negotiate. But that was not based on Budhini's trip to Delhi, or her plea. People come up with crazy things, trying to drag the DVC's name through the mire.'

'But . . .'

Rupi couldn't help but feel that Vijaykumar, being a DVC employee, was trying to hide something.

Vijaykumar must have understood that confusion. 'You could ask Budhini in person. Don't take my words into account. Ask her directly,' he said.

Rupi and Suchitra found it hard to accept new facts about Budhini, especially because they rebutted every other thing they knew about her so far. Vijaykumar was a spokesperson of the DVC, but it was he who dismissed their misconceptions about Budhini's death. News reports had said, 'Budhini died last year, disconsolate to the end. She was in her late sixties.' This was information that had been considered authentic. But, clearly, the truth was still a matter of dispute.

Vijaykumar said, 'It was Budhini's husband, Datta, who wrote to Rajiv Gandhi. Datta is a gentleman and a learned person. During those days, they were in a bad state. The coal factory where Datta was working closed down. He couldn't do labour-intensive work because of his worsening lung disease. They couldn't make a living out of the little money Budhini earned once in a while. I have spoken to Datta about this in detail. It was at a point when they had no options that he decided to write a letter to Prime Minister Rajiv Gandhi. And that proved to be a turning point.'

*

The road to Telkupi was packed with tourists. Suchitra wanted to visit Telkupi one more time, walk through the ghostly temples there, click pictures of the hot water springs. They had all the time in the world till Budhini returned. Maybe, their investigation would end.

'Can we go there once again?' Suchitra asked.

'What's there to see? Anything important?' Vijaykumar asked.

'It's not like that,' Rupi corrected him. She said she had studied the temples of Telkupi in detail, the hot springs and the tribal villages girdling them. The villagers still mourned the losses of the submerged forest temples and the disease-curing hot springs.

'I was taken there by an officer of the archaeology department, Mr Abhijit Mallik. According to him, the archaeological value of those temples was beyond speculation. There were a lot of grievances. The Santals gave the first complaint to the archaeological department in 1957, when they started realizing that their temples were sinking, slowly but surely. However, Abhijit Mallik openly admitted that the archaeological department showed no interest in the matter. There was no other way. Dams were being constructed to check the most gruesome of floods. The lives of hundreds of thousands of people are more critical than ancient temples. Don't you consider the lives of hundreds of thousands of people to be more critical than ancient temples?'

'Therefore,' Suchitra continued, 'we would like the DVC's PRO to accompany us to the ghost temples of Telkupi.'

'I have absolutely no objections,' Vijaykumar smiled.

Suchitra sauntered around the ghost-like temples that jutted out from the middle of the dam that had been covered over time by a rumbling spout of mud, boulders and gravel beds.

'I would like more detail, with a little more clarity,' strolling behind Suchitra, Rupi Murmu told Vijaykumar. 'I know about Datta's letter and how some journalist happened to see it, and how it changed everything.'

'That's right. Rajiv Gandhi agreed to step in when they brought the letter to light. He gave orders to the DVC to take Budhini Mejhan back immediately. However, we couldn't locate her. The DVC searched for her in Purulia, Asansol, Kumardubi and Dhanbad. We looked far and wide, in almost all the places we heard Budhini had stayed. Like what you said, some people told us that Budhini was no more. The DVC found itself at a loss. Proceedings of the case were dropped at some point. It was at that time that Datta contacted the corporation. The moment Budhini reached the DVC; the corporation gave her the appointment order.'

'The DVC took her back after twenty-three years!'

'Yes.'

'Why did they suspend her for so long?'

Vijaykumar didn't answer that question. Instead, he said, 'Budhini is settled now, thanks to the DVC. The corporation gave her land and monetary help to build a shelter. She has a pension these days. Moreover, it's been agreed that someone from her next generation will be given a post in the corporation, it doesn't matter after how many generations.'

'Even so.'

33

'This road takes you to the DVC colony,' Vijaykumar said taking a left turn. 'Budhini's house is over there.' It had taken them a while to get there from the Panchet guest house.

This road! Rupi Murmu's mind sprinted forth. I know this uneven tarmac route with its battered margins. Not that I have walked through these roads somewhere in the past, but it feels like I have lived here. I wish I could walk down till the end of the lane wearing a white panchi and parhan, with profound joy in my heart, picking up one of those yellow leaves that come fluttering down in the breeze. If you follow me as I walk, you will see the three yellow genda flowers I am wearing in my hair, close to my right ear. Since I have worn my panchi a little high-waisted, you will see the golden border of it rubbing against my shin. You will also see the silver anklets I am wearing. I stand here in the bright openness and look blithely at the darkness on the other side. The path crawls through a green cave created by the luscious canopy on both sides. Suddenly, a rumbling surge of wind scatters a handful of dead leaves, giving me goosebumps. I see a flock of sheep coming out of the green cave like small, little clouds. I am an eight-year-old girl skipping and hopping through the sheep, playing on her tiriao.

'All these buildings you see on your left are the workers' quarters,' Vijaykumar said.

Though the road was narrow, there were open areas on either side where the goats were grazing. Except for the birds, it was silent.

'Budhini's house is on the right side,' Vijaykumar said.

As they got closer, they could see the wind rocking the bamboo. The ground was clothed in bamboo leaves. Every step you took, you could hear the rustle. The giant banyan tree on the roadside marked the thin trail leading up to Budhini's house. With the autumn leaves falling, the tree seemed quite impassive.

'Let us get off here,' Vijaykumar stopped the car.

'I can't believe the rate at which my heart is beating,' Rupi Murmu told Suchitra, who pressed her palm. Her own hand was cold and moist.

Tread softly on the carpet of bamboo leaves donned in a golden hue. It is a valley of unbroken silence.

Red and yellow flowers popped out of the hedgerow of thorns and plants around the house. Opening the bamboo gates, Vijaykumar walked in. 'Please wait here. I will go and tell her.'

Shade, cold and silence! Holding each other's hand, with their fingers interlocked, Rupi and Suchitra waited. Suchitra said she had never waited so anxiously for anyone. Rupi merely nodded.

The courtyard was somewhat large in size. A dark, humid world of plants flourished around an old well in the corner, which was visible from the entrance itself. Two structures that looked like houses jutted out from either side of the well. They had doors that opened into the courtyard. The verandahs, broad in size, seemed to be slightly elevated on the right side. A creeper with blue flowers and long tendrils spread across the left side of the verandah, its scent diffusing into the fresh air. The creeper filled up the vacuum with cool green shade. Bright sun rays fell on the structure on the right.

Rupi and Suchitra saw a woman sitting on the left side of the verandah. Showing no particular interest in the visitors, she crossed the courtyard and went to the house on the right side. She came out after a while.

'Ma is resting,' she said.

'Asleep?' Vijaykumar asked.

'No, just lying down.'

She went inside and came back with two red, plastic chairs.

'Please sit down,' she said and disappeared into the house on the left side.

'Ratni,' Vijaykumar said. 'Budhini's daughter.'

She was in her late forties. There was not even the faint ripple of a smile on her face. The courtyard, verandah, well and its surroundings were swept and tidied, everything neat and spotless. Though the walls were whitewashed, there was not a single picture on any of them. Ratni brought a pot of water on a tray.

'I hope everything is okay with Budhiniji?' Vijaykumar asked.

'Yes, she is fine,' Ratni replied in a shallow voice, as if she didn't care.

'They,' Vijaykumar said pointing to Rupi and Suchitra, 'have come from Delhi. They came all the way to write about Budhiniji.'

'What's there to write now?'

'It is not like what the others have written.'

'They all write the same.'

Hearing a door open, Ratni went inside. They had to wait a lot longer. 'This is strange and quite unusual. Usually, Budhini doesn't keep people waiting. She finds tourists very amusing and likes to crack jokes with them,' Vijaykumar said.

Budhini took some more time to come out. She was clad in a white, creased and faded soft cotton sari, draped in the typical Bengali style. A woman wearing the river! The door opened and let the river flow out. Rupi Murmu stood up holding her breath. The woman who descended the steps was not alone. It was as if she was accompanied by a deluge of hundreds of millions of people who had been uprooted and ousted from their own soil; of the vast forests and hundreds of villages and farms that existed no more.

Budhini Mejhan stepped into the courtyard, smiling with her toothless gums on display. It was a figure brawnier and more vivid than the one Rupi Murmu had longed to see. Within that short time, Suchitra had already clicked a lot of pictures of Budhini.

'Haven't I told you, Budhiniji, these girls are from Delhi?'

'Yes, I know.'

'They want to write a book about you.'

'What's there to write about me?'

'Your life.'

'It's all in the past. What's past is past. There's no point talking about it now. I don't want to remember and I don't want to tell you anything about it.'

'Would you like to go back to your village even now?' Suchitra asked.

Before Budhini could answer that, Ratni came with a tray of tea and biscuits.

'Please have tea,' Budhini said.

'How long has it been since you retired, Budhiniji? Do you remember?' Despite knowing the answer, Vijaykumar asked her, as if to help Rupi and Suchitra.

'Fifteen years.'

'It's been fifteen years since Dattaji passed away, isn't it?'

'It hasn't been fifteen years,' Ratni said.

'I don't think that he has passed away. He is still with me,' Budhini said. She talked about Datta with great reverence.

It was in Purulia that Datta had told her about the possibility of a married life between them.

'Budhini Mejhan, I know you are a child. It's to save you that we are on the run here. But in the eyes of people, you are a woman, and I am a man, strangers to each other. Besides, we belong to two different castes. Everywhere we took refuge, people wanted to know how you were related to me. Were you a daughter, sister or wife! If you are none of these to me, they won't let us live. The law also doesn't permit it. I see two ways in front of us. Either I leave you to your destiny, or I marry you and we live a life of our own. It is not something a man of my age may ask a child. I am not even sure that I see you as my wife. You decide. I leave this to you.'

'Ma won't stop once she starts talking about Baba,' Ratni put the teacups on a tray.

'I was afraid of their people,' Budhini continued. 'Would the bhadralok leave him alone? Would they spare me? One day, he asked me whether I was frightened of his sacred thread. And then he removed it from his body.'

'Now you have a pension and a house. Your life is somewhat peaceful, isn't it, Budhiniji?' Vijaykumar asked.

'Ah!' Budhini said, sounding indifferent.

'How do the Santal people behave with you these days, Budhini Ma?'

Before Rupi could complete her question, Ratni intervened: 'Santals?! Which Santals are you talking about?' And then saying that Ma was exhausted, she retreated into the house with the teacups.

'I don't want to blame anyone. I have no love or hatred for anyone,' Budhini said and stood up. 'I want to lie down for a while.'

'There's no use asking again. Budhiniji must be tired by now,' Vijaykumar said apologetically.

Though she was tired of the questions, she posed for Suchitra. Showing her toothless gums, she smiled like a little child.

'Budhini Ma, our nation has wronged you. To make it right . . .'

'Nation! What nation? Which is my nation?'

Glossary

Aadi Bhoota: Water

Aagan: November

Agrahara: A Brahmin community. 'Agraharam' is a name given to the dwelling place of Brahmins in India

Alpona: A design drawn at the front of the house using rice flour and colours. It is considered auspicious

'A peacock on my rooftop': Peacocks feature in Santal songs as a symbol of feminine sexuality

Bagna: Son-in-law

Bagwaan: A long cloth worn by men around their waist

Bahu: Daughter-in-law

Baju: An ornament or a piece of decorated thread tied around the arm below the shoulder and above the elbows

Bala-sakam: Silver or brass bangles

Banam: A stringed musical instrument

Bavuji: Aunt

Beta: Child, son

Bhadralok: A Brahmin community

Bither: The sacred place inside the house where Bongas dwell

Bitlaha: Excommunication

Black cow's milk: Gruel or rice porridge

Bongas: The Santals believe that the dead people transform into invisible Bongas who guard the village and its people. A Santal's world is inseparable from Bongas

Boysakh, Jenth, Ashad: May, June and July

Climbs up the big fig tree: A way of denoting adultery

Dadiya: Paternal grandmother

Dadu: Paternal grandfather

Damaadi: rice water

Danda jhumka: An ornament worn by women

Deadly flower: The poisonous flower symbolizes a brother who is arrogant and bossy

Dhak and dhamak: Two different percussions

Dhobistan: A place where the washermen and women go to wash clothes

Dida: Grandmother

Diku: A man from outside the clan. An outsider

Five and Six: The Five and Six are short-tempered Bongas in whom the Santals take more than casual interest compared to the other deities

Genda: Marigold

Gormen: The government

Gosae Era: Another deity of the sacred woods. Its symbol is a mahua tree

Hadiya: An alcoholic drink made from rice

Haram: An old man

Haram Budhi: An older woman

Hasa-sakam: Mud bangles worn by married women

'In the Flood': A short story by the famous Malayalam writer Thakazhi Sivashankara Pillai

Itil paini: Anklet

'I will make you swig a river': This denotes sexual intercourse. It is a way of the women challenging the men, saying they will tire them out

Jaher: The sacred grove where the Bongas dwell

Jaher Era: The deity of the sacred grove. Sal trees symbolize all the three powerful Bongas of the jaher, including Marang Buru and Five and Six

Jal, Jungle, Jameen: Water, forest and land

Jalpita: Meat-filled balls of steamed dough

'Janamdada flew away': 'Father has died'

Jathedars: Landlords

Jog Manji: Second chieftain

'Johar . . . Jaher Nayo': A song sung in praise of Marang Buru

Johar Ol-Chiki: Ol-Chiki is the Santali alphabet

Kalsingh and Bhutrang: Two angry Bongas. It is difficult to please them

Kanta: A decorative ornament for a hair bun

King Dasaratha: Dasaratha is described in the Ramayana and Vishnu Purana as the king of the Koshala kingdom and the father of Hindu god Rama

Lotta, batti and kanda: These are pots of different sizes

Magh and Fagun: January, February and March

'Makes bagna drink water . . . in the absence of the son': All these imageries indicate adultery

Manji: Chieftain

Manjithan: A thatched shrine where the spirit of the Haram Bonga dwells. This shrine is situated in the exact centre of the village. Haram Bonga was the first chieftain or manji of the village

Marang Buru: The most superior Bonga, the deity of the mountains

Milk tree: Mother. The Santals call their mothers milk trees

'Mughpudi, ayile ki hobek': 'Why did you come here, you whore?'

My child's baba would fly away': Santals never use the word 'death'. They either use the phrase 'fly away' or 'going beneath the ground'

Naike: The priest of the village

Oja: Sorcerer

'Our milk tree, uprooted': 'Our mother has passed away'

Pagra: Earrings

Panchi and parhan: A traditional Santali woman's clothes. It includes a long piece of cloth to drape around the waist and one to go around the shoulders

Paranik: An official in the village panchayat office

Phuli: Nose pin

Ramaphal: Soursop

Raybar bapla: A marriage with the consent of the community

Santal Pargana: Divisions and community localities in the region

Sarana: The Santals do not believe in any religion. They follow a philosophical doctrine known as Sarana

Setta: Stray dog

Silha: An ornament worn above the ear, on the hair

Sima Bonga: The angry Bongas who are always in a state of unrest and are considered the Bongas of the margins. These Bongas couldn't leave the borders or enter the village. The husbands of witches, those who committed suicide, or were killed or died in accidents turned into these marginalized evil Bongas

Sitaphal: Custard apple

Sosuma: Mother-in-law

Sosur: Father-in-law

Tamaks: A drum-like instrument

Tarkari: A curry made of roots and vegetables

Tiriao: A flute with seven holes

Tunki dipil bapla: A marriage ceremony of the poor people. The bride carries a small basket on her head and follows the groom to his house. Then they live together

Selected Bibliography

Articles and Websites

1. 'Recovering Budhini Mejhan from the Silted Landscapes of Modern India', Chitra Padmanabhan, 2 June 2012, *The Hindu*, https://www.thehindu.com/opinion/op-ed/recovering-budhini-mejhan-from-the-silted-landscape-of-modern-india/article12846589.ece
2. 'Tribal "Wife" of Nehru Is Outcast, Driven to Poverty', 2001, www.ambedkar.org
3. 'Price We Paid for Nehru's Development Model', V. Balachandran, *Sunday Guardian*, http://www.sunday-guardian.com/analysis/price-we-paid-for-nehrus-development-model
4. Translator's Preface by Gayatri Chakravorty Spivak in *Imaginary Maps* by Mahasweta Devi.
5. Land Acquisition, Rehabilitation and Resettlement Act, 2013.
6. The first Five-Year Plan presented by Pandit Jawaharlal Nehru in 1951.
7. 'Why Do We Want Cheap and Abundant Electricity in India?' asked B.R. Ambedkar, as the chairman of the Policy Committee on Public Works and Electric Power, reports in *Dainik Bhaskar*.
8. *Mathrubhumi*, 21–27 May 2017, Book 95, Issue 10.

9. 'The Pathalgadi Rebellion', Amarnath Tewary, 14 April 2018, *The Hindu*, https://www.thehindu.com/news/national/other-states/the-pathalgadi-rebellion/article23530998.ece

10. 'The Temple Sites at Telkupi (Bhairavasthan): Jaina Architectural Remains Submerged by Panchet Dam in Jharkhand and West Bengal', Bulu Imam.

Books

1. *The Adivasi Will Not Dance* by Hansda Sowvendra Shekhar
2. *The Mysterious Ailment of Rupi Baskey* Hansda Sowvendra Shekhar
3. Novels by Mahaswetha Devi
4. *The Hill of Flutes* by W.G. Archer
5. *Santal Folk Tales* by P.O. Bodding
6. *Santali: A Look into Santal Morphology* by Arun Ghosh
7. *Profile of a Pioneer*, Damodar Valley Corporation
8. *Energy India*, Damodar Valley Corporation
9. *Maithon*, Damodar Valley Corporation
10. *Concern for Community*, Damodar Valley Corporation

Acknowledgements

I would like to acknowledge the generous help I received with this translation from many different quarters.

Above all, I would like to thank Ambar Sahil Chatterjee for his courtesy and generosity. This translation would not have been undertaken, much less completed, without his supervision and generosity of spirit.

Special thanks are due to Manasi Subramaniam for her critical and painstaking readings of the manuscript. I am deeply appreciative of her conscientious editorial guidance. A special thank you to Aslesha Kadian at Penguin Random House India as well, who lavished on the manuscript more loving and meticulous attention than I could have hoped for.

I owe my warmest thanks to my husband, P.K. Sreenivasan, and daughter, Medha Sreenivasan, who was there at every step.

I benefited from the wise and generous concern of a number of friends. They know who they are, and they know how grateful I am to them. But three individuals merit special thanks: Achu Ullattil, for his heartwarming hospitality and support; Vinitha Shiva, for her endless love and patience; and Nishima K. Vijayan, for her unending enthusiasm.

Sachu Thomas helped me check against the Malayalam original and read through the final version for English rhythms and nuances.

Lastly, I am particularly indebted to my mother, Sarah Joseph, for reading and checking the first draft of this translation for accuracy, and for her wise comments. I feel privileged to have the good fortune of being her translator and to have her as my guiding spirit.

None of them, of course, are responsible for any errors or infelicities of language. That responsibility lies with me.

—Sangeetha Sreenivasan